cyber nation

PAX BOOKS $17.00

cyber nation

Erica Blaney

Hodder
Children's
Books

A division of Hachette Children's Books

A Catalogue record for this book is available
from the British Library

ISBN 978 0 340 95032 6

Typeset in Bembo by Avon DataSet Ltd,
Bidford on Avon, Warwickshire

Printed and bound by CPI Bookmarque, Croydon, CR0 4TD

The paper and board used in this paperback by Hodder Children's
Books are natural recyclable products made from wood grown in
sustainable forests. The manufacturing processes conform to the
environmental regulations of the country of origin.

Hodder Children's Books
a division of Hachette Children's Books
338 Euston Road, London NW1 3BH
An Hachette Livre UK company

To Darren, who never stopped believing

Acknowledgements

There are so many people who have made writing this book possible. I'd like to thank all those whose kind acceptance of the state of the house, in the knowledge that greater things were afoot, allowed me to leave the vacuuming for another day (I'll let you know when that day arrives). Thanks too to Rob and Patti, members of the Canterbury Freecycling community, who donated a computer when mine performed an illegal operation and shut down for ever.

I am indebted to my agent Lindsey Fraser and editor Emily Thomas for all their help, advice, confidence, suggestions, hard work and encouragement, and for being so good to work with.

I really appreciate the help my daughter Lydia gave me with 'computer speak'; and her friends Holly Austin and Emma-Louise Day, who read an early version and said nice things about it. Thanks go to my parents Peter and Jane, and my children Lydia, Phillip, John and Tim, without doubt the best and most encouraging family in the world.

Finally, I am hugely grateful to my husband Darren, who let me weep on his shoulder when things were going badly, and got as excited as I did when they were going well.

Prologue

The planet Clandoi is a curiosity.

Thousands of years ago, its North Pole was thrust into permanent darkness by a collision with a massive comet, prompting the Frenchman who discovered it to name it *Le Clin d'Oeil* – 'The Wink'. The impact left a huge crater scarring the planet's surface, and shattered the comet into a billion pieces: a tiny remnant revisits Clandoi every fifty-six years.

But that is not what makes it unique.

It is a tiny world, hardly qualifying as a planet. You can walk edge to edge in half a Clandoi year, and a whole year is only three hundred and forty-one days long. Somebody aged sixteen on Clandoi would be nearer fourteen on Earth.

But that is not so odd.

The North Pole on Clandoi is fiercely cold, and getting colder. Land suitable for farming is shrinking fast: there are harsh Edicts to control the population because there is not enough food to go round, nor will there be in the foreseeable future. The lowest caste, the Wayfarers, are forced to give up most of the food they produce as 'taxes' to support the Appaloosians and the Pelegians; although if nothing is done soon, all of them will starve, whatever their caste.

No, what makes Clandoi one of a kind is this: *it has an edge*.

This edge, known as Worldsend, is made of cloud. It is solid and real and encircles the flat planet completely: you can travel that far and no more. It reaches high up, and higher, and is called the Ne'Lethe. In the Beyond, the void after the Ne'Lethe, nothingness goes on for ever and ever, though some do believe that a tunnel exists that leads to a larger, warmer world.

This is what has been taught to children on Clandoi for generations: this is what is still taught to the few who are left.

Not that there are many.

Not that much is taught.

Because the Ne'Lethe blurs more than geographical reality: the edges of history are also hazy. Nobody knows of anything that happened more than three hundred years ago.

The superior Appaloosians are not concerned: they deny the fact of history altogether. They are fond of technology, of here, and of now. Today is yesterday, rewritten.

The Wayfarers dislike committing anything to writing, so have lost much knowledge. They believe that there used to be a sun and two moons, perhaps even stars, but they are all gone now. One day they will return, to be hung on the Ne'Lethe by morning joy birds, and the ice will melt and the fields be fertile again.

As for the Pelegians, the highest caste of all: well, nobody exactly knows what they think. Nobody knows anybody who has ever actually seen one. They must exist, as they wrote the Edicts; they invented the cyberclinic, and dictate who may be saved in it and who may not: but what they look like is anyone's guess.

That is how life is on Clandoi.

Unless somebody remembers . . .

1

'Damny Pelegians! I wish you were dead, damny dead.'

Solly stormed through the darkness, fury ripping through his veins.

'Sacry cyberclinic! Diably, damny Appaloosians.'

He didn't mean Lalune, of course, though she was an Appaloosian.

He did mean her parents, though.

'Sacry, inferny Toayef! Damny Threfem! I hope you rot in a swag's den until you turn into swags.'

His lungs agonized in the cold. He began to clamber up the little hillock over the cyberclinic. A lock of blond hair escaped from his hood into his eyes, so that he couldn't see where he was going: his foot caught in something, the strap on his snowskate snapped and he was hurled face down into the snow.

'Devilly snowskate!' he sobbed, wrenching it off his foot. 'I'll feed you to a tubal worm, use you as snarg bait.'

He flung it away from him, howling, 'I hate you! I hate you all!'

After a while, he wiped his eyes with his mitten and got to his feet again. He limped over to grope for his snowskate in the dark – even in his rage he realized that he couldn't afford to lose it – and carried on. He had to walk more slowly now; his booted left foot sinking deep into the snow every other step.

Behind him he could hear the sounds of morning. The raucous blast of the daybreak horn. The creak of the Great Gate. The hunters calling their snowcamels. Solly's snowcamel, Star, would be with them. *He* was part of the team.

The thought made Solly clench his fists savagely. Only yesterday he had heard for the third time in a year that he was not considered an experienced enough hunter to be allowed a licence.

'Damny, inferny Forcyef!' he screamed at the cyberclinic, and at the Appaloosians, who sat on the Board of Sanctions and Permits. 'What do you know about hunting, anyway?'

There was an outcrop of rock in front of him at the entrance to Cirque Hallow, a little shrub-filled dimple in the side of the hillock. Solly hurried on towards it. He heard his father, Brise, shouting orders. There was a brief pause while one of the hunters – probably Tache – prayed to the Being for a successful hunt. Then they were off, the sledges hissing along a tubal worm track.

Solly huddled behind a dead tree, feeling the snowcamels' paws shaking the ground beneath him. Despite their name they weren't white: apart from a leathery 'umbrella' on their upper halves, the heavy animals were covered in shaggy black fur. They were called snowcamels because they could survive for days eating just snow, which they guzzled down their long necks along with any dead vegetation in it. The umbrella, covered with green symbiotic moss, was a feature of most vertebrates on the planet Clandoi.

They were heading in the direction of the lake; at least two days away, maybe more if the ice had grown. Their thundering paws made snow cascade on to Solly's head as they passed: the tinkling of icicles hanging from the branches echoed the jingle of harness.

Solly waited for the darkness to swallow the last swish of the sledges. The silence clung to him. He was all alone. The hunters would be gone for days. His mother was at work in the cyberclinic.

He had lost Lalune for ever.

Bitterly, he kicked out at a fallen branch — and suddenly found himself grabbed by the ankle, swung up into the air, and left hanging there helplessly.

2

The girl lies in near silence, tightly curled hair spread around her face, dappled skin glistening in the pale light. The only sound is the endless trickle of a whispering computerized voice.

On the wall over her head somebody has fixed a plaque stating her name: Tuef Seventeen. It is incorrect. Those who loved her called her Lalune.

A silvery tunic covers the wires and tubes that invade Lalune's body. This one keeps her temperature constant. This one monitors her heart; this one her lungs; this one her kidneys.

Lalune does not breathe: her lungs are filled with oxygen-rich orbal oil. Orbal oil also fills the glass pod in which she lies. She is in it and it is in her: orbal oil is her world.

Sometimes she dreams: about memories of a life once lived; about the ceaseless flow of mind-knowledge.

And she dreams of Solly, in her death that is not death.

Next to the pod that entombs Lalune is another; another is next to that; and another; and another. More corridors lie alongside this one. The light is too weak to show how many there are; but the markings above the elevator show that there are twenty levels.

The ghostly vault is womb and tomb to ten thousand besides Lalune. One day they hope to be woken up to a new, warm world: a fertile world free from ice, and pain, and disease.

They are known as the Sleepers.

3

After a few minutes of kicking to free himself, Solly realized that he was only making the rope around his ankle tighter. He stopped, and concentrated on breathing and staying conscious.

Half an hour crawled past. The night gradually relinquished its hold and a weak light bleached the sky.

Solly's nose was blocked and his throat was dry; his mouth kept trying to water it, but only succeeded in sending a trail of frosty dribble into his eye. His left foot was numb; his right leg ached with the effort of keeping it in the air. He felt that at any moment his head would explode: the blood rushing past his eardrums sounded like a small underground river. It was so loud that at first he didn't register the voice.

'Come now, Angelus; surely if what you are saying were true, one could begin walking in one direction and eventually one would get back to the place one started from?'

Solly jerked on his rope. The voice had come from immediately behind him.

'Now, you know that can't be the case. I've *been* there. I've *seen* it with my own eyes.'

If the speaker's companion had answered, Solly hadn't heard him.

'No, I'm afraid we shall have to agree to disag— Gracious heavens above us, what have we caught here?'

Hurried footsteps approached.

'Hmm. *Homo Sapiens Juvenilia*, I do believe. And I was so hoping for a pudgia for dinner.'

'Let me down!' screamed Solly, writhing about enough on his rope to catch a glimpse of a very short man with a wild grey beard and huge bushy eyebrows that stuck out as far as his nose.

'Hmm. Let him down, he says, Angelus,' said the little man thoughtfully. 'But what I say is, what's he doing in our trap? Dinner was supposed to be in the trap, so it was.'

'I ain't your damny dinner!' shouted Solly. 'Let me down!'

'Now there's the thing,' explained the old man. 'This trap was meant to catch a pudgia for dinner. If it catches something else, we generally eat the something else.'

'You ain't eating me!' yelled Solly furiously. 'Let me down right now!'

'Now there's another thing,' said the man. 'How? How, indeed, do we get him down, Angelus? This trap was made for a pudgia, not for a great lumbering *Homo Sapiens Juvenilia*. How do we know we won't break the trap? Or, indeed, the boy? Land on your head, you will.'

'I don't care, just let me down,' bellowed Solly. He was starting to feel sick, and doing it whilst still upside down was too awful to contemplate.

The man took off a mitten and felt inside his pocket.

'He doesn't care, he says, Angelus. You're my witness to

11

that. If he breaks his head open, *he* said "I don't care". Remember that.'

The rope was looped over a branch and tied on to the tree trunk close to the ground. The man brought out a knife and cut it. With a yell, Solly flung his hands over his head to protect it, and crumpled in a heap at the man's feet.

'Are you broken in any way?' enquired the man, more out of interest than sympathy, Solly felt.

Solly moaned and sat up. Pain shot through his wrist and a wave of dizziness flooded him. He retched violently.

'Heavens preserve us, he's been sick on my boots!' said the old man, wiggling his eyebrows furiously. 'What do you think, Angelus? Broken arm? Broken leg? Broken mind?'

'Broken everything,' groaned Solly. 'How am I going to get home? I want my ma.'

'Your ma will have to wait,' said the man. 'Got to patch you up first. Got to get you back to the cave and undo the damage. Now there's the thing. How to get him back, Angelus? If I had your wings I could pick him up and fly.'

Solly glanced around for the elusive Angelus, but saw nobody.

'I ain't coming nowhere with you,' he said. 'I want to go home.'

He tried to stand up, but his ankle buckled and he sat down again hurriedly.

'You've broken my leg!' he said weakly. 'And my arm. Pa's going to kill me.'

'Then I'm probably the safer option,' said the man

absently. He was doing something to a fallen branch. 'There: a crutch. You have one good leg? Good. Try it, go on.'

He helped Solly up and picked up the broken snowskate. He was surprisingly strong for such a small man. He was almost a dwarf in size and in looks, with his beard spread over his chest, and his head hidden beneath a furred hood made of what looked and smelled like swag-skin.

Nobody wears swag-skin, thought Solly contemptuously. Swags were huge, unpleasant creatures that looked and stank like a pile of rotting carpets. They were one of the few animals whose skin was non-taxable, since nobody in their right minds would use it.

'Now, then, homeward,' said the man. He took Solly's arm to help him along, and Solly yelped in pain.

'Apologies, I had forgotten about your arm,' he said. 'Tell you what: I'll lead, you follow. Not far . . . not far at all.'

Solly knew he wouldn't get very far on his own. Reluctantly, he limped along behind the strange little man, who was humming happily to himself as he led the way deeper into Cirque Hallow.

'Who are you?' he asked after a while.

'Now there's the question,' said the man. 'Who am I, indeed? Hear that, Angelus? He must be a student of philosophy, to start with such a big question.'

'I mean, what's your name?' said Solly irritably.

'Most people call me Aube.'

Solly's eyes widened.

'You're the Seer!' he exclaimed. 'I thought you lived

on the other side of the world.'

'I'm *a* Seer,' Aube corrected him. 'One of many. Angelus constantly reminds me of that. And we have many homes. But we haven't been back here to the Twilight in a long time. Fifteen years, I believe.'

'Where is this Angelus?' asked Solly, looking all about.

'Oh, he'll be about somewhere,' said Aube vaguely. 'He comes and goes. Now then, here we are.'

He waved his mittened hand at a small wall of rock. At first Solly could see nothing in the early-morning gloom; then he noticed the very small entrance to a cave. At its highest it only came up to Solly's knees.

'I'll never get in there!' objected Solly.

'Nonsense!' said Aube. 'Just roll in. Like this.'

He dropped to the ground and rolled through the entrance. There was a muffled thud as he landed.

'Just one minute and I'll strike a light for you.'

Solly heard the sound of a flint-box being struck, and saw a flicker of yellow which steadied and brightened into a strong blue light as Aube lit a lantern filled with orbal oil.

'Come in then, Solly,' said Aube cheerfully. 'Mind the drop.'

Solly tensed.

'How do you know my name?' he asked. 'I never told you.'

'I know Revas, your ma,' said Aube, his voice strange and echoey through the opening. 'You were born last time I visited Twilight. Now there's the thing: I gave you your name! Named after the sun. There was a reason for that. Mind you, I would have done anyway with that hair.'

14

Solly wanted to disbelieve him.

'If you know that,' he said, 'tell me, who else was there the day I was born?'

Aube chuckled.

'Your pa, of course, sick with worry over your ma.'

He wasn't there then, thought Solly. Otherwise he'd have said about Lalune being born, too . . .

'And the moon-girl's parents,' Aube went on. 'She came the very same day, just two hours earlier. I named her, too. First time I've ever named an Appaloosian: first and last, I dare say.'

4

Lalune dreams and dreams.

Her eyes are half open, her star-shaped pupils dilated, and her dreams are memories of a life once lived.

Dreams are her life now; all she has, just dreams and memories. Lalune is completely unaware of her surroundings. She has no feelings, no thoughts of her own: nothing but her mind-knowledge.

She dreams of Solly, in her death that is not death.

There is no order to her memories: Appaloosians do not believe in the constancy of history. Each day is a great wheel turning, always coming back to the place it started, laying the new day over the top of the old, intermingling events, colliding them, weaving them together.

It is something that no longer bothers Lalune now that she has become mere tissue in a sterile container.

Nothing troubles her now: not wondering what happened that made her race deny history; not wondering what terrible event they are trying to hide from themselves.

She used to try to imagine time in a line, as the Wayfarers do, with a beginning and an ending – she used to, in the days when she had some say over her thoughts. Now she just sees the wheel turning, turning, turning, causing her to drift into the night-time beyond dreams.

Lalune is becoming too relaxed.

She turns on to her side. A light should be shining faintly, but it has flickered out some time ago. She is at risk of sliding so far into dark unconsciousness that there will be no return.

But the central computer will not allow her to drift towards a lingering, painless death.

Lalune will not die. She is too necessary for that. Even now, the monitors are sending out warnings. Soon the drugs feeding through her tubes will be rebalanced.

She will not die. Not yet.

And she carries on dreaming of Solly, in her death that is not death.

5

Solly sat painfully and stretched his legs out in front of him. He lowered himself gingerly into lying position, pushing his makeshift crutch through the opening first before shuffling under the rocky overhang. He didn't trust the Seer's cheerful 'mind the drop' – which was fortunate, as the drop was immediate and at least half his own height. Instead he sat up carefully and let himself fall down on to his good foot.

He was in a small tunnel with a slatted wooden floor to allow the melted snow to drain away. Aube had hung his boots, coat and hat on some bone hooks at the far end. An orbal-oil lantern lit a small doorway covered by a swag-skin curtain.

Solly hobbled along the tunnel, sat down, and took his outside boots off. His foot began to throb. He couldn't take his coat off with one arm, so he kept it on as he pushed the curtain aside, wincing with pain.

'Come in, and welcome,' beamed Aube, bringing both him and the orbal lantern inside. Without his hat, his head was revealed to be completely bald. He was wearing a woollen robe cinched in at the middle with a piece of frayed rope, and thick, rough trousers underneath. Round his neck hung a sliver of yellow stone on a silver chain.

'I've set some water to heat up; I dare say you could do with something hot inside you.'

Solly gritted his teeth as Aube eased his coat off and told him to sit down on a small bed.

'Hmm. Have to get a proper look at that arm, I shall,' said Aube. 'And the leg, too. Need a better light to see by. Not much oil left, anyway.'

He took his pendant off and picked up a small metal box. Inside was what looked like very fine white sand. Holding the yellow stone flat in one hand, he poured some of the sand on to it. Immediately, the sand started to glow and a few grains near the edge began to jump as if they were being heated up. Aube lifted the pendant up to his lips and gently blew the sand off it. It swirled upwards and hung in the low ceiling of the little cave: a cloud of pure light, much stronger than the light of the orbal lantern, which Aube now extinguished.

'What is it?' said Solly, curiosity overcoming his antagonism.

'Fire dust,' said Aube. 'They mine it somewhere in the Glimmering, I believe. Only don't ask how it works, because I don't know. Quite safe, though; quite safe.'

Aube knelt down and started to take off Solly's soft indoor boots and socks.

'Why were you at my birth?' said Solly. 'Ow, that hurts!'

'Now there's the thing about Seers,' said Aube. 'We See things. I Saw a thing and I had to come and tell it to you. Only as you were a bit young, I told your ma instead. Wriggle your toes.'

'But what did you See? Why didn't anybody tell me?'

19

'Not the right time, I dare say. Point your toes . . . good, now flex them.'

'Ow!'

'Just a sprain, I think,' said Aube. 'Though I dare say your ma might want to X-ray it just to make sure. Still work at the hospital, does she?'

'They don't do X-rays any more,' said Solly. 'There's only us Wayfarers left now, and we can't pay, so they shut all that stuff down.'

'Hmm,' said Aube. 'Let's look at your arm then.'

The arm hurt a lot more. Solly had to swallow hard to stop himself being sick again.

'What did you See?' he asked again, to take his mind off the pain.

'Your journey to find the Key,' said Aube. 'That's definitely broken, that one. I can put a splint on it, but you'll want your ma to see to it properly.'

'What key?' said Solly.

' "What key?" he wants to know, Angelus,' said Aube, heaving himself up off his knees. 'The Key of Being, of course. Don't you listen to the songs? I think that water must be hot enough by now.'

'Oh, *that* key,' Solly said. 'Well, you can forget about that for a start. I'm not going chasing after some pointless Wayfarer artefact when I should be here . . .' He suddenly thought of Lalune. Doing what, exactly? When they were small children, they'd planned to run away to Worldsend and marry: they could hardly do that now, could they?

Aube was clearly astounded by his words.

'Pointless artefact? It's the key the first Wayfarer

had stolen from him when he parted ways with his brother . . .'

'Probably a hundred people have had the same prophecy, and haven't found anything,' said Solly derisively. 'And *you* think *I'm* going to find it? Always supposing it actually exists, that is. All by myself, without the huissier finding out I'm travelling without a permit, because they won't give me one, you know.'

'No, no, no, not all by yourself,' said Aube, throwing a handful of leaves into a teapot and pouring hot water over them. A pungent smell filled the room. 'You and the moon-girl. I named her, as well, you know. There should have been a third; there's normally three, but I never did find him. Or her.'

'Well, you've got it wrong, old man,' Solly said, his dizziness and nausea making him aggressive. 'I ain't going nowhere. And neither's Lalune. Not now, not ever. Because they've taken her away, and put her in the damny cyberclinic, and she ain't coming out for a hundred years, and I ain't never going to see her again, so where's that leave your sacry prophecy?'

As his voice rose, he stood up – and promptly fainted.

6

As the stimulating drugs flow through Lalune's veins, her memories and dreams grow more disturbing.

She remembers the day her mother got the news.

Outwardly she was submissive, as she always was, though her face paled and flushed and paled again rapidly.

Even now she trembles in her pod, and little ripples fly over the surface of the orbal oil.

Her mother was beautiful, exultant, waving her arms, unable to stand still.

Blood whooshed in Lalune's ears as she concentrated on not fainting, clutching the back of her father's chair so hard that afterwards her hands ached for hours. The chair became the only thing that mattered.

—I half thought they wouldn't let us, you know, because of your low status, Threfem.

Threfem inclined his head a little to one side at this. She never meant to hurt.

—They will come and clear the house for us, said her mother, showing them the etched acetate that had brought the news. — No point in keeping everything: when we are woken we shall have all new clothes and furniture.

—We enter so soon, murmured Father, his shoulders drooping.

—*Once you are in, you are in, said her mother, snatching the acetate back.*

Lalune was finding it difficult to breathe and her mother asked if she felt entirely well.

—*You didn't tell us you'd applied, Lalune said in a low voice, eyes cast down, concentrating on the chair still.*

—*I wanted to give you a surprise, darling, her mother said, her feet dancing in her excitement.* —*Besides, what if I had told you and they hadn't let us? You would have been so disappointed.*

Her mother did not know her at all.

Lalune thought of the cyberclinic, all those chilly pods side by side under indifferent lights. Her memory skips her forwards to their tour of the clinic, *Forcyef proudly showing them around, and later being helped into her pod, the needles piercing her skin, the sensation that she was pitching head first into a pit so cold and deep that she was going to drop for ever, all the time expecting to hear the crunch as her body hit the ground, but never reaching . . .*

—*I've bought our suits already, said her mother, showing them.* —*I couldn't wait. Silver-white for you, Lalune. The silver in the material actually cleans them: isn't that clever?*

She liked Lalune to wear white, for youth and purity. She was the only child in Opita, after all. Unless you counted Solly.

Lalune would have preferred black: mourning for the life she was about to lose.

—*How do they know they can wake us?*

—*Darling, they have been working on the technology for ever, said her mother confidently.* —*There's no point in braiding your hair now, though it's much neater that way. It carries on growing, apparently. Imagine, it'll reach your knees when you come out again.*

There was no point in asking how long that would be. It was that Appaloosian paradox again: there is no such thing as time. Lalune tried to forget the picture of the wheel, tried to imagine time in a line, and the years stretched out before her endlessly.

Solly, *she thought.*

He'll get older, and I'll be exactly the same.

Except for my hair, which will carry on growing.

How old will he be when I come out?

Will he still be alive, *she wondered, and tried to imagine what it would be like to be not alive . . .*

And once again she was falling into the pit, struggling for breath as the air in her lungs was replaced by orbal oil.

Her memory shifts once more . . .

She was crying, holding Solly and sobbing. They didn't speak. There was nothing to say. They knew that nothing would be all right ever again.

They had less than an hour to say goodbye. Once you were in, you were in.

They had so little time. Her father shuffled his feet nervously nearby, hugged Revas and Brise. They would never be allowed into the cyberclinic: they were Wayfarers.

This was it, the instant when Wayfarers and Appaloosians parted for ever.

—*We'd better get back,* Threfem *said awkwardly, before we are missed.*

Lalune drew in a deep breath, wiped her eyes dry, brought herself under control. She would not cry again.

She asked Revas for some scissors, cut off a lock of her hair, gave it to Solly. He went to do the same.

24

—*No point, she said.* —*I can't take anything with me. Just memories and dreams.*

Like in death, *she thought.*

—*Remember me, he said.* —*Dream of me.*

She dreams of him now, in her death that is not death.

7

When Solly came to he was still in the little cave, but he was alone. The fire dust still hovered above his head, but was slightly dimmer now. He could see some of the tiny grains winking out from time to time. He tried to sit up, and was sick again.

The cave was not big: about twice the size of the tunnel that led into it. Dust was piled in the corners, as if Aube hadn't finished cleaning it yet after his long absence; and everything smelled a bit mushroomy. The Seer had, however, done a good job of blocking up the draughts: it was warm and Solly was sweating in his many layers of clothing. There was a curtain covering another door at the far end, and a fireplace; but for some reason that Solly couldn't work out, the fire was hanging in mid-air. The furniture was sparse: just the bed with its fur throws, a table and a chair.

The orbal-oil lantern was still on the table where Aube had left it. It was a roughly made orb of pewter and glass – a well at the bottom to hold the oil and a twist of wire holding the rag wick. It was nothing like the beautiful filigree silver ones Revas had inherited from her grandmother, set with sapphires to reflect the blue flame.

A few cooking pots hung on the wall. Two alcoves had

been gouged out of the rough stone walls; one held a small amount of dried food, the other some flat rectangular objects Solly didn't recognize.

There was a picture on the wall above his head. He twisted round to have a better look at it. It was of a luridly coloured sun, moon and comet, surrounding what looked like a pointed glass building the same size as the planet it was built on. Another moon was underneath the planet.

For some reason it seemed important, though he couldn't think why.

Solly wondered what privy arrangements the Seer had. On the floor next to the bed was a chipped mug full of the infusion Aube had been making for him before he passed out; fortunately he'd missed it when he was sick. He picked it up and smelled it suspiciously, but thought he recognized the herbs: painkillers. His arm and ankle were both aching badly, so he drank it down in one mouthful, making a face as he swallowed: it was cold and unsweetened. Then he peed into the mug and lay back down again. He fell asleep almost immediately.

8

When Lalune was six she was permitted to attend a ceremonial banquet. The Appaloosians held many of these, usually in honour of instruction, or reason, or some other concept: without any history, perhaps they needed something to assure them of their humanity.

The clerks had sweated for days over the seating plan: nobody must be offended by being set lower than their allotted position. Lalune was with her mother: she was six, the only child there. Father, a lower rank, was some way off. She would rather have been with him: her mother was tense, fussing about her appearance, her posture, her manners.

Her mother had bought them matching white suits for the occasion; Lalune was trying to hide a grease stain with her napkin when the officer opposite her spoke.

—So, what do you do with your days, Tuef?

She was confused momentarily: Tuef was her official name, the one on her certificate of citizenship, and she rarely used it.

—Answer nicely, Tuef, said her mother, pinching her leg so that she gasped.

—I am receiving an education, sir. Begging your benefaction.

Her front teeth were missing so that she lisped.

—And what are you learning? he asked.

Her new clothes itched. she tried not to scratch her neck as she answered.

—*Today I have been 'sperimenting with grain man* . . . *management systems,* she said, stumbling over the big words despite her best efforts.

Her mother cleared her throat quietly.

—*Sir,* Lalune added hastily.

He looked amused.

—*And what does experimenting with grain management systems entail for a six-year-old?*

—*I've got a big room full of tubs of grain, sir,* she told him, wide-eyed with this burden. Her tutor had said that it was difficult to grow grain on Clandoi, and many proper grown-up scientists were also carrying out this research. —*I'm growing them with different amounts of water and light.*

—*And what have you discovered, child?* asked the lady next to him, a fat administrator with grey-and-brown skin.

Lalune flushed, realizing that four or five others were also listening in. She scratched her neck, dabbed her mouth with her napkin, remembered the grease stain, and jammed the napkin back into her lap.

—*Stop fiddling and answer politely, darling,* said her mother sharply, before scattering an apologetic glance around.

—*Grain needs more light to grow better, ma'am,* Lalune said. —*Twilight has good soil and lots of water, but not enough light.*

—*Bravo,* said the man, giving her a silver coin as a reward, and her mother beamed with relief.

She was not sure what *bravo* meant, but the man smiled, and the administrator nodded at him; so encouraged by this she carried on earnestly.

—*Too much water makes the seeds go all slimy and soft, and not enough makes them not germil* . . . *germ'nate, but mostly*

29

the water in the soil is 'xactly right to make it grow. The problem is always the light. I think that the Wayfarers are right, she said, too interested in her subject to notice the tightening of her mother's lips. —They say that once there used to be a great big light hanging from the Ne'Lethe, a sun, that made it warm and light so the grain could grow . . .

. . . slap . . .

Her mother coughed and asked the administrator about her work, but Forcyef was staring thoughtfully at her . . .

Suddenly in her dream she is back at home. The slap came then, not at the banquet, and in her dream happens over and over again. Her rapid pulse alerts the central computer and a soothing confusion of sedatives makes her memories fuzzy.

. . . slap . . .

Father lifted a hand as if to stop her mother, but lowered it again, saying nothing.

—Never . . . slap . . . ever . . . slap . . . do that again, her mother hissed . . .

But she was receding, her voice echoing from far away.

—Never mention those . . . people again, especially at an official banquet, especially in front of Administrator Forcyef . . . slap . . .

—Toayef, my dear, said Father . . .

And from far away Lalune watches her mother's face crumple tearfully.

—Don't you realize the power those people have? she sobbed, and Threfem patted her nervously on the arm. —I've worked so hard, and now she's ruined everything, everything . . .

Threfem put his arms around her.

30

Lalune observes herself with them remotely, separated by a mist of time and space, sees her own hand reaching out towards her mother.

. . . slap . . .

—*And you are never to see that . . . slap . . . boy again. Never, you hear me? You are never to listen to those wicked filthy lies they tell . . .*

Her six-year-old self knew that she must have done something truly dreadful, though she didn't understand what.

—*Now she's ruined everything, everything . . .*

Did her mother scream these words then or later? It doesn't matter. It is happening to somebody else entirely, her memories have become muddled.

—*Now she's ruined everything, everything . . .*

And she stood up straight and silent, accepting her punishment, determined not to cry, though one tear did escape . . .

. . . *Solly* . . .

9

Solly woke again to the sound of voices.

'Touch of concussion, I dare say,' Aube was saying to a cloaked figure next to the fireplace. Solly wondered if it was Angelus. 'Missed that. *You'd* have seen it. I was more concerned about his arm. He used it to break his fall.'

'We need to try and get him home,' said the figure.

'Ma?' croaked Solly.

'Solly!' she said. 'What have you been up to?'

'Breaking myself,' he said, trying to return her smile, but his mouth went all wobbly, and he turned his head sideways. *It's the shock*, he thought fiercely.

She crossed the room swiftly and he buried his face in her brown curls. After a while, he gave a big shaky sigh and she gave him a handkerchief.

'You're missing work,' he said, blowing his nose.

His mother laughed. 'I finished over an hour ago.'

'Have I been asleep that long?'

'All day,' said Aube. 'In between vomiting on my floor and peeing in my cups.'

'Sorry,' said Solly, going red. 'I couldn't get up. I'd have wet myself . . .'

Then he stopped, seeing the twinkle in the Seer's eyes.

His mother was feeling his forehead and looking at his

32

wrist with a worried expression in her brown eyes.

'How do you feel, Solly? Can you get up now?'

He felt as weak as a baby. He sat up dizzily.

'You've bandaged my foot.'

'Aube did,' she said. 'Day or two in bed and you won't know the difference. Try and stand on it.'

Solly tried. It hurt, but the bandage and the crutch together at least made walking possible.

'I'll never be able to walk home,' he said.

'I brought Lalune's old sledge,' said Revas. 'Threfem did say to use anything we needed.'

Aube and Revas helped him into his coat and boots. Revas wound a handle on the side of the flint-box until the flint sparked and lit a bit of oiled rag which she used to light the lantern again. Aube took the chair out into the passage so that Solly could use it to climb out.

Outside, the twilight had deepened into night. Apart from their lantern, the only light in the whole world was the one on the Great Gate.

Aube carefully manoeuvred the sledge on to a tubal worm track and pushed off. Tubal worms were huge creatures seven or eight times as long as Solly. Like snowcamels they were covered in moss, from which they got many of their nutrients. The rest came from tunnelling through the snow. The snow and anything present in it – dead animals, vegetation, rocks and minerals leached from the ground below – was funnelled into their bodies by their huge jaws, and crushed in the massive teeth that lined over half of their bodies. They could move at incredible speeds, leaving behind them a worm cast of ice; long and straight, and guaranteed to be smooth and free from rocks: a perfect track for the Wayfarers' especially shaped sledges to run along.

Solly, Revas and Aube shot down the hill, the freezing wind tugging at their clothes and furs. The lantern flickered and went out. By the time they reached the end of the track, a short distance from the Great Gate, tiny icicles were hanging from Solly's eyelashes, though he felt as if he were on fire. Aube braked gently. Revas carefully helped Solly up and walked him towards the gate.

'Passes, please,' said a voice. It was Wuneem, a sour-faced Appaloosian huissier, or guard. Appaloosians were as human as Wayfarers, but they looked very different, with their bitonal skin and the star-shaped pupils in their eyes. Wuneem was particularly ugly, as Appaloosians go. His skin was greyish-brown, with patches in an ugly shade of yellow scattered randomly all over.

'Begging your benefaction,' murmured Revas, as she fumbled under her coat and handed him an egg-shaped silver pendant. Solly did the same, but Aube only had the yellow stone, and it didn't hold all the computerized data of a pendant pass.

A Wandering Automated Security Patrol (WASP) had backed its striped body into a recharging unit next to Wuneem, its wings folded back along its back. Solly couldn't help thinking how unnatural it looked with just the two: most birds like pudgias had three, while flutteries and other insects had one.

Wuneem dangled the pendants in the beam of light coming from its front end, then looked at Aube in a nasty, enquiring way.

'Can't go in without a pass,' he said.

'Now there's the thing,' said Aube. 'I live out there, I do. Never had need of a pass before. I don't have one.'

'Outcast, are you?' jeered Wuneem. 'Cave-dweller? Don't think we want your type in here, do we now?'

'He's a Wayfarer Seer,' said Revas. 'Can't you give him a temporary pass?'

'Temp'ry pass?' said the huissier. 'Don't recall such a thing as a temp'ry pass. Though I do recall an Edict against Seers and outcasts and cave-dwellers.'

'Huissier Wuneem,' said Revas, trying to keep her temper, 'my son had a serious accident today and this Seer probably saved his life. Please let him in, so that I may give him a hot drink before he goes home in this cold weather.'

'Um . . .' said Wuneem, grinning horribly. 'No.'

Solly was shivering and felt himself begin to sway. Revas grabbed his shoulder.

'Very well,' she said sweetly. 'Then, in order for us not to be in breach of Edict 17009.7, we shall have to leave our sledge here, as we are not allowed to ride it inside the compound, and I have to help my son to walk. Which means that according to Edict 119.4, you will have to follow us home with it, as you cannot let us leave it here, and, according to Edict 320.1, you have to help us, as we are incapacitated. Which is a shame, because that means you'll be deserting your post, which according to Edict—'

'All right, he can go in,' said Wuneem sulkily, opening the small doorway that was part of the bigger gate. Solly noticed him release the WASP to follow them.

'I am indebted by your clemency, Huissier Wuneem,'

said Aube, and he sounded as if he really was. 'May all heaven's blessings fall on you and your wife, especially in these times.'

He leaned forwards confidentially as he said the last few words.

Wuneem looked startled.

'How did you know about my wife?'

Aube gave a little bow.

'Now there's the thing about Seers, Huissier Wuneem. We *See* things.'

When they had walked a little way, Revas said, 'What's wrong with his wife?'

Aube chuckled.

'I have as much idea about that, m'dear, as you have knowledge of all those Edicts, I suspect.'

Revas giggled. Solly looked back at the WASP nervously. It had reached the end of its range and was circling slowly in order to turn back, but could probably still hear them.

'What are you talking about? You *are* a proper Seer, aren't you?'

'Sometimes,' said Aube. 'Sometimes I just let people think I am.'

10

Lalune drifts down again in a sea of narcotics, and her dreams are blurred and sweet.

She dreams of her third birthday . . .

Father had got a little sledge for her and he took her out to play on it. He showed her a tubal worm track and they hauled the sledge on to it and whizzed down the hill over and over and over again. Her nose was red and her fingers and toes were numb and she couldn't feel her ears and she was so happy she nearly burst. But then afterwards he took her to play with Solly, and Revas gave them hot, sweet drinks, and she was even happier and wished she could stay there for ever and ever . . .

And, she remembers before that, when she was so young that things like walking and talking were still new accomplishments: sitting on Father's shoulders high, high above the world, her stubby legs in their white synthetic trousers wrapped around Father's neck, the wind attempting to blow her hood off. She shivered in delighted terror as Father tottered down the narrow streets in his nailed boots. He had taken her to work with him: he was not supposed to, but it was his turn to look after his baby daughter, and the Wayfarer hunt had returned the day before: the Edicts required that he visit them within twenty hours.

He nearly slipped, and she squealed and giggled, not realizing her danger. She howled as he pulled her down to safety.

—*Carry!* she commanded, holding up her short arms, and he smiled and twinkled at her.

—*Nearly there, moon-girl*, he says. —*Can't you hear them singing?*

The voices were coming from a nearby house. It sounded like angels, and she was reminded of the silver face of her own angel, who smiled down on her every night. Father hummed along happily and knocked on the door.

Her stomach growled as a savoury fragrance burst out on a gust of warm air.

—*Threfem!* cried several voices, and they were pulled inside the crowded room. She hid behind Father's legs, but somebody pulled her out again.

—*Oh, you precious thing*, said a big white face – not an angel after all, but a Wayfarer. —*Come and play with Solly.*

A cup of berry juice was thrust into one hand, a chewy bar of dried fruit into the other, and a tiny boy appeared. He had long blond hair and the bluest eyes she'd ever seen. Her memory makes him fifteen suddenly, dressed in his outside gear, the hood pulled back – which is how she pictures him always. He scowled at her, that first time, and she stuck her tongue out and crossed her eyes at him, and they both laughed great guffaws, their friendship forged in the age-old childish ritual of face-making.

11

Solly's home was in Opita, a walled village that had been built when the cyberclinic had been an ordinary hospital in need of workers. Like all Wayfarer houses it was dome-shaped: inside, one round main room had a few tiny chambers leading off it, hidden behind curtains. The ice pit, where they stored the meat and uncured furs that Brise brought back, led off from one end of the porch, and the privy from the other.

The leather curtains were the same creamy-white colour as the painted walls, the stone floor was dark grey, and Revas had saved scraps of dyed leather to make into colourful rugs and cushions for the chairs. There were no windows: there was no point. There was never enough light for windows to make any difference, and they would have let a lot of warmth escape.

In the middle of the main room was a fireplace: the chimney above it was also an oven, and above that was the smoking cupboard, where Revas hung salted meat and fish to preserve it. A clepsydra – a clock that worked by water trickling over the mechanism – hung on the wall. It was made from filigree silver hung with sapphires, like Revas's orbal lanterns, and was divided into the twenty hours of the Clandoi day.

Solly's bedchamber was big enough to hold his feather-stuffed bed and a shelf, no more. On the shelf was the lock of hair that Lalune had given him when she said goodbye. Revas had given him a leather pouch to keep it in. The bed coverings were made of the thick blue-grey fur of blue poleys. Revas and Brise shared a room that was only slightly bigger, and their furs were the white skins of giant poleys.

Other chambers contained clothes, weapons, tools, and any goods they had made to sell. When Revas wasn't at work, she spent most of her time making clothing from fur and leather, necklaces from bone and teeth, and weapons for Brise to hunt with; and since Solly wasn't allowed to hunt, he often helped her. At the moment there was a big table behind the chimney, spread with leather boots and ornate combs they were making from the skin and bones of a snobrella, a white bird the size of a goose. They were one of the few Clandoi birds to have only one umbrella-shaped wing, instead of three, like a helicopter. They weren't at all common in Twilight, and though Appaloosians mostly wore synthetics, many would pay a lot of blackstone for snobrella-wing boots. They were monogamous birds, fiercely protective of their own; Brise had hunted for its mate too, though he'd never found it. Quite besides its value, a lone snobrella could be a danger to humans.

The only other chamber in the house held nothing but a chair and a small round table with a curious dip in the centre.

Aube and Revas helped Solly out of his outdoor clothes and sat him down at the table. Revas lit an orbal lantern.

'Aube, could you boil some water, please, and bring me the green box from the cupboard over there,' she said, unwrapping Solly's bandage. His arm had puffed up and was beginning to show a delightful array of colours.

'This finger: does it hurt?' she asked him, touching one of his fingers, which was sticking out oddly.

Solly gave a screech of pain.

'And what about when I do this? . . . And this?'

'Don't keep touching it, Ma,' gasped Solly. 'It *all* hurts. Just make it stop hurting.'

'What I really need is to have a look inside.'

Solly shrieked again.

'Don't cut me open, Ma!'

Revas laughed.

'I need an X-ray, silly. Look, I'll put a bandage on it for now, and I'll try to smuggle you into the cyberclinic tomorrow and have a proper look.'

'Hmm. Are there no doctors?' asked Aube.

Solly gave a grim laugh.

'Not for us Wayfarers.'

'Tache and I look after the Wayfarers,' explained Revas, unrolling a clean bandage. 'All the Appaloosian doctors entered the cyberclinic months ago. They bring one in if one of the Sleepers needs one, but we have to look after ourselves.'

She started to bind Solly's hand carefully.

'Why would the Sleepers need anything done?' asked Solly. 'I thought the Bubblenet did everything for them. Ow, Ma: be careful.'

'Maybe they just come in to check the equipment.'

'I heard rumours about this cyberclinic, even as far

41

away as Worldsend,' said Aube. 'Tell me – what exactly happens there?'

Solly gritted his teeth as his mother tied off the bandage.

'Some Pelegian guy invented it because of the food shortages. It's for the Appaloosians, not for us. It's supposed to freeze 'em in some oil – orbal oil, I think, and while they're all in there waiting for the ice to go away and for somebody to invent a way for us all to eat *air* or whatever, they're all being turned into supergeniuses. They're connected to the Bubblenet and all the information on there's being downloaded into their brains.'

'There you are,' said Revas, getting up. 'You're all done.'

'Hmm. And how long are they to be in there?' asked Aube, wriggling his eyebrows and staring intently at Solly.

Solly turned his head away from the light. A memory suddenly popped disconcertingly into his head: Toayef, Lalune's mother, had been ill, and her father had taken Solly and Lalune with him to a remote farmhouse where he had to collect taxes. They had travelled by snow skimmer, and he remembered Lalune's hat flying off and her long curls streaming out in the wind, her cheeks pink, her dark-blue eyes sparkling, the star-pupils dancing. He was mortified to find his eyes filling again. *It's the concussion*, he told himself. He squeezed his eyes shut tight and tried not to think about her.

'Might as well be for ever,' he growled, and sniffed.

'Nobody knows,' said Revas, pouring hot water over herbs to make tea. 'When the climate changes and we can grow crops again. Could be ten years, twenty, a hundred.'

Solly suddenly swept a pile of combs off the table.

'It's not fair!' he shouted. He lurched up from the table and leaned his head on his arm against the wall. 'It's not damny fair!' he repeated, his shoulders shaking.

Revas finished making the tea and began picking up the combs silently. Aube observed them both thoughtfully. After a while, Solly wiped his eyes on his sleeve and picked up the last of the combs.

'Sorry, Ma,' he grunted. He gulped his hot sweet tea thirstily, without looking at anyone.

'You'll stay and eat?' Revas said to Aube.

'Hmm. That would be most welcome, my dear,' said Aube, 'especially since somebody broke my pudgia trap.'

'Why don't you visit Lalune, Solly?' said Revas. 'It's not as if you'll be any use helping me.'

'You can visit Lalune?' asked Aube in surprise. 'And there I was thinking she's all frozen.'

'She is,' said Solly, getting up from the table. He limped over to the little alcove that held the table and chair. 'Bring a chair. I'll show you.'

Taking the silver pendant from around his neck, he held it over the dip in the table for a moment before dropping it in. Immediately, a large pearly bubble sprang out from it, glowing with a silvery sheen. Sparks of light zigzagged across its surface and indistinct shapes started to appear. When they reached the surface Solly said, 'I've just got to focus it: this bubblescreen's *ancient*.'

He placed both hands on the sides of the bubble and gently manipulated it until he could see a cartoon-like face clearly at the top.

'Welcome to the Bubblenet,' it said blandly. 'My name

is Kenet. When you need assistance, please say my name, or simply ask a question.'

'Take me to Tuef Lalune Seventeen, Cyberclinic, Opita, Twilight,' he said. 'Tuef's her official Appaloosian name,' he explained to Aube over his shoulder. 'If you just ask for Lalune they don't recognize it, because it's Wayfarer.'

The animated Bubblenet helper bowed; and after a few moments of confusion, during which colours swirled across the bubble, a three-dimensional figure appeared. It was blurred, but undoubtedly it was Lalune, lying in her glass pod.

She could have been dead.

'You can leave messages for her and see what she's dreaming about.'

'Gracious heavens above,' said Aube. 'And you can visit anybody you like by this method?'

'Yes,' said Solly listlessly. 'Only this is it. It's not like you can *talk* to them or anything. Here, you have a go. I'm tired.'

He slipped out of his seat and hobbled back into the main room. Revas looked at him and felt his forehead.

'Bed, I think,' she said. 'I'll bring you some soup and something to help you sleep. You're going to be in pain tonight.'

Solly allowed himself to be undressed.

'When's Pa coming home?' he asked.

'In a few days,' said Revas soothingly. 'Now you be quiet and get some rest.'

12

When Lalune and Solly were ten some traders arrived and there was a fair. Father wanted to take her with him when he went to collect the taxes from the traders, and her mother must have been in a good mood as she agreed.

In her pod, a little smile hovers around Lalune's mouth, and she sinks down into this memory deliciously. She turns on to her side and her pulse once again becomes dangerously slow.

They met Solly there with his ma and pa, and father bought her a little pair of boots from Revas. They were made of soft blue poley leather, lined with fur and covered in little coloured beads that clicked together when she walked.

—The beads are made from bones, Solly told her ghoulishly.

She didn't believe him. Who would? The idea was gross. Solly laughed and threw a snowball at her . . .

And because she is dreaming it flies in slow motion, and when it hits her it is warm and soft, and soon they are chasing each other around the fair, their feet not touching the ground, their voices sounding distant, because she is watching the pair of them from above.

People stopped what they were doing because it was so rare to see children any more. One of the traders had a stall selling hot herbal tea and he gave them some for free, sweetened with berry juice. They found a bench and sipped it together while they got their breath back. Steam from the drinks swirled around their faces, and somebody was playing a flute.

—I'll have to go soon, when father has finished his business, she said.

—One day we'll get married, Solly said, then you'll never have to leave ever again.

She laughed indulgently because Appaloosians never marry Wayfarers, but she didn't tell him this.

Father brought them some fluffy pink stuff on plastic sticks.

—Candyfloss, he said. —Ever seen it before?

Neither of them had. She buried her mouth in it. It was warm and gooey and grainy between her teeth, and little strands of it floated around her mouth as she chewed.

—It's almost as nice as toffee, says Solly.

He had pink all round his mouth and was so sticky that she couldn't help laughing, and when she had finished she jumped off the bench and hugged him goodbye, and she trotted home to show her mother her new boots, and her mother wrinkled her nose and the next day she couldn't find them and her mother said they'll turn up, but they never did, so her mother replaced them with some Appaloosian ones decorated with real wooden buttons . . .

And Lalune winces as a sudden rush of stimulants pours into her veins, because she must not die, she is necessary, and her heart beats faster and her mind becomes more and more aware of the world outside her pod . . .

13

Solly slept badly and woke early to find that Aube had left some time in the night. Feeling ghastly still, he gulped down some tea. He didn't feel like eating. Revas helped him to dress.

They left for the cyberclinic before day broke, using the back ways through the Wayfarer houses where there was less danger of being spotted by a WASP. There was one panicky moment when Revas pulled him into a doorway, thinking they'd been seen, but it was just the guards being changed.

Revas worked as a cleaner in the cyberclinic. It was one of the few jobs that Wayfarers could get. At fifteen, Solly should have been working too, preferably as a hunter like his father, but a recent Edict had announced that all such matters went before the Board of Sanctions and Permits. On his last application, Solly's lack of experience had disqualified him: the time before that there apparently had been no need for more hunters, and before that they'd claimed he was still too young.

How he was supposed to get the necessary experience nobody could tell him.

Revas smuggled Solly into the cloakroom, where

they took off their outdoor clothing and found her cleaning trolley.

'I'm going to have to think of a way to get you to the X-ray unit,' she whispered. 'It's in the operating wing, but they've closed that down. Get in the trolley: there are WASPs everywhere.'

The trolley was a sort of mobile cupboard with a bin at one end and a broom clipped to one side. Revas took most of her cleaning equipment out of the cupboard and removed the shelf. There was just enough room for Solly to squeeze in, though the door wouldn't shut properly. He held on to it tightly and felt a slight jolt as Revas started to push.

They glided out of the cloakroom and into a gloomy corridor. The overhead lights flickered dimly through the crack in the trolley door. Solly caught an occasional glimpse of the glass pods they were passing. The Sleepers inside were sometimes turned away from them, sometimes curled up in their sleep, and sometimes lying with their eyes open, the star-pupils dilated and unseeing. At least, he hoped they couldn't see. He pressed himself further back into the trolley just in case.

After a while Solly heard the high-pitched whine of a WASP as it flew down the corridor. He stayed absolutely still. He had no idea how the things knew you were there; if it was body heat he would be found out for sure: he was burning hot. Revas turned the trolley to one side and pushed the door end up against something, perhaps because she knew that it couldn't detect him like that. He heard the rustle of her overalls as she pulled out her pendant for the WASP to scan, and sighed with

relief as it whirred off again. He peered out of the trolley
– and gasped.

Lalune was floating only a hand's width away from
him. Her beautiful Appaloosian skin was like dark
chocolate on the backs of her hands and round her
hairline, and as pale as milk on her face. One arm was
stretched out towards him, and he could see the blue
veins in her wrists. She could have been sleeping: he felt
he only had to touch her and she would wake up, and
everything would be all right again.

But those days were gone, never to return.

'She's not dead, darling, remember that,' said Revas
gently, seeing where he was looking. 'She still has a life to
live. One day.'

'But mine has ended,' said Solly bleakly, and thought:
She was my only friend and they took her away from me.

'Look,' said Revas, 'this lightbulb has blown. The
storeroom is in the operating wing: they'll have to let me
to get a new one. We've found our way in.'

Solly squashed himself back into the trolley and Revas
hurried him into the elevator. They went up a floor and
walked along another corridor. Revas knocked at a door.

'Come!'

She opened the door, leaving the trolley outside.
Through the crack in the cupboard door Solly could see
the glow of a bubblescreen. A fat Appaloosian woman
with grey-and-brown skin was talking into it. Solly felt a
familiar dislike. This was the woman who'd turned him
down for a hunter's licence.

'Reference number?'

The woman nodded curtly at Revas.

'Twelve B(M) Nineteen? . . . It's rare for your own to be unavailable . . . Ah, I see: well, under those circumstances we would try to find a close match . . . Yes, we have ten thousand to choose from – ha, ha . . . Yes, I shall be in touch.'

She touched the screen, deflating it, and looked at Revas suspiciously.

'Yes?'

'Begging your benefaction, Administrator Forcyef Eleven–oh–three . . .'

'Granted.'

'One of the lights has gone in Sleeper Unit Level One. Might I have a key to the store cupboard?'

Forcyef looked annoyed.

'I don't have time to go running about opening cupboards for people all day.'

'If you gave me the key, Administrator, I could bring it straight back.'

Forcyef smiled at Revas nastily.

'Yes, I'm sure you would love to have the key, Cleaner Revas,' she said, 'so that you could help yourself to the stores. But I'm afraid that the Edicts dictate that only personnel of Grade Seven or above should have access to governmental property, and that includes the store cupboard. I myself am Grade Eight. And you are . . . Oh, I forgot: you haven't even got a grade, have you? Cleaners don't, do they?'

She got up and waddled to the door.

'I shall open it myself, *Cleaner* Revas,' she said. 'I shall be able to keep an eye on you that way.'

How will we ever get to the X-ray machine now? thought

Solly in despair, his head pounding.

Forcyef led the way swiftly down the corridor. Revas found it hard to keep up, what with Solly's weight in the trolley and having shorter legs. Appaloosians were a lot taller than Wayfarers. Solly cursed Administrator Forcyef silently.

Forcyef was wearing a large keyring at her waist, with a gleaming bunch of egg-shaped keys. Each one was a different size and colour, and contained computerized information to open the doors and cupboards. From Solly's position, she looked as if she had some crazy plant growing out of her hip. She pushed a button on the door to the operating wing and a drawer slid out. She selected an insignificant-looking bronze key and dropped it into a dip in the drawer. The door whispered open and shut again when they had walked through.

Solly shivered despite his fever. It was cold in this wing. The electricity had been off for a long time.

Forcyef lit an orbal lantern. The corridor was long and wide, with doors on either side every few paces: she walked halfway down and unlocked a large storeroom. Revas entered.

'Come on, Cleaner, hurry up,' barked Forcyef.

Solly had to turn his head so that the Administrator wouldn't see his breath condensing in the cold air.

'I'm sorry, Administrator; I can't find the proper lightbulbs,' said Revas, her voice muffled. 'We're supposed to put special dim ones in the corridors, so that the Sleepers don't get too much stimulation—'

'Stop making excuses,' snapped Forcyef. 'Just pick up any old lightbulb and get out of there.'

Revas picked up a box and came out, her face pink and angry.

When they got back to the door of the operation wing Revas swung her hips so that her skirt caught on something. Solly saw her lean over to free it, and as she did so, slip the plastic packaging from the lightbulb into the doorframe. When the door shut behind them it didn't shut completely, and Forcyef didn't notice. Solly grinned. *Clever Ma.*

Forcyef led the way to Level One.

'There really is no need for you to—' began Revas.

'I know when you are up to something, Cleaner Revas,' interrupted Forcyef.

She watched Revas remove the faulty bulb, and snatched it from her. Revas screwed the new bulb in. Solly's trolley was pushed right up against the pod again so that he had a clear view of Lalune's face.

When the bright new lightbulb was switched on she flinched.

'Well, it seems to be in order this time,' Forcyef was saying with a scowl. She leaned up close to Revas and hissed maliciously in her face, 'Has that boy of yours got himself a job yet, Cleaner Revas?' before stalking away.

Solly clenched his jaw.

'Indebted by your clemency, Administrator,' Revas called after her. 'I shall have to clean this passage now,' she muttered. 'She's bound to check up on me.'

Lalune was trembling, sending little ripples through the gel. Her foot was tapping against the side of her pod.

'Ma, look at Lalune,' whispered Solly. 'I think there's something wrong with her.'

'It's the light,' Revas said anxiously. 'She's over-stimulated. I don't know what I can do for her without finding a better lightbulb. Look, I'll push you back to the operating wing, but I have to come back here. Will you be all right on your own? I wedged the door open, did you see?'

She pushed him back as far as the operating wing before hurrying back to Lalune's corridor. Solly removed the packaging Revas had slipped into the doorframe, went in, and lay down on the floor – which felt wonderfully cool against his feverish body.

He seemed to wait for ages. WASPs whined passed at intervals. He prayed that they couldn't see through doors.

His head felt like it was about to burst and his arm throbbed. He wanted to doze off, but didn't dare in case Revas arrived and he didn't hear her.

At last he heard somebody at the door and got up to open it.

But it couldn't possibly be his mother.

Because whoever it was had a key.

14

Lalune's invigorated heart is pounding. *Ba-boom, ba-boom.*
Somebody somewhere doesn't want her to die.

Her body is working far too hard. Her awareness of it
competes with her memories.

—*Seventy-eight per cent of five hundred and four? Father is
saying in her dream.*

—*Three hundred and eight-three point twelve? she hazards,
trying to ignore the rushing of blood around her body.*

*He shook his head and glanced hesitatingly behind her, where
her mother was braiding gold beads into her hair so tightly that
tears stung her eyes.*

In this dream she is older, much older, and it is more
recollection than dream. The drugs are rushing her on
and on through it at double speed.

*Her mother's feet were tapping restlessly. She was waiting for
some important news and had no time for patience.*

Lalune's foot is tapping the side of her pod.

—*And ninety-three point twelve?*

—*Good. Now, then, twenty-four per cent of two hundred
and fifty-nine?*

*This time she had nearly worked it out when her mother
pulled her hair, and she yelped.*

—*I was doing mathematics like that in my head at half your*

54

age, her mother said, slathering her hair with mousse to tame it.

—Sixty . . . sixty-two point one six.

—Good. Now then . . .

The bubblescreen beeped in another room and her mother leaped to her feet to answer. In a moment she would be back in, beautiful and exultant, waving her arms, unable to stand still, brimful of the news that would take away Lalune's life. But that was still a few precious minutes away, and for now Lalune sagged against the table, loosened her hair where her mother had pulled it too tight.

Her heart is still beating hard, but not in her dream. She is very aware of her body's agitation, and she turns herself over restlessly in her pod.

She is far younger than anybody else in the cyberclinic, and the Bubblenet is having trouble adjusting her drugs correctly.

—Have another look at the equation, moon-girl.

She stood behind father and looked over his shoulder obediently.

—I disappoint her. I'm sorry.

—No. No, of course not, he said, too hastily. —She just . . . well . . . you know . . .

—I do try.

—Obviously not going to be a tax official when you're older, are you? He grinned, trying to cheer her up.

—Or a technician like mother, she said ruefully. —I'm better with words.

—Sadly there are few jobs that use words.

—No. We have no stories to tell, like the Wayfarers, she said. —Why don't we, do you think?

—Stories are to explain things, he said. —We have nothing

to explain, no history, each day is the same over again. There is no need for stories.

—*I should like to write stories. I would write down what happens on each day, to see just how much each day is the same.*

—*Don't let your mother hear you say that sort of thing,* he warned her.

—*I won't, she said, and her heart pounded . . .*

But she will not die, not yet . . .

And her dream whisks her back a year, and into the snowcamel barn. *She was trying to make Solly tell her the Wayfarer stories. She shivered in her expensive synthetic coat, and he lent her his because it was not work, raking straw and dung. And when she got home it was late, and there was straw in her hair, and her mother cried as if she'd been betrayed, which is somehow worse than if she had slapped her . . .*

—Now she's ruined everything, everything . . .

15

Quickly, Solly chose the nearest door and shut it behind him. He seemed to be in an old scrubbing-up room. There was a large sink, a row of dusty operating gowns, and some swing doors.

But the door began to open. There was nowhere to hide in here. Solly went through the swing doors. He was in an operating theatre. He had seconds to find a hiding place. He looked around wildly. There was a large bin next to a cabinet. Another row of gowns hung above it. He sat down behind the bin and pulled a gown over his face.

He had a tiny slit to see through. Somebody backed into the room, pulling something after them. Several more people came in too.

'How long will it take, Dr Dollysheep?' asked a voice. Solly recognized it: it was Forcyef.

'About half an hour,' replied another voice — male this time, with an unusual, nasal accent.

'It's not as if we have to worry about anaesthetic or aftercare . . .' said Forcyef with a laugh that sent a shiver down Solly's spine. Half an hour? His mother was bound to come back before then, and then . . .

'We *will* need anaesthetic,' said the doctor. 'Otherwise

they go into shock, and that doesn't do the components any good.'

'You're the doctor.'

The people were very busy round whatever it was they'd brought in with them. Solly couldn't see much. He heard a hiss, like a lid being taken off a vacuum flask. Voices murmured: he could only catch some of the words.

'No, leave it under . . . keep the temperature constant, please . . . hold the light steady . . .'

They were using an orbal lantern, which was lucky for Solly, as it left him in shadow. The pain in his arm was torturous. His bottom started to ache on the cold floor. What was taking them so long? He tried not to imagine what would happen when his mother walked in.

Somebody dumped a large plastic box down right next to him, startling him. He held his breath so they wouldn't hear him breathing. Then he realized that sooner or later he'd have to let it go, and that would be even noisier, so he let it out again slowly.

He peeped out. The people were still there, but they were laughing and the atmosphere had changed. Obviously the difficult bit of what they were doing was over.

Somebody asked a question, which Solly didn't hear.

'No, it can be deleted,' replied Forcyef.

'No, there is still some usable material,' objected the doctor in a sombre voice. 'Besides, I prefer to sew them up again afterwards.'

'Really, Dollysheep: your compassion is rather misplaced,' said Administrator Forcyef snidely.

'I can't use them for research if I don't,' explained the doctor. 'Or teaching. Sew it up, please, somebody.' He walked right over to where Solly was hiding, and started to strip off his gloves and apron and drop them into the bin. Solly shut his eyes just as he used to as a toddler, believing that it would make him invisible. He was so hot now he was afraid that the doctor would feel the heat from his body. There was some more fuss around the table, and other people in the room came over to the bin. He could smell blood. Somebody kicked the bin accidentally and it jolted his arm. He bit his lip hard to stop from crying out.

Then he felt the gown he was hiding under moving to one side.

'We ought to get the cleaners in here,' said a voice. 'Look at these things – filthy!'

Sweat dribbled down his face. He was just wondering whether they'd be too surprised to chase him if he jumped out now and ran for it, when Forcyef said, 'I'll see to it later. Don't really want any Waifs poking round in here. Had one in earlier for the store cupboard as it was.'

The gown was dropped once more. Somebody picked up the plastic box and everybody left the room.

Solly sighed – very quietly – with relief. He heard them for a while washing in the next room, then the door opened and shut again. He stayed where he was, listening for any noise that might show that somebody was still there, but there was none. Very cautiously he got up, tiptoed to the door, and slipped back out into the corridor. He went back to the main door and opened it just a crack. There was nobody waiting in the passageway. He stood next to the door, wondering what to do.

16

Pain becomes Lalune's focus. It forces through her closed eyelids and into her brain.

Help me . . . she thinks silently.

But there is nobody to hear her.

She is in distress. To stay within safe limits she must be neither too conscious nor too unconscious; neither too warm nor too cool; the lights must be neither too bright nor too dim. She has already once become dangerously close to slipping too far into her coma, and her system is awash with correcting drugs. Now the bright light is making her terrifyingly aware of the world outside her pod.

Please help . . .

Sounds enter her consciousness. The hum of a floor polisher. Footsteps up and down the corridor. The wires going in and out of her body. The feel of the orbal oil on her skin. The beating of her heart.

She shifts uneasily in her pod. Messages are conveyed to the Bubblenet. The drugs dripping into her are changed once more.

But the change will be gradual, over several days, and she is still too stimulated.

. . . Somebody . . .

17

After about ten minutes Solly heard a scratch on the door. He opened it, and Revas crept in and gave him a hug.

'There were people here,' he whispered as she lit a lantern and led him down the gloomy passage.

'I saw them,' said Revas, opening a door. Solly saw dusty medical equipment and an examination couch. 'Lie down here. What were they doing?'

While Revas got him ready for the X-ray, Solly told her what he'd seen and heard.

'I didn't know this place was used any more,' said Revas. 'Perhaps one of the huissier needed an emergency operation.'

'But why wouldn't they want the cleaners to come in and clear up after them?' asked Solly.

Revas shrugged.

'I have no idea,' she said. 'Now, I've got to leave you alone for a few minutes to turn the power on. There's no electricity in this wing at the moment.'

She left the room, taking the lantern with her. Solly lay back and waited in the dark. Even lying down his head was spinning. After a few minutes the main light blinked suddenly, hurting his eyes. Blue lightning

crackled over everything before disappearing into a
bubblescreen table.

18

Blue lightning snapped through the Bubblenet.

Pain convulses Lalune's body, tormenting every blood vessel. She writhes, opens her mouth, but there is no air in her lungs, only orbal oil. She tries to escape the agony.

Is there nowhere she can go, nobody she can alert?

With a terrible surge of clarity she knows that she will die very soon unless she herself does something.

There is no time to think. Lalune flings herself into a wire. Quick as thought, she flies to the central bubblescreen, finds her file and forces the correcting drugs into her body.

19

'I hope nobody noticed that,' said Revas nervously when she returned. 'Caused quite a power surge. Now, darling, lie back and relax.'

Revas took several X-rays of his arm, and also of his head and ankle, just to be sure. She turned off the power again and went to develop the films. Solly dozed off.

After a long while, Revas returned and Solly woke up, feeling dazed.

'No wonder you're feverish,' she said. 'The break's infected. You must be in a lot of pain. I'm going to have to get somebody to come and help me to set it. And I am going to have to cut you open, I'm afraid.'

Solly whimpered.

'Will it hurt?'

'There's still some medicines here. I've borrowed something to put you to sleep, and some antibiotics too, in case my herbs don't help.'

Solly got back into the trolley, feeling very sorry for himself. Revas rolled up the X-rays and gave them to him to hold. She pushed him out of the operating wing and into the nearest elevator.

'I'm supposed to be cleaning the elevators today,' she

told him in an undertone as she got out cloths and cleaning stuff. 'If somebody comes in here I want to be caught at my job, otherwise I'll be fined. Remember the WASPs: don't get out of the trolley until we get back to the cloakroom, just in case.'

She sprayed some cleaner on to the mirrored walls and began cleaning them.

Suddenly the elevator jolted and began to move.

'It's just somebody needing the elevator,' whispered Revas, shoving Solly's end of the trolley against a wall.

The elevator jerked to a halt. The door slid open.

'Ah, Cleaner Revas, not finished yet?' said a sarcastic voice. It was Administrator Forcyef. Solly balled his good fist.

'Begging your benefaction, Administrator, doctor, but I've nearly finished,' said Revas politely. 'Would you like me to leave so that you can all get in?'

'No, it was you we wanted to see,' said Forcyef, in what Solly thought was a very self-satisfied voice. 'This is the one, doctor.'

Solly froze in fear. They'd been caught!

'Cleaner Revas?' said another voice. Solly recognized it. It was the doctor from the operating room.

'Yes, doctor.'

'I believe you changed one of the lightbulbs on Level One today?'

'Yes, doctor.'

'You used a hundred watt bulb. Regulations clearly state that fifteen watts is the maximum.'

Solly's rage was so hot he felt dizzy. Forcyef had done it on purpose! She'd lied! He wanted to get out of his hiding place and smash her smug grin down her smug throat.

'I am sorry, sir, but I did try to tell—'

'I'm afraid "sorry" is not enough, Cleaner Revas,' said Forcyef smoothly. 'You could have caused serious harm to our patients.'

'It was only through the vigilance of Administrator Forcyef that your error was noticed,' continued the doctor.

'I shall fine you this time, Cleaner Revas,' said the Administrator. 'But regard this as a final warning. One more slip-up and you will lose your job.'

'Yes, Administrator,' said Revas dismally. 'I am indebted by your clemency.'

They left the elevator. Revas finished her cleaning in silence before trundling Solly back to the cloakroom.

'Indebted by her clemency!' he burst out. 'She set you up! How could you let her, Ma?'

'How could I not let her?' she said quietly, though Solly could see that she too was fuming. 'I need this job. Administrator Forcyef could sack me any time she wants, for any reason, including accusing her of negligence, or sabotage, or whatever. Put your boots on, let's go home.'

'How much will they fine you?'

'Probably ten days' wages.'

They couldn't afford it, Solly knew. Revas tied his boots on for him and helped him into his coat.

20

Lalune tried to scream: *What have I done?*

Tried but failed. She couldn't make a noise. She couldn't control her voice.

She was no longer part of her body.

She had left it; she could see it lying in its pod.

Don't be so devilly stupid, you damny useless girl. How can you not be part of your body?

But she wasn't. If she had been, she could have shut her eyes, taken a deep breath, and looked again, more calmly this time.

As it was, she could only look, and try to work out where she was.

I'm inside the monitor, she thought fearfully. *I'm inside the monitor, looking out. I have to get back. I have to get back.*

She blundered about; and after what seemed like hours but was actually only a few minutes, she managed to find her way back into her physical body. Terrified, she forced herself to lie still and quiet, trying to convince herself that this was normal. But she could tell that she and her body, though they occupied the same space, had somehow become detached.

Thoughts tumbled around in her mind.

What have I done?

I was afraid because . . . because I was dying. The Bubblenet wasn't adjusting my drugs quickly enough, so I left my body to do it myself. I didn't even think about it. I just did it.

What if I'd never been able to get back?

I could've died.

But I didn't. I'm still alive.

I'm also conscious.

Then . . . *I wonder if I could do it again?*

Even as Lalune was thinking it she found herself back in the monitor. This time it wasn't nearly so scary. This time she knew she could get back.

It's the power of my thoughts! I left my body by just thinking about it!

She did it again a few times, keeping a close eye on her monitor just in case her heartbeat sped up or her blood pressure rose, or anything else nasty happened – but nothing changed. She was all right.

She remembered the terror she'd felt in the pit of her stomach when her mother had told them that they had been accepted for the cyberclinic. She'd imagined something like death.

No: worse than death.

But this didn't feel like death.

Perhaps this was all part of the cyberclinic experience. Nobody had said anything about this, but then none of the doctors had been in the cyberclinic themselves. They probably didn't know. This was probably happening to everybody so that they could learn from the mind-knowledge more efficiently. Appaloosians were into efficiency.

Or maybe this was part of the waking up at the end:

she was waking up from the inside out, and her body would follow on soon.

Except that I'm not in my body. I wonder what part of me this is — my consciousness?

What am I when my body sleeps?

Perhaps it's my soul?

She liked that thought. Appaloosians have no soul. Everybody knew that — even Wayfarers, and they were the ones with all the really weird beliefs. But Wayfarers had souls, part of themselves that would live on after they died. Her body wasn't exactly dead, but she was definitely living without it.

It's a bit bizarre, though, being a soul without a body, she thought. *There's no* me *to look at. It's like there are places where the hands of my soul should be. I feel like I can hold them up in front of where my eyes should be and see them . . .*

Suddenly she could see them.

I can see my soul!

Lalune shut her soul's new eyes for a moment, then opened them again.

She was still there. She hadn't disappeared.

She held both hands up. They looked as if they were made of light. She could see them and see through them at the same time. She could even see inside them: there were her bones, there was translucent blue blood pulsing through her veins. As she stared closer and closer, her eyes magnified what she could see as if she was looking down a microscope. She could see hair follicles, skin cells, blood cells.

She looked down at her body. It was all there, clothed in the silvery tunic her mother had chosen.

She had wanted black.

Her thought rippled through the material, and now it was black.

Can I feel? she wondered, and immediately began to sense a steady breeze blowing over and through her. It was a few moments before she realized that it wasn't air that she could feel, but light. It was flowing in streamers from her hands and arms, and she could feel tiny prickles as minute particles rushed past her and round her and through her. She sniffed, and smelled hot wires and plastic: she stuck her tongue out and tasted metal. She laughed, and jumped: this time she could hear her own voice, echoing strangely in the . . .

In the where, exactly? Apart from her body, she could see nothing.

And as soon as the thought entered her she *could* see suddenly. She was inside some sort of ball. The walls were darkly iridescent and honeycombed with small round holes.

'What is this place?' she wondered out loud; and then screamed in terror as a voice spoke out of nowhere.

'Welcome to the Bubblenet.'

21

Revas asked Tache's wife, Lumie, to help her operate on Solly's hand.

He was ill for several days afterwards. Occasionally he would half wake up and find either Revas or Lumie sitting by his bedside, and he would swallow some tea or weak soup before slipping into delirium again.

Then one day he woke up properly, feeling as if he had been on a long journey. His bed had been moved into the main room. Revas, looking weary and grey, was fast asleep in a chair next to him with her head on his pillow. Solly sat up gingerly. His arm had been bandaged with a broken spear for splints to keep it straight and still. The bit he could see looked bruised and shrunken. His head ached a little still, but his ankle appeared to be better. He felt as if he hadn't eaten for a month. He had certainly drunk though, because he was in desperate need of the privy. He tried to ease himself out of the bed without waking Revas, but when he put his weight on his legs they folded under him and he landed on the floor.

'Solly?' said his mother sleepily, then more urgently: 'Solly!'

'I needed to pee.'

'Solly, you're awake!' she cried, and to his

embarrassment burst into tears. She ran round to pick him up and hug him.

'There's a chamber pot under the bed,' she said after a while, pulling back from him and blowing her nose. 'I won't look.'

When he had finished, she brought him a bowl of warm water to wash in, and some soup.

'How long have I been ill?' he asked, swallowing the thin soup greedily.

'Days and days.'

'Is Pa back yet?'

'No. I expect they had to go further than they thought to find anything to hunt.'

'Any more soup?'

Revas poured him some.

'I shall have to see if I can't sell some of those combs and boots we made. We're nearly out of food.'

Something about the way she said it made Solly look at her sharply. Something was wrong.

'Did they fine you a lot at work?' he asked.

'Now, don't you worry about that—' she began, but he interrupted her.

'Ma, tell me.'

'Forty days' supply of blackstone and grain,' she said after a pause.

Such a wave of anger washed over Solly that his head span. The cleaners were paid in blackstone and grain. Blackstone was fuel: wood was scarce, and only hunters were allowed to use it to burn. The Appaloosians owned the blackstone mines, though it was the Wayfarers who went down them. And grain would not grow anywhere except Brume and Worldsend, the seed strictly regulated by Edicts. The Wayfarers were completely dependent on the Appaloosians for both.

'I swear, if I ever meet that damny woman . . .'

'Solly, there's no point in getting angry,' said Revas.

'But she's being so unfair . . .'

'Lie down, Solly.'

'I hate her, Ma. And so do you.'

'Yes, I do,' said Revas. 'But poisoning yourself with hatred will destroy you not her.'

Solly sat back, still raging.

'I didn't mean to fall asleep,' Revas said, yawning and glancing at the clepsydra clock. 'Lumie will be along shortly. I've asked her to eat here tonight. She's been very kindly looking after you while I've been at work.'

Working for no wages, Solly thought bitterly. He lay down and watched his mother tidying the room. The short conversation he'd had since waking had left him feeling utterly exhausted.

22

The shock sent Lalune's amazing soul body spinning into the side of the chamber, and dusky rainbows shimmered up and down and all around her.

'My name is Kenet,' continued the voice.

'Kenet,' said Lalune with a shaky laugh. 'Of course.'

Everybody knew Kenet. She was a two-dimensional animation designed to give minimum information and maximum annoyance. At least, that's what Threfem had always said, though he'd said it with a twinkle in his eye.

And now, here she was, face to face with Lalune.

'When you need assistance, please say my name, or simply ask a question.'

'I'm *inside* the Bubblenet?'

'Welcome to the Bubblenet,' said Kenet again, staring ahead glassily. Her voice was lifeless and had a strangely nasal accent. Her body was flat and not particularly well drawn. Her eyes were too big, and her nose was too small. She wasn't even Appaloosian: her skin was olive all over instead of being bitonal; her pupils were round, not star-shaped; her bobbed hair was straight and black, the pointed ends sticking out to one side absurdly. 'Would you like me to define "Bubblenet"?'

'No,' said Lalune peering into the opening next to her.

'Thank you.' It was the beginning of a long, undulating tunnel. Its walls were translucent, and through them she could see the gentle movement of other tunnels spiralling and swirling around each other in all directions. Her eyes magnified the tunnel; in the distance was another chamber exactly like the one she was in.

She looked into another opening. This tunnel was a short cul-de-sac with something familiar-looking in its centre.

'Hey, that's me!'

It was her pod. There was a string of light travelling into her head. Without being conscious of having moved, Lalune was suddenly near enough to see that it was made up of words.

'. . . *a large brown root, sometimes single, sometimes divided into three parts . . . decoction of the leaves opens obstructions of the liver or spleen . . .'*

'It's the mind-knowledge from the Bubblenet,' said Lalune, fascinated. Now that she recognized it, she could hear the words and see the pictures in her head as they were downloaded.

'Would you like me to define "mind-knowledge"?' said Kenet.

'No, thanks.'

Another line was travelling in the opposite direction: data about her physical well-being. Lalune followed it back into the main chamber and out again down a tunnel that came off it almost vertically downwards.

She was about to pursue it when she suddenly thought: *All the tunnels look exactly the same. Will I be able to find my way back?*

She looked around her chamber, remembering how she had first seen it was there. Before she had thought about it, it hadn't been there, not that she could see anyway. Neither had her body.

'Kenet, can I change the look of this chamber?'

'You can program your page to your own taste,' said Kenet. 'Would you like me to display some options?'

'No, I'd like to design it myself, thanks.'

Lalune shut her eyes and thought for a moment. If she could imagine the perfect place, what would it be like?

'Trees. I love trees. But no snow. And lots and lots of flowers: orange and yellow and white and red and blue.'

Lalune opened her eyes. The chamber was still ball-shaped, but the walls looked like living, growing trees, heavy with blossom, winding in and out of the openings. Except that it was all flat, like wallpaper. The flowers gave out such a strong fragrance that she sneezed.

Somewhere to sit would be good, she thought – and there was a chair in front of her. She went to sit down on it, but it kept drifting away from her. She concentrated for a moment, and managed to stick it in place, though it was upside down. It didn't seem to matter. *No gravity*, she thought.

'Now for my pod,' she said, and made the chair move towards the tunnel where her body lay. 'Green velvet, I think. And candlelight.'

She had seen candles occasionally in Solly's home, when they had run out of orbal oil for the lanterns. They smelled a little, being made of animal tallow, but she needn't have the smell here. She shut her eyes, concentrated, and when she opened them again her pod room was lined luxuriously in green, and lit by a flickering indistinct light that came from nowhere in particular. She giggled.

'I forgot the candles to go with the candlelight!'

The candles appeared.

'Kenet, is there a map to the Bubblenet?' she asked.

'There is no map to the Bubblenet,' said Kenet. Her voice was irritatingly impersonal. 'Just tell me where you would like to go, and I can take you there.'

'All the same, I'd like a map,' said Lalune. You always had to use exactly the right form of words with Kenet. 'Uh, show me what the Bubblenet looks like.'

A glowing orb spun into the space in front of her. In the centre was her pod, and the tunnels she had already looked down sprang out of it like tentacles. She put out her hand and the orb shrank into it.

She was ready to explore.

23

When Lumie arrived, Solly woke up again.

'Praise the Being: you're better,' she said, her wrinkled old face beaming. 'And today of all days. I've brought you just the thing.'

She rummaged in her bag and brought out a small something wrapped in bright foil.

'Open it,' she said with an encouraging nod. 'I got it from a trader a few months ago; a present for my grand-niece, over at Brume. But I don't suppose I shall see her a while, and your need is greater.'

Solly scrabbled awkwardly at the wrapping. His hands, like his legs, didn't seem to be working properly yet. Eventually he managed to peel the wrapper off.

'Oh, wow; thanks, Lumie.'

'What is it, Solly?' asked his mother.

He held it up for her to see.

'Toffee!'

Sugar was so expensive that Solly had not seen a toffee since he was six, when Lalune had had a large slab for her birthday. She'd shared it with him in the snowcamel's barn, and Toayef had been so angry when she found out that Lalune hadn't been allowed out for three days. Even though she'd allowed Threfem to give Lalune a Wayfarer name, Toayef was never happy with her associating with a Wayfarer child.

The toffee stick was about as long as his finger. Solly broke a bit off and chewed it blissfully. His mother smiled and rumpled his hair before going back to the meal she was preparing for herself and Lumie.

Solly lay back and watched drowsily. It was comforting having his bed in the main room. The sounds of Revas and Lumie talking in low voices, dishes clinking gently, the warmth of the room, and the trickling of water in the clepsydra all combined to soothe him into a half-dreaming state. He found himself inside the picture he had seen in Aube's cave, only he was the sun and Lalune was the blue moon. They were staring at something that Solly couldn't quite see. He was straining his eyes trying to make it out when the front door opened with a bang, jerking him awake again, and a huge man burst into the room.

'Pa!' cried Solly.

24

Lalune started to glide along the wires of the Bubblenet. It felt very odd. Everything she did was done by thought. She didn't have to move her legs, and the orb-map slid along without her having to hold on to it. And there was no gravity. She soon lost all sense of 'up' and 'down', and without the orb-map would soon have been lost.

She was full of the thrill of an explorer entering land never seen by human eyes. She couldn't look in enough places at once. There was so much to see, to feel, to hear to smell, and even to taste. But she had no need to sleep, and the days became like hours.

The most insignificant things fascinated her: she spent ages just examining light. The shorter wavelengths, like ultraviolet light, felt dense and syrupy, and tasted sweet: longer ones ware light, feathery and salty. Radio waves were like sliding on bitter-tasting wet silk.

Fantastic lights and sounds surrounded her. Rainbows dazzled her, both in front and behind; sounds resonated right through her. Worms made of pure darkness squirmed along the sides of the tunnel.

'This is amazing,' she shouted, though there was nobody else there. 'And it's all mine! I'm a queen!'

She stopped and imagined a bottle of sparkling

mead-wine into her hand. Holding it high above her head she said in a loud voice. 'I name this realm "Cybernation",' and smashed it against the wall. Splinters of glass and golden splashes of wine expanded outwards in slow motion, filling the tunnel before melting away.

She wished she could have shared the moment with Solly. *But he must have grown up years ago*, she thought despondently, imagining him out hunting, marrying somebody else, having children and grandchildren.

When we were little we promised to marry each other.

It was just a childish fantasy: she always knew that Toayef would have found her a more suitable husband.

Even if he was fifty years older than me. Which he would have to be, she thought wryly, *since there are no other children that I know of.*

Perhaps that's why she was so keen for us to enter the cyberclinic. To get me away from Solly. Well, it worked. Mother always gets her way.

Something whined past her at an incredible speed, breaking her out of her melancholy.

'What was that?'

'That was an electronic message,' said Kenet, making her jump by appearing suddenly beside her, quite unruffled by the breeze. 'Would you like to know how to send one?'

'No, thanks,' said Lalune. She had a better idea. When the next e-mail passed her she leaped on to it for a ride.

'Wheeee!' she yelled.

It was better than a snow skimmer, better than sledging, better than anything she had ever experienced

81

before in her life. She stood up and stretched her arms out on either side, and sang . . .

. . . and arrived in the message tray of a bubblescreen.

To Administrator Forcyef Eleven-oh-three, from Commander Toobe-ef Eighty-nine.

Somebody had been waiting for the message: it was opened immediately.

. . . received with approval the news that the first stage has been begun. The enthusiasm with which you planned and implemented the program has not gone unnoticed . . .

Could she be seen?

. . . approved your request for additional huissier . . .

Lalune hastily extinguished her new body.

. . . need for both speed and caution, as so large an influx will arouse natural suspicion . . .

Invisible once more, Lalune began to look for a way out of the strange bubblescreen.

. . . essential that the next stage be carried out with absolute efficiency . . .

There was a tunnel opening right behind her. She emerged from it, recreated her body and returned to her pod, very shaken.

Solly would have loved that e-mail ride, she thought when she had recovered her composure. She tried to imagine him older, perhaps becoming the leader of the hunt, like his father. She tried not to imagine that perhaps he might be dead by now.

'I wonder what the date is,' she said out loud. Appaloosian minds found no difficulty coping with the fact of dates, even though there was no history. Today was, after all, yesterday rewritten: yesterday no longer existed.

'There is a calendar and a clock in your monitor,' said Kenet. 'Would you like to see them?'

'All right,' said Lalune, a little apprehensively. But when they appeared she stared blankly. 'No, that can't be right. Check it again.'

'The reading is correct,' said Kenet.

'But . . . but it can't be,' said Lalune.

'The Bubblenet clock is accurate to point zero zero zero one of a second,' said Kenet. 'It is checked regularly and precisely.'

'But . . . according to this, *I was only asleep for a few days.*'

25

Brise was just like Solly, but older and bigger. He had an untidy mass of fair hair, eyes as blue as if they'd been chipped out of a glacier, and the build of a snowcamel. Perhaps because he spent most of his time in the open air, he always seemed to fill any room he walked into to capacity.

He had taken off his outdoor boots, but still had on his coat and over-trousers.

'Oh, Brise, you've brought in half the snow on Clandoi!' scolded Revas, after she had hugged him tight.

Brise chuckled and allowed her to pull off his coat. Underneath he was wearing several necklaces of carved teeth and gleaming gems. Revas and Lumie gasped.

'Where did you get these from?' said Revas. 'They're beautiful!'

'Got caught in a blizzard for days,' he said. 'That's why we're so late back. We just sat in a cave, carving. Tache found the gems, Lumie, probably a trader's stash from decades ago. The bag they were in had nearly rotted away. He's got a bagful for you, too.'

Lumie gave a little breathless squeak.

'Tache! I must get home to him . . . do you mind?'

'Go, Lumie,' said Brise. 'But come back! There's

some feasting to be done.'

Lumie left. Brise took off a gorgeous purple necklace and slipped it over Revas's head.

'That one's for the most beautiful wife of any hunter I know. The rest you can sell. And for Solly . . .'

He glanced at Solly in his bed.

'What's happened to you?'

'Had an accident,' Solly said in a small voice. 'The Seer laid a pudgia trap. I got caught in it.'

At first Solly thought his father was angry. He pressed his lips together and turned his head away from him. Then he noticed that his shoulders were shaking. Revas's mouth started to quiver, and all of a sudden both of them were howling with laughter at his expense.

Solly wasn't sure whether to be relieved or offended.

'I wish I'd been there to see it!' gasped Brise. 'Hanging upside down, were you?'

Solly grimaced and nodded.

'I had to wait until Aube came to collect his dinner.'

'What a thing to come back to,' chuckled Brise. 'And on your birthday, too.'

'My birthday!' said Solly, astonished. He turned to Revas, who was looking sheepish. 'I didn't know I'd been ill that long. Why didn't you say?'

'I didn't know you were going to wake up today, or that Brise was going to come back. I had thought to save it for a while anyway, but as you're both back . . .'

She disappeared into her bedchamber and came back with a parcel wrapped in red plastic.

'Happy birthday, darling.'

'A present!' said Solly in genuine surprise. He knew

they couldn't really afford presents. He started to unwrap it clumsily. His fingers behaved as if they were made of rubber, and the splints got in the way, but at last he was able to tear off the last of the plastic and hold his gift up reverently. It looked like a long leather belt. It had a golden buckle in the shape of a sun, and a row of loops and pockets to hold hunting tools. The leather was soft and white, and had been burnished until it glowed.

'A hunter's bandoleer!' he breathed.

'Try it on then,' said Revas.

Solly pulled the belt over his head. Revas fetched a small mirror so that he could admire himself.

'Look at me! I'm a real hunter now! Thank you, both of you. It must have taken you for ever to make it.'

Revas tweaked the bandoleer straight, though it didn't need it.

'It's for next time you apply for that licence,' said Brise, as if his promise could actually make a difference. 'I have something else for you too. Can you manage to get yourself to the ice pit?'

'Can I?' Solly pushed his blankets away. It wasn't often that he got presents, and he'd already had toffee that day. Dear Lumie must have remembered what day it was, even if he hadn't. 'It's my arm I hurt,' he said, swinging his legs out of bed. 'And my head.'

Even so, he was still unsteady, and Brise had to prop him up.

'Shut your eyes,' said Brise, holding the curtain to the ice pit dramatically. 'Now, open.'

Solly opened them. Behind him he heard Revas catch her breath.

In front of him, filling the ice pit to overflowing, was a shimmering, iridescent leather hide.

'A snarg!' said Solly in awe. 'You caught a snarg!'

He stroked it reverently. Snargs were the largest, fiercest fish known on Clandoi. They had far more meat than any other fish, being so big; but it was the hide that was most precious. It was both thick and light, and had a beauty that never faded. But best of all were the scales that ran along the back. Deeply anchored in the skin, they were almost impossible to dislodge, making perfect armour for whoever wore them: important for any hunter, with all the dangerous animals he might have to face. If they were stroked in one direction, as Solly was doing now, they became sleek and smooth: but stroked the other way they stood out forty-five degrees, and sharp enough to cut.

'Not just one,' said Brise proudly. 'Three! Did you ever hear of that before? Three snargs on one hunt! And a giant poley! With Tache's gemstones, it was the most successful trip I can ever remember.'

'And it's cured already?' asked Revas.

'Not just cured,' said Brise, reaching under the topmost fold and pulling out a package. He gave it to Solly, who opened it with trembling hands.

'Snowskates! Oh, Pa! My old ones broke.'

Because of the scales, snowskates made of snarg hide let the wearer climb the steepest slopes easily and slide down them like the wind. Solly had never owned anything so precious. He found himself dropping to the floor with a plop.

Brise took out two enormous hunks of meat and handed them to Revas.

'Start roasting these, my love,' he said. 'We'll have the whole of the hunt turning up soon. Here's snarg meat, and a poley roast, and mubble caviar, and we'll have mead-wine. There'll be stories and poems, and you, my love, shall sing, and we'll even let Solly tell the story of how he fell into the Seer's trap.'

26

Lalune felt as if she had been winded.

'That means I've got a hundred years, maybe more, before they take me out of this place!'

A hundred years, completely on her own. She sank down on to the shimmering floor of the Bubblenet.

Surely she couldn't be the only one of the Sleepers who was awake? Perhaps she could make a few visits.

At least Solly will still be around, she thought suddenly, cheering up.

'Kenet, could you take me to Solly, Opita, Twilight, please?'

'Access to Human Component Solly, Opita, Twilight, is authorized,' said Kenet, and Lalune was taken there in an instant.

Solly's bubblescreen, however, was turned off, and by the look of it hadn't been used for a long time.

He's probably got his licence, she thought. *He's off catching pudgias and things. Forgotten me already. I can't say I blame him: it's not like he was expecting to ever see me again. But he's only visited me twice. Once when I first came in and once two days ago.*

He didn't even leave me a message. Lalune tried to ignore the hurt, and sighed. *A hundred years!*

'Perhaps I should look in on Father and Mother before I get too depressed. Kenet, take me to see Threfem Seventeen, please.'

'Access to Human Component Threfem Seventeen is authorized.'

It took no time at all to reach her father's pod. Lalune gazed down at him through his monitor. He looked calm and peaceful and – she shivered – *dead*.

'Hello, Father.'

Was it her imagination, or did he move slightly in response to her voice?

'It's me, Lalune.'

'*Lalune.*' His lips weren't moving, but it was his voice.

'Father!' she said joyfully. 'You're awake too . . .'

He ignored her.

'*Tuef Lalune Seventeen. Age fifteen Address: Opita, Twilight . . .*'

'Father?'

'*Occupation: not applicable, minor . . .*'

Lalune felt dismayed. He wasn't awake after all, just reciting information about her in response to her name.

'*Reasons for entering the clinic: to be with her family . . .*'

'Father, no, I want *you* with *me*,' cried Lalune, beating on the side of his pod. But neither her hands nor the pod were real, and they shattered into a million pixels: and he didn't wake up.

I bet Mother's awake, she thought despondently, guiltily hoping that she wasn't. *That would be just my luck. I'm not sure I could take a hundred years alone with her, and no escape. But Mother always gets what she wants.*

90

She changed her tunic back to silver, and even found herself brushing it down, as if it could possibly be dirty.

But she needn't have bothered. Her mother too was unconscious. Lalune leaned against the cold pod and whispered to herself.

'Why me? Why am I awake, and nobody else? Surely what had happened to me must have happened to others? I should search for them. Begin with this corridor until I find somebody. Yes, that's what I'll do.'

She started to look, calmly and methodically checking each patient. The whole of her floor took her nearly half a day, and she found nobody.

But that's only one level, she told herself. *There are nineteen more. There's got to be somebody.*

Afraid of missing Solly, she checked that he hadn't visited her while she'd been busy.

He hadn't.

She carried on looking. At the end of each corridor she checked on him again, and soon she was in a pattern: investigate one corridor for wakeful Sleepers; check on Solly: investigate a corridor; check on Solly.

A feeling of desperation knotted inside her stomach.

Solly never visited her, not even once. And nobody else showed the slightest sign of having been woken up.

She continued looking at the next level down, and the one after that. As she slowly descended deep into the bowels of the cyberclinic and she *still* found nobody, her search became more and more feverish.

She didn't need to sleep, so she couldn't be tired; but she began to make mistakes, forgetting where she'd got to, and missing people out; and she had to go back several times to recheck them.

But I've got time! she thought drearily. *I've got a hundred years to spare!*

And she carried on.

And on.

Several levels below her own she found an empty pod. She drifted round it, puzzled. She was sure she remembered her family being hurried over their decision to enter the cyberclinic due to a shortage of places. Surely they wouldn't have left empty pods like this?

She had no answer to that.

And where was Solly?

Lalune began to fill with self-pity and anger.

And fear.

'I can do practically anything I want to do, know anything I like, be anywhere within this world of wires and information that I choose to be,' she fumed desperately. 'I can make it all into whatever I fancy, then change it all in an instant. I thought I was queen of this world, this Cybernation; I'm much more than that: I am its god. But what is the point if I can't share it with anybody, and I can't make Solly come to me?

'And what about these empty pods?

'Damny Solly! I bet I could get back into a coma if I tried. Then he'll come along and find out that he missed me. That'd show him!'

She pushed the thought away immediately, but the longer time went on, the more it persisted.

A hundred years on my own. Wouldn't I be better off unconscious?

Half guiltily, half defiantly, Lalune began a different search: how to put herself back to sleep.

27

The Wayfarers were gathering. Everybody brought something to eat, and a song, poem or story to share.

They all seemed to know it was Solly's birthday, and soon his bed was piled with knives, jade spearheads, and even a miniature crossbow, to put in his bandoleer. He and Lalune were now both sixteen Clandoi years old, by which time most Wayfarers would have been working already.

He had never had so many presents in his life. He stammered out his thanks to each person, and everyone assured him that it was nothing, and that they were sure he'd soon be joining them.

Revas had made him a better splint out of the flat snarg bones, but he would still have to wait a while before he could take it off.

When everybody had helped themselves to an enormous plateful of meat and a flagon of mead-wine, the singing and storytelling began. Revas brought out her guitar, and a hunter named Soir had a flute, and Revas sang 'The First Wayfarer':

> *Two brothers together did journey away,*
> *Across stars and mountains a year and a day,*
> *But the time did come when they parted their way,*

And the Wayfarer went on.
And the Wayfarer went on.

He stopped for a rest, and more's the pity,
He was lulled to sleep by a mystical ditty,
And his brother took from him the Key to the City,
And the Wayfarer went on.
And the Wayfarer went on.

But when he discovered his loss 'twas too late,
He returned, and he beat his hands raw on the gate,
But to be the outsider was ever his fate,
So the Wayfarer walked on.
So the Wayfarer walked on.

The Key that divided brother from brother,
Shall one day unite them again with each other,
With the sun for a father and moon for a mother,
And the Wayfarer will return.
And the Wayfarer will return.

There were cheers and claps. Tache recited some ancient Wayfarer poems. Brise, who was a master storyteller, recounted the story of the recent hunt. And as promised, Solly got to tell of his adventure with the pudgia trap. He was beginning to get over his embarrassment: all the other Wayfarers seemed to find it as amusing as Revas and Brise had.

More mead-wine was poured out. More food was served. The guitar was passed around for others to play. Solly's bed was pushed back against the wall to clear a space for dancing.

As Solly gazed around the room, he was filled with a

sudden envy. The hunters were very kind, and were trying so hard to make him one of them: but he wasn't, and the way things were going he never would be.

He felt exhausted and was glad that he could lie down in his bed. Revas caught him yawning so hard that his jaw cracked.

'It's Lalune's birthday too. Why don't you go and leave her a message?' she whispered.

People were starting to break up into twos and threes to talk, and looked like they would stay around for another couple of hours. It would be a while before he had enough quiet to sleep. And he hadn't sent a message to Lalune since Aube's visit. He nodded.

His bed had been pushed so hard against the doorway to the bubblescreen chamber that the curtain covering the entrance looked like an extension of the wall, and he had the merest gap to squeeze through. Only the slightest chink of light leaked into the little chamber.

He booted up the bubblescreen.

'Welcome to the Bubblenet,' said Kenet as usual. 'My name is Kenet. When you need assistance, please say my name, or simply ask a question.'

'Take me to Tuef Lalune Seventeen, Cyberclinic, Opita, Twilight.'

There was the normal moment of chaos, and Lalune's face appeared on the screen. Solly was about to open his mouth to leave her a birthday message he knew she wouldn't hear for a hundred years, when the most unexpected thing happened.

'About time too!' she said.

28

Solly was so shocked that he fell off his chair. Lalune giggled. She looked as surprised to see him as he was to see her, but her face was also full of relief.

'Lalune!' he said, scrambling back up again. 'I thought you were . . . er . . . asleep.'

'I woke up,' she explained airily, as if waking up out of computerized hibernation was something that happened every other day. 'At least part of me did. My body's still there, in the cyberclinic.'

'But how? How long?' Solly went very red. 'I haven't visited you for ages . . .'

'Yes, I noticed.'

'It wasn't the same,' he said defensively. 'I looked at you a couple of times, but you were just lying there. Might as well have been dead. And anyway, I've been seriously ill. I could've died.'

He added the last bit to make it sound a bit more impressive, but Lalune didn't seem to notice. She grinned at him happily.

'So, what's going on there? Sounds like a party.'

'Yeah — the hunters came back today. They're all round to celebrate. And did you know it's our birthday?'

'Is it?' said Lalune in surprise. 'I haven't been keeping track of time.'

Solly showed her his bulging bandoleer and the new snowskates, and told her his adventure with the pudgia trap, and Aube's prophecy.

'How did *I* end up in a Wayfarer prophecy?' she said, laughing. Solly told her the story of the first Wayfarer, which he knew she'd heard before, but he told her anyway, just to have something to say while he looked at her. Then Lalune told *him* all about the wonders of the Bubblenet, which he didn't hear at all, he was so busy wondering if this was a dream.

'I've missed you so much, Lalune,' he said, interrupting her flow.

Lalune looked deeply self-conscious and a little ashamed. She opened her mouth, looking as if she was about to confess something terrible, but she never had a chance.

There was a thunderous knocking at the main door to the house.

'What on Clandoi was that?' she said.

Solly pulled back the curtain a crack. He saw Revas getting up to open it, and heard voices.

'It's Wuneem,' hissed Solly to Lalune. 'You'd better dim that light, if you can. If he finds you awake he'll only make trouble for you.'

'I heard you were back from the hunt, Brise,' Wuneem was sneering in the main room. 'I wouldn't like to think that you had forgotten to go to the tax office.'

'They've only just got back,' said Revas.

'We were coming in the morning, like we always do,' said Soir, bristling.

'Since when have taxes been *your* responsibility, Huissier Wuneem?' demanded a young hunter called Vasseurl, with a flash of her dark eyes.

'Since I was promoted, yesterday,' said Wuneem. 'They've been looking for somebody with the "right qualities" to replace Tax Officer Threfem Seventeen. I must say I was surprised. He'd always had such a good reputation. I didn't realize things were so . . . *lax*.'

Behind him, Solly heard Lalune gasp at this slur on her father.

'How dare he!'

'What do you mean, "lax"?' demanded Brise hotly.

'I mean, giving you people time to deal with things so that you can work out what not to declare,' said Wuneem. He strode into the room and Solly saw him poking at a food bowl contemptuously. 'I'd like to bet that cured hide lying out there wasn't to be included. Is it usual to keep them in the food store? I think not.'

Solly could see that Brise was having difficulty keeping his temper.

'I would have declared it,' he said, '*and* paid what's due. I know the Edicts.'

'Knowing isn't keeping,' said Wuneem. He strutted to the open door. 'Tuefem! Fordyef! Load it up!'

Solly heard movements in the hallway and heard his mother somewhere out of sight saying, 'Hey, that's the *whole hide*!'

'No! You can't!' cried several voices. 'Leave it!'

'Oh, but I can,' said Wuneem in an oily voice. 'I'm the Tax Officer. Not only does Hunter Brise owe us tax on that hide; I'm fining him for non-declaration. He can appeal if he wants.'

Brise sprang to his feet, red faced and furious.

'I was going to declare in the morning!' he shouted. 'We all were. Ask them. The other hunters. We'd already worked out the tax . . .'

He was running to the doorway as he said it. Some of the other hunters got up with him.

'Give . . . it . . . back . . .'

Solly looked on, horrified, as Wuneem raised his gun.

'No!' screamed Revas.

Wuneem hammered the gun hard into Brise's skull and the great man sank to the floor.

There was an awful silence.

'Cuff him,' panted Wuneem, wiping the sweat from his forehead. 'And the others. All of them.'

He tucked his gun into his belt with a satisfied smirk, then stood back as dozens more huissier poured into the room.

There were shouts and screams. The Wayfarers were obviously not going peacefully. Solly, terrified, drew back into the chamber and pressed himself against the wall. He shut his eyes, waiting for the curtain to be flung open, and for strong arms to grab him.

29

Solly felt as if he had been hit in the stomach. He could hear his mother's voice moaning in pain. Any minute now they would find him too. Lumie was sobbing; crockery was being smashed; furniture was being thrown about.

He dragged oxygen into his lungs as though if *he* stopped breathing, no breath would ever be taken again on Clandoi.

There were horrible crunching noises of Wayfarers being beaten. Then came a lot of dragging sounds. The cries and groans gradually faded, and finally silence fell on the little house.

Solly dared himself to look through the gap in the curtain.

They left me behind.

The curtain over the doorway was pulled so tight they had mistaken it for another bit of wall.

He slid to the floor and tried to steady himself, hardly able to believe what had happened.

'Solly?' whispered Lalune nervously.

'They took everybody away,' he said hoarsely. 'All of them, gone.'

'But, why?'

Solly couldn't answer: he felt as if he was trying to swallow a huge lump of meat whole. He peeped back out into the room, lit only by the dying glow of the fire. The front door was open; snow was drifting in. The floor rugs were sodden with filthy, snowy footprints. Bedclothes had all been thrown over the floor and trampled on. Pots had been thrown into the fireplace: it was full of shards of shattered and blackened pottery. Drawers had been emptied out wantonly. Revas's medicine jars had been smashed. Her precious guitar was in pieces.

'I should have helped them,' he said with difficulty.

'What could you have done?'

Solly fumbled with his bandoleer.

'I've got a crossbow and all these knives. I should have shot them.'

'All of them? On your own?' said Lalune, trying to be realistic and gentle at the same time. 'When all those hunters with really big muscles who *haven't* just recovered from a serious illness couldn't defend themselves?'

Solly bowed his head and said nothing. He felt so tired and weak and shocked, he was afraid he was going to cry.

'You have to hide,' said Lalune.

'What about Ma and Pa?'

'You leave them to me,' said Lalune. 'You need to get yourself away. Wuneem isn't a complete idiot. It won't be long before he notices that you're missing.'

'But what can *you* do?'

'Remember, I'm connected to the Bubblenet: so are all the cameras. I'll find them in no time.'

Lalune's voice sounded confident, but her eyes gave away her dread.

'I don't know where to go,' said Solly despairingly, his hands over his eyes. Even in the dimness Lalune could see the wetness, and she ached for him. 'I don't know what to do. I should have helped them . . .'

'Get together some food, warm clothes, and all your hunting stuff,' she ordered, seeing that Solly needed her to take charge. 'Where do they keep the sledges?'

'In the snowcamels' barn outside the Great Gate,' said Solly. 'But I don't think I could manage one: they're built for about ten adults.'

'Couldn't Star pull one?'

'Not by himself. And they'd have to be blind and deaf not to spot four snowcamels pulling a full-size sledge.' A thought occurred to him. 'Ma used yours when I had my accident.'

'Good idea,' said Lalune, considerably relieved. 'Father gave Revas a key to our house, didn't he? You haven't much time: daybreak is in an hour or so. You'll have to stay there for the day, but they'll never think of looking for you in an Appaloosian house, and it'll give you a chance to sleep. When night comes, you'll have to try to get out of Opita. Where can you go? What about that Seer you were telling me about? The one with the prophecy.'

Solly nodded. Aube would know what to do.

'He went back to his cave, I think.' The lump returned to his throat. 'I won't be able to speak to you again.'

'I know,' whispered Lalune.

Solly was no longer trying to hide his tears. He moved closer to the screen so that they were facing each other, and he pressed one hand on to the screen.

'Maybe never again.'

'You'll find a way,' said Lalune, lifting up her hand and spreading it against his. 'I'll be waiting for you.'

30

They've taken Ma and Pa.

Solly tried to block out the voice in his mind with action. He dressed in his warmest clothes as quickly as his injured arm would allow, and felt his way to the front door in the dark. Brise's hunting pack had been emptied and cleaned and repacked in readiness for the next hunt. Solly dragged it inside and filled it with as much food as he could find. He put a little dried meat into his bandoleer, to eat on the move.

He nibbled a bit of his precious toffee: the strong sweet flavour spread over his tongue and down his throat, though nothing but his mother's arms could have warmed him at that moment. He slipped the remainder into the pack. He picked up the pouch containing the lock of Lalune's hair and put it safely in the smallest pocket of his bandoleer. He struggled into his over-trousers and coat with difficulty, as the bandage made his arm fatter; pulled on the bandoleer, snowskates and pack, and crept out of the house.

They've taken Ma and Pa.

He stood still for a moment, trying to adjust his eyes to the darkness, but he might as well not have bothered. Appaloosians didn't waste precious electricity on

105

streetlights for Wayfarers. No chinks of light peeped out from behind drawn curtains. No lights lit up important cultural buildings. The ambient light of towns and cities did not light up the cloudy dome overhead. The night was as dark as a night could be.

Solly added his silence to the silence of the night, sliding his feet carefully over the slippery road, worrying about leaving tracks. It was actually a relief when sleety snow began to fall on any marks he made: though it cooled him drastically, his chilly body could never match the iciness inside.

They've taken Ma and Pa.

Whenever he could he went by the back ways, feeling his way along the walls with his mittened hand. Though it was way below freezing he didn't dare have his hood up for long, as it would block out the sounds of his enemies. He pulled it down at every corner to listen. A bitter wind sprang up, making his ears sting.

Nobody seemed to be about.

Even though he tried to be quiet, he seemed to fill the whole world with noise. He breathed short, shallow, noiseless breaths, and clenched his jaw to stop his teeth from chattering in the icy coldness.

They've taken Ma and Pa.

After a lifetime, he reached the clinic. This was the most dangerous part. He couldn't walk behind it as it was built right into the huge perimeter wall of the settlement, and there was a huissier in front guarding a wide space that ran all the way up to the wall on the other side. Solly could see Lalune's house right over there. The huissier had a perfect view all the way.

The daybreak horn sounded. Solly began to be afraid that he would have to stay outside in the sleet all day. The huissier was good. His back was lit by an orange glow from a brazier of some kind, but he was keeping it well back so that he didn't lose his night vision. He never once dropped his guard, and he never stuck to a predictable routine. The sky grew lighter and lighter, and Solly grew colder and colder. His arm ached, but not as much as his heart.

The sleet stopped. Beneath the fur hat Solly could see the huissier's eyes roving about the wide space in front of him, probing into the shadows. Occasionally he would send a WASP across to the Great Gate, but he trusted his own eyes more. Sometimes he would walk to the end of the clinic, but his eyes were always busy in front and behind. Even if Solly made it to the next nearest hiding place without being seen, there was no doubt that the huissier would notice the shadows change and would investigate.

They've taken Ma and Pa.

Solly thought of what Brise the hunter might have done. He could almost hear his voice: *Wait for your opportunity, Solly. Don't be tempted by impatience. Become one with the night. Embrace the stillness of the ground with your body. Take the sharpness of the air into your sight. And may the Being make your pathway smooth.*

Thinking of Brise made him feel stronger inside. He could do this. He *would* do this. He would make Brise proud of him. He ignored the numbing cold of his limbs, and carried on watching and waiting.

It was another hour before he got his chance. Though

dawn had arrived, the Ne'Lethe had darkened again with the promise of more sleet. Once or twice the huissier had stamped his feet and looked at his watch. He was coming to the end of his shift. Solly wiggled his fingers and toes, trying to will the warm blood back into them.

There was a movement at the door. Another huissier guard swaggered out to face the first. They saluted each other and the first one marched back inside. The new guard turned round and with gloved hands dragged the brazier forwards. Solly could see the blackstone burning brightly, and wished he could warm his hands at it too.

Then the huissier looked about him furtively, reached behind one of the shrubs next to the doorway, and heaved out something large and unwieldy. He lifted it up, and in the light from the fire Solly saw exactly who it was and what he was putting into the brazier.

It was Wuneem, and he was about to burn a stout tree limb.

He was burning wood! Wood was a restricted resource for Wayfarers, and even Appaloosians treated it with respect. Brise had once told him that when they were out hunting sometimes they had to use wood when they ran out of blackstone, and it never felt right.

Wuneem was looking extremely disgruntled. Solly allowed himself to grin. Either he'd been demoted again, or everyone possible had been pulled on to guard duty. That was good. There was no way he was going to be as vigilant as the first huissier.

He'd already made one mistake. The light from his brazier had considerably decreased his circle of vision.

Solly shielded his face from it so that his night eyes weren't affected. Very carefully he pulled a ball of string out of the bandoleer. It was made from the silk of an insect like a cross between a jellyfish and a butterfly, with one perfectly round wing, and dozens of trailing legs. The silk was as strong as rope, but so fine that it was almost invisible. Silently, he made a loop in the end of it and tied it around a nearby drainpipe. Finally, he took a piece of dried meat out and dropped it on the ground.

Wuneem hadn't made the same careful assessment of his surroundings as the first guard had. What was the point? Even if there had been anybody left to attempt it, nobody would try to cross the distance with *him* there. It was impossible. He stamped his feet, rubbed his hands together over the brazier and spat, making enough noise to cover the whole hunt trying to cross. Some small birds were hopping around near the perimeter wall and he pretended to shoot them.

After five minutes he marched right across the space to the far wall. Unwinding the string as he went, Solly ran silently across to the doorway, dropping to the ground behind a shrub just as Wuneem was turning. He crouched there as Wuneem returned to his spot. It began to sleet and Wuneem retreated further into the doorway, turning up his collar. If he were to turn and look down right now he would see Solly straight away.

But he didn't turn. He squinted up at the clouds, scowled, and warmed his hands again. The smell of burning wood wafted over Solly and he curled his lip.

A piece of wood shifted and there was a sudden flare of light. Solly saw something glinting in the snow.

Keeping a careful eye on Wuneem, Solly slowly took a long curing hook out of the bandoleer. Wuneem shuffled his feet. Solly stretched out and snagged the object. Wuneem shivered and puffed impatiently. Solly flicked his prize back towards him, stuffing it straight into a pocket. He didn't have time to look at it. Wuneem might move any minute. Besides, he knew what it was. He unwound another length of string and prepared himself to spring up at a moment's notice.

Wuneem stayed under the shelter of the doorway until the sleet slowed to a gentle patter. Then he slouched out and walked away from Solly, towards the far edge of the space, slapping his hands on his sides for warmth. Solly darted out and dashed to another bush.

Birds were twittering near to the dried meat Solly had dropped, where Solly's string was wrapped around the drainpipe. When Wuneem was nearly back, Solly tugged on it and it broke free. The rusty drainpipe groaned, and instead of returning to the doorway Wuneem walked unhurriedly over to investigate. Solly made a dash for it, winding the string up as he went.

Wuneem didn't even see it as it snaked past him. As he reached the drainpipe, a bird swooped to the ground in front of him. He pushed at the drainpipe – which complained again – seemed satisfied, and returned to his post.

Solly lay panting on the other side, safe in the gloomy doorway of Lalune's house. He had made it! When he had recovered his breath, he edged round to the back door and used the key that Threfem had given to Revas.

He was in.

Thankfully he collapsed on to the floor and felt in his pocket. He pulled out the object he had picked up outside the clinic and poured it into his lap, watching it blaze purple, blue and white through his fingers.

It was his mother's necklace.

31

Lalune watched Solly turn off his bubblescreen, feeling as though she had a great bowl of tears inside her chest that wouldn't spill, however much pain she felt.

All her life she'd had to train herself not to cry, and when she had created her soul body she hadn't even thought she might want to. Now that she needed to she couldn't.

Oh, Solly.

She sat in her chair staring at nothing, filled with grief at the knowledge that there was nothing she could do.

These were Appaloosians — my own people — who did this.

It was so cruel. She and Solly had found each other, only to be separated again. Lalune began to shake as the thoughts drummed into her mind. She would probably never see him again. Her loneliness had vanished when Solly visited, but now once more the years stretched out in front of her, a never-ending night.

And Solly? Solly had lost everything and everyone he loved. He was in danger, and she couldn't protect him.

She had never felt so utterly useless.

'Come on, Lalune: you're not helping anyone just sitting here,' she said at last, dully. 'You made a promise to find out where Solly's parents have been taken and look after them. You can at least do that . . . Kenet, I need to go to HIVE.'

' "HIVE" is the Holographic Intruder Verification Equipment centre, where WASPs are made and monitored,' said Kenet, appearing suddenly with her flat stare.

'I know, my mother worked there,' said Lalune, snapping even though it wasn't Kenet's fault — she couldn't help having no personality.

'HIVE requires Grade Eight clearance,' said Kenet. 'You do not have that level of clearance.'

'I'll work on that one when I get there,' snarled Lalune. 'Just take me there, would you?'

Immediately, she was in a long stretch of tunnel that looked exactly the same as any other wire inside the Bubblenet.

'You are now outside HIVE,' said Kenet.

'Where is it?' said Lalune, seeing nothing.

'HIVE is inside a high-security area,' said Kenet. 'It has a single entry portal requiring Grade Eight clearance. You do not have that level of clearance.'

'If I reprogrammed the appearance of my pod just by thinking it, surely I can get past any security measures they've put in here,' Lalune said, prowling up and down the wires. 'After all, I'm *inside* the Bubblenet.'

But the tunnel was polished and flawless. Lalune could see no entry portal at all. She tried feeling the walls for inconsistencies, but her pixel soul hands were useless at that kind of detail. She stared hard with her magnifying eyes, but if there was an entrance it was well hidden. Unhindered by gravity, she crawled along the ceiling, but there was nothing there.

Kenet was no use either: she just stared straight in front of her with a 'Can I help you?' smile on her face like an idiotic question mark. Except that she *wouldn't* help: Lalune knew that if asked she'd just tell her she didn't have the necessary clearance. Lalune felt like slapping her, but it wouldn't have achieved anything.

There was nothing to do but to carry on looking. After an hour her soul eyes were aching. After two, only the memory of Solly's tears stopped her from giving up altogether. She slumped to the floor for a brief rest, then jerked in shock and lay down with her ear flat to the ground.

She'd heard a voice.

'*Forcyef's Army.*'

Not a real voice from the real world, but a digital recording, repeating a coded phrase.

'At last! A voice-recognition lock.'

'*Forcyef's Army.*'

It occurred at only one point on the floor of the wire: a point so tiny that if she had sped by quickly she would have missed it altogether. She listened to the recording several times. Then she mimicked it exactly.

'*Forcyef's Army.*'

A large aperture opened beneath her and she swam through.

She didn't see Kenet break herself in two identical animations, only one of which followed her.

32

Solly placed Revas's necklace carefully in the pouch containing Lalune's hair, and lay down on a bare mattress clutching it. Although he was dropping with weariness, for a long time sleep wouldn't come, and when it did it was chased away by dreams of Wuneem striking his father, his mother moaning in the background.

By mid-afternoon he was wide awake, and he lay resting until it was time to go, trying not to think too much.

They've taken Ma and Pa.

A raucous horn blast announced the closing of the Great Gate for the night in thirty minutes. Solly heaved his pack on and let himself out, wincing as fresh pain shot through his arm. He filled a skin water bottle with snow and placed it close to his body to melt. It wouldn't make much water, but he didn't need much.

It was nearly dark outside and the temperature was dropping rapidly, but the cold fresh air revived him and, in spite of having slept so badly, he felt alert.

He crept round to the shed where Lalune's two-man sledge was kept, wrapped in a protective skin. He tied the pack on to it and pulled it out of the shed.

He glided silently behind the houses towards the Great

Gate. There would be a guard there as normal with a WASP, as well as somebody outside the clinic, so he had to be careful.

The workings of the Great Gate were out of sight up some steps. Leaving the sledge in a shadow, he climbed up. His snowskates only just fit. He stopped at a huge hinge. Just above him was the horn, which was due to give a second blast any minute. He took out the skin water bottle and carefully poured half of the water into the horn. It turned to ice as he watched. Then he did the same to the hinge.

He returned to the sledge and hid. He didn't have to wait long. There was a muffled squeak from the horn. He saw the silhouette of the huissier on the gate come out of his gatehouse and stare up at it, scratching his head. He went back inside; there was another squeak, and he came out again. Solly watched him wave to the huissier outside the clinic and shout: 'It's all frozen up!'

The huissier on the door walked across to the gate, just as Solly had hoped he would. Nothing could be much duller than guard-duty. He probably appreciated the unexpected diversion.

As soon as he was out of the way, Solly pushed the sledge into the shadow made by the gate, and peeked out. The two guards were deep in discussion, their backs to him. They'd sent the WASP up to examine the horn. Solly pushed the sledge round the corner and behind a bush, and then stopped dead.

One of the guards had disappeared. He could be anywhere: he might spot him any moment.

Despite the temperature, Solly started to sweat. The

116

bush was scarcely cover, it was so small, and the sledge was sticking out, looking obviously *un*bushlike.

There was a clang, and the guard emerged from the gatehouse with a steaming cup. While he climbed up the steps to pour it into the horn, the other lit a cigarette and watched. Solly sidled out of the gate, trembling with relief. By the time they had discovered the frozen hinge as well he would be long gone.

The snowcamels were kept in a barn a little way away from the Great Gate. They began to *huff* loudly as soon as they picked up his scent. Solly wasn't too worried about this as none of the Appaloosians ever went near them, and wouldn't have known the difference between the friendly *huff* they gave to friends and the resounding *hoo-hoo-hoo* reserved for strangers.

Star was only just out of puppyhood, but even so he stood taller than Solly. He jumped excitedly and Solly scratched him behind his ears.

'Ready for an adventure, Star?' whispered Solly. 'You've got to be quiet, though. Like when you're hunting with Pa, see?'

Star wrapped his trunk around him affectionately. Solly led him to Lalune's sledge. The other snowcamels tried to come with them.

'No!' he whispered urgently, pushing them back inside.

But the snowcamels were far stronger than he was: they had only recently returned from a long and strenuous hunt, and they hadn't been fed all day. They huffed at Solly and nudged him out of the way as they went to forage for food.

Star tried to go too, but Solly managed to catch him

and harness him to Lalune's sledge.

'I know you want to be with them,' said Solly, clumsily tying a bale of seaweed on to the sledge with stiff fingers, 'but I need you. We've got to find Aube's cave.'

33

Lalune was in a chamber full of light: light that bounced from the walls and floated around in huge discs that shone like flat bubbles, each a different colour. For a minute she was so dazzled she couldn't think.

'What is this place?'

'You are in the iris scanner leading into HIVE,' said Kenet. 'It requires Grade Eight clearance. You do not have this clearance.'

'It's so beautiful,' breathed Lalune. 'I never realized that eyes had so many different shades.'

Soft browns gave way to deep purples, to muted greys, to brilliant blues, to delicate greens, to severe blacks; the list was endless. Most of them had star-shaped pupils.

'How do I get through it?'

'This iris scanner requires Grade—'

'Grade Eight clearance,' said Lalune irritably. 'Yes, I know.'

A tiny aperture suddenly opened nearby. It blacked out again for a few seconds and one of the irises rolled in front of it. There was a click, and the aperture opened wide for no more than a second before disappearing again. Somebody had just used the scanner.

'I see,' said Lalune, 'I need to move an iris across to that hole.' She chose the nearest one, a golden iris with glints of green and brown, and tried to pull it; but her hand went straight through it. She got behind it and blew, but the iris swayed mockingly. She glared at it and it shrank away from her.

'I wonder,' she said, 'if I can move *me* by thought, can I move an iris too?'

Concentrating very hard she telekinetically pulled it towards the lens. It slid forward: the aperture opened and she slipped through.

34

After what seemed like years, Solly and Star reached the rocky outcrop that marked the entrance to Cirque Hallow. The night was absolutely black. They hadn't been seen. Solly unharnessed Star from the sledge and hauled it into some bushes: he wouldn't be able to get it through the rough snow under the trees.

'Come on, boy.'

Star *huffed* and bounded ahead into the Cirque. Solly wasn't completely sure of the way, but he knew it was somewhere near the top. There were a number of narrow animal tracks leading in the right direction, so he chose one at random and set off.

Fortunately, the Cirque was small enough for him to find fairly quickly what he thought must be the low cliff where the cave was, though it was a lot further to the left than he remembered. He groped about its soily slopes until he felt rock; he felt along the rock until there was nothing but space under his hands: Aube's cave.

'Aube?' he called. 'Are you there?'

Warm air worked its way through the cold layers of skin on his face. He stumbled forward, hands held in front of him. There was a noise: a flint-box was struck. Then a blue flame fountained from somewhere beside him – not the cave – and he heard a voice saying, 'Well, heaven bless us all: it's the boy, Angelus. Come on in, we've been expecting you!'

Solly bent down to see if the Seer was looking out of the cave mouth, but he was nowhere to be seen.

'Over here,' came Aube's voice again, and Solly saw another flash of blue, and Aube's face beaming at him from the cliff-side as though he was looking through a very dirty pane of glass. Solly couldn't remember any windows being there.

'Come in,' said Aube again. 'I've put the kettle on.'

'Stay here, Star,' said Solly. Star sat down with a *huff*, and laid his head on his front paws.

Aube wasn't in the corridor. 'Hang your coat up, there's a good fellow,' he shouted from the main room of the cave. Solly removed his outdoor clothes and pushed aside the swag-skin door. The Seer was sitting down at his little table, looking into a curious shiny object made of a highly polished piece of black wood about the thickness of Solly's arm.

'Janus mirror,' explained Aube cheerfully. 'Made from the wood of a Janus tree, you know. Picked it up in Brume. Supposed to be used to see into other dimensions: trouble is, one has to actually *get* to the other dimension to leave the other half there. Still, it works just as well leaving it in the doorway. See who's visiting. Convenient. Saves having to get up all the time.'

'You were expecting me,' said Solly.

'Ah, well, that's why they call me a Seer, you see,' said Aube, heaving himself out of his chair. 'Cup of tea? Fast asleep I was, got woken up by a dream. Violence and sorrow in Opita. Are you hungry? I had the feeling it was more than a dream, then blow me if I didn't See you coming, all packed up for a long journey, so I got ready to leave at once. Still, time to eat before we go, hey? How's that arm?'

He plonked a large mug of hot tea on the table in front of Solly, and went back to the stove to stir something that smelled delicious. Solly realized that he was starving: he hadn't eaten since the hunt celebration.

'Thanks. It's getting better.'

'Do you want to tell me what happened?' Aube said gently.

So Solly told him, his voice cracking at the worst bits. Aube listened while he dished up a rich stew, occasionally saying things like, 'Gracious heavens', or 'Did you hear that, Angelus?'

'Then Lalune said I should come to you,' Solly finished heavily. 'I didn't know what else I could do.'

He gulped down an enormous mouthful of stew and told himself that it was the heat making his eyes water.

'Well, I have to say I didn't See all that coming,' Aube said. 'What now, hey, Angelus?'

'I was hoping *you* would know what to do,' said Solly.

'Have to get you away first,' said Aube, rising and going to his bed, where he was halfway through filling a pack. 'Though who's to say they're not rounding up Wayfarers everywhere else as well?'

'Where will we go?' asked Solly.

'I'm thinking Latrium, perhaps. Now there's the thing. Odd things happening there. Too many comings and goings for my liking. Besides, the further away I am from the Great Darkness the better I See. Who knows, I might See your next step, hmm?'

'Latrium? At Worldsend?' said Solly. He was feeling terribly tired again.

'Yes. But the correct question would be "Why?", not "Where?", I think,' said Aube.

'What do you mean?'

'If we are merely running away, dear boy, we face a lifetime on the run,' explained Aube. 'Is that what you want? We should have to live out in the open, always moving from place to place, ever alert in case we're detected, and never knowing when, or indeed if, return is safe. I'm not young, either: you'd probably have a good fifty years on your own. We would never know the truth about your parents, and you would certainly never see the moon-girl again.'

'What else *could* we do?' asked Solly helplessly, thinking of Lalune all alone.

'You're forgetting something,' said Aube, putting a flat rectangular object into his pack. 'You are the child of the prophecy. One of them, anyway. Fulfil that prophecy and, well, I don't say that your troubles will be over, but things would be far better than they are now.'

Solly didn't know what to say to that. How was finding some key going to help anything? And wasn't Lalune supposed to be with him?

Aube had made a pile of the rectangular objects on the table. He started to put the rest back in an alcove. Solly picked one up. The nearest thing he'd ever seen like it was an acetate printout from the bubblescreen, but that was only ever a single transparent sheet, and this was made of a hundred or more sheets of something whitish and opaque, all bound together between two pieces of leather.

'Books,' explained Aube. 'We don't generally write things down, us Wayfarers, do we? I don't have a bubble-screen: I like to jot down the Wayfarer stories and songs.'

'What's this stuff they're made of?'

The pages were filled with tiny writing, which Solly had difficulty in reading even when he held it close to his face.

'Paper,' said Aube. 'Sort of mashed-up wood. Like the stuff stingwings build their nests from. Now then, I think we have a journey to start.'

35

Lalune had reached HIVE and was looking down at it through a bubblescreen. It was a storeroom for WASPs with a dust-free workroom down one side. Toayef had once worked there as a senior technician. Rows and rows of WASPs were slotted into recharging units on the wall, and bubblescreens hung in clusters from the ceiling, like grotesque glistening fruits. Normally, one or two technicians would have been maintaining and controlling these bubblescreens, each of which showed views from half a dozen WASPs. Other people would have been cleaning and repairing the WASPs themselves on the long white benches.

Today, however, it was empty. There was nobody left to be watched.

Once when Lalune was very small, Toayef had rashly taken her to work, and she'd spent the afternoon learning how to plug a WASP into a recharging unit and take it out again using the remote bubblescreen. But then Toayef had been called to some emergency and Lalune had got bored. She'd made her WASP fly round and round the head of the huissier on guard-duty at the Great Gate. The whole Bubblenet had been swept for viruses and had crashed before anyone had realized that Lalune was to blame.

She must have been five when that had happened, but the memory was still fresh.

Later, when she'd been sent to bed in disgrace, her cheek stinging from the slap her mother had given her, she'd heard tears; sobs of 'I worked so hard . . . this is how she rewards me . . . how's this going to look . . .' and Threfem's troubled voice, comforting his wife.

Why did you always do that, Father? Why did you never stand up for me? Or for yourself?

Lalune resolutely brushed the memory to one side. It hardly mattered any more.

'Kenet, where do they send prisoners?' she asked, and Kenet appeared, her expression as fixed as normal.

'Please pick one of the following options,' Kenet said, staring glassily ahead. ' *"Transportation of prisoners, twenty-first century." "Transportation of prisoners, seventeenth, eighteenth and nineteenth centuries."* ' Her words unfurled in bold shimmering letters. ' *"Accommodation for prisoners in Peleg City." "Accommodation for prisoners in Opita." "Sentencing of—"* '

'That one,' said Lalune. ' *"Accommodation for prisoners in Opita."* ' The rest meant little sense.

'There are one thousand, seven hundred and two entries under that heading.'

'Oh, just show me the first,' said Lalune wearily.

' *"Crime in Opita is rare,"* ' said Kenet's mouth, but somebody else's voice came out of it. ' *"Wayfarers caught in petty crimes are typically flogged, fired, and returned to their own kind to be dealt with. It has not been common practice to hold them, as this would have been deemed an inappropriate use of*

Appaloosian resources. However, should the need arise, for instance in the case of the murder of an Appaloosian, a Wayfarer would be held in the Appaloosian prison cells until arrangements have been made for their execution. Appaloosian criminals typically have their entry procedure into the cyberclinic accelerated, and are held in prison cells in the Appaloosian accommodation block before being—" '

'Thank you,' interrupted Lalune. She didn't enjoy the way Kenet made it sound like the whole cyberclinic was a prison.

The tunnel here was dotted with hundreds of narrow openings, leading she guessed either to a WASP or to its recharging unit.

' "Cyberclinic, Level One",' she read above one group of openings. ' "Perimeter Fence." "Snow Skimmer Hangar." Ah, here we are: "Accommodation Block, Level One." '

36

Nobody went voluntarily into the Great Darkness. Something horrible was supposed to live at the centre. Animals, birds and fish all avoided the place. Humans, both Wayfarers and Appaloosians, would go round it for days rather than enter. The Twilight was as close as anybody ever went.

But that was where Aube was suggesting they went.

'Nothing there to harm us. Many a time I've crossed it and never once have I been attacked. And it will be an excellent place to hide.'

'I'm not afraid,' said Solly.

All the same, as Star dragged the sledge into the silence that marked the end of the now-blackened Twilight and the beginning of the Great Darkness, Solly began to shiver – and not just with cold. He fingered the pouch containing Lalune's hair and Revas's necklace, which he had put inside his mitten.

At first he let Star lead the way. But the poor animal started to behave as if they were approaching some malevolent thing, after a while stopping altogether. Solly got out of the sledge, but after ten minutes of pulling him, wild-eyed and flat-eared, Aube suggested they try a light.

'He might feel safer,' he said. 'And I don't suppose we're

in sight of the clinic any more.'

'I didn't think to bring a lantern,' said Solly.

'Hmm. And fire dust will only drift away,' said Aube. 'Never mind. A fire it will have to be.'

'A fire?' said Solly, imagining the Seer lighting it on the back of the sledge.

'I'll make a levitant fire,' said Aube, taking off his gloves.

He struck his flint-box and lit his pipe. When he was satisfied with it, he took a pouch from one of his many pockets and took out some tiny slivers of wood. He gently fed them into the bowl of the pipe, until it seemed that the whole thing would catch alight, and Solly picked up a handful of snow in case Aube's beard caught fire. Just before he threw it, however, Aube took one half of the Janus mirror out of another pocket and tipped the contents of the pipe on to it. There was a *pop* and Solly blinked in astonishment. The slivers of wood had enlarged into sizeable logs, which were crackling with orange flames, and the whole thing was encased inside a bubble.

'You did that before,' said Solly, holding his hands out to the sudden warmth. 'In your cave, after I had my accident.'

'Safer than leaving an open fire and no one to watch it,' said Aube. 'And we can attach a string to it, which is very handy just now.'

He pinched the bubble between his fingers and thumb, and deftly tied some fluttery silk string on to it. The fire bobbed in the air like a giant balloon. Star sniffed at it.

'Follow the fire, Star,' said Solly encouragingly.

The snowcamel was still uncertain, but he knew fires. The hunters always had them, and they meant warmth and feeding time, and they kept away the fierce creatures he helped hunt in the daytime. With Solly holding the bobbing levitant fire in front, and Aube laying a comforting hand on his side, he began to walk on through the eerie silence more confidently.

The fire lit only a short distance in front of them, but even in its poor light Solly could see that the landscape was changing. They came across piles of stones and odd boulders stranded on top of the ice, with snow lying deep on top of them. It was like walking through an abandoned building site. In one place, soil had been blown into a deep ravine and trees had taken root. There must have been a landslide, for all the trees stood at different angles: all were dead, as was everything in this barren land.

'How could trees grow here in the dark?' he whispered to Aube, as if they were walking through a graveyard and he didn't want to disturb any ghosts.

'Maybe it wasn't always dark,' said Aube. 'There's a legend of—'

Star interrupted him with a loud *huff*, straining forwards as if he could smell something familiar.

'What is it?' said Solly. He patted Star on the nose while Aube moved in front to see.

'I can't see anything,' he said quietly. 'But I've heard the stories about what lies at the centre of this place. Keep Star under control now.'

Star thumped the ground with his foot, as he did when about to be fed. Solly tightened his grip on the harness. 'Something's supposed to live there, isn't it?'

'So I have heard,' said Aube. 'In the exact middle of the

world, at the place the compass points to. The legend is that it lures anybody and anything that comes near it to its death. Hmm. Where's the wind coming from?'

'You knew that and you still brought us here?' Solly whispered furiously.

'Behind us,' said Aube, ignoring him. 'That's good.'

'You've got a very strange idea of the word "good".'

Aube got out some fire dust and lit it. Star whined and pulled forward. The fire dust swirled round in front of them, giving an eerie glow to things that hadn't seen the light in hundreds of years. Star pawed the ground and started forward again.

'I can't hold him,' panted Solly.

'Let him go.'

'Let him go?' cried Solly. 'Are you mad? Something out there wants to kill him. And us. And nobody would ever find our bodies.'

'Hmm. Keep hold of the rope and run with him, then. If it's what I think it is, we'll be able to stop him in time. I've seen one before.'

Star pulled up so abruptly that Solly skidded forwards and fell over. He looked back at the snowcamel, who had raised his trunk into the air and was sniffing with a puzzled expression. Solly got up slowly. Ever since they had entered the Great Darkness silence had surrounded them, but now it seemed that they had moved beyond the other side of silence. Solly could feel it vibrating in the ground beneath his feet, pressing down on his body, screaming in his ears. Star flattened his ears to his head and dropped to his knees.

'What is it?' shouted Solly. His voice was thin and

132

small, as if the air was already so saturated with sounds they couldn't hear it couldn't fit any more in.

'Look!' shouted Aube, pointing straight ahead.

Solly could just make out in what was left of the fire dust the bottom of a tree so massive that several dozen people could have fitted inside its hollow trunk.

'A tree?' yelled Solly, wrapping the harness round his good arm and clamping his hands to his ears. 'How can a tree do all this?'

'It's a Janus tree,' cried Aube happily. 'Like the one the mirror comes from. Exists in several dimensions at once. Marvellous, hey, Angelus? We mustn't go any closer.'

'I can't stop Star,' shouted Solly. 'He's too strong.'

The snowcamel had stood up again and was moving forwards towards the tree. Solly and Aube hauled back on the rope as hard as they could, but Star didn't even notice them. The nearer they got, the worse was the effect on their ears. Solly felt his head would explode. He screwed up his eyes, and through his lashes he thought he saw tentacles of darkness thrashing about: darkness that was darker than the night.

'I've never seen one so strong!' shouted Aube delightedly.

'Aube, it wants to eat Star!' bawled Solly. 'Stop admiring it and help me!'

The tentacles were clearer now. Solly could see them without half shutting his eyes. They weren't made of anything material: every so often one of them would pass through the straining snowcamel. Each time it did, he dragged them forwards a bit more.

'Star, please stop. Please,' begged Solly.

Star took no notice. The air was charged with electricity: all the hairs on Solly's body were standing up on end.

'Pull harder!' shouted Aube.

'I'm pulling as hard as I can already.'

As Star towed them even further forwards, one of the dark tentacles flicked forwards and sliced into Solly's head, and he was flung out of the world . . .

37

Lalune directed her soul down the opening for one of the Level One WASPs. At the end was the image as seen by the camera, distorted by the lens so that near things loomed very large and far away things were tiny.

The first five levels held the most sumptuous accommodation she had ever seen. She could see part of a bed through an open door: it was made from an unbelievable amount of wood. The WASP didn't have a particularly wide range of vision, but she found that she could 'think' it up and down and from side to side to see further, and caught tantalizing glimpses of more wooden furniture, beautifully carved and polished.

Most of the Appaloosians she had ever known had lived in houses outside the cyberclinic. Lalune couldn't remember ever having been here. Her own house, according to her mother, was the height of luxury; but it was nothing compared to this: just the wood for the bed would cost a year of her parents' combined wages, and that was before a craftsman had been paid to carve it. No Wayfarer had ever got this far, that was for sure: she wouldn't find Brise and Revas here.

The next level down appeared to hold a leisure facility. A few Appaloosians Lalune didn't recognize were walking the corridors in exercise-clothes, and a leopard-spotted woman came out of a shower room with a towel wrapped around her head.

A sign outside another door announced that it was a film room, and that the next showing would be at sixteen hundred hours. Lalune had only ever seen films shown over the Bubblenet, and it puzzled her that here was a communal film room that she'd never been told about. But then, she had been the only child – the only Appaloosian child, Solly didn't count – so they would hardly have made films just for her.

Another level was what appeared to be a health centre, though as far as she knew all the health facilities had been shut down when the last of the Appaloosians had entered the cyberclinic.

'How come I never heard about this place?' she wondered. 'And who are all these people?'

Everybody she could see was a complete stranger. It was as if she had accidentally entered a completely different world. The carpets looked lavishly thick. Soft music was playing. It was far richer than anything she'd ever experienced.

'Hey, I know *them*!' she exclaimed. Her old doctor, Dr Dollysheep, was sitting in one of the consulting rooms, talking earnestly to Wuneem's wife.

She carried on looking. There was a restaurant, and another level that was one huge meeting room, with piles of chairs – again made of wood – at one side.

Under that level she was back to corridors: this time they were grey, and two huissier guards stood there, smoking and chatting idly. The rooms off the corridor

136

had barred windows in the doors, and Lalune could hear faint groans coming from them.

'This is it.'

She was inside a WASP that was plugged into a recharging unit on the wall.

'Left!' she willed it, trying to turn it so that she could see inside the nearest room, but the window on the door was too small.

There was a commotion from the end of the corridor. She twisted the WASP towards it. A group of Wayfarers was being led in. Their hands were tied together behind their backs and their mouths were gagged. As they passed, one of them turned her face up to the camera so that Lalune could see that a purple bruise was spreading over one of her eyes. Lalune stared at her, appalled.

It was Revas.

38

Star and Aube, the Great Darkness, and the cold all disappeared.

Solly was standing in a field of swaying herbs. The smell of them was intoxicating and he breathed in deeply. Clouds of white flutteries lifted in synchronized leaps from the flowers, and a warm breeze brought him the chattering sound of a shallow stream somewhere nearby.

Apart from that, he could hear nothing. He felt no fear, only wonder and peace. He didn't question the oddness of what had happened. It all felt so right, somehow, as if this was the place he had been heading for all along. He was about to sit down and do nothing when he saw that he wasn't alone.

A few paces in front of him stood an immense and magnificent Appaloosian woman, her skin green and creamy-white. He was sure she hadn't been there a moment before. She was wearing an emerald-green cloak and had long nut-brown hair that streamed out as if she was underwater, and she was holding out her hand to him. Though she was smiling, her eyes were terribly sad.

The eyes of a dying person, Solly thought.

She opened her mouth to speak, only instead of words, bubbles came out of her mouth, which drifted towards him lazily. He laughed, and laughed again at the bubbles coming out of his own mouth, and when her bubbles reached him he was not at all surprised when they broke over his head and he heard the woman's voice coming from them.

'Come closer.'

It was the most beautiful voice he had ever heard.

Solly took a step closer. A tiny voice coming from very far away tried to tell him that he mustn't, but the woman was so lovely and her smile so tragic, and she wanted him with her so much: how could he refuse her?

He took another step towards her. The voice in his head grew fainter, screaming at him to fight it, but he didn't want to, because the woman had turned around and he wanted to see what she was doing.

He took another step and she moved aside, holding something high up above her. Then, with a sound like the air itself being torn apart, she slashed downwards towards the ground.

It didn't seem at all strange to Solly that a tunnel suddenly appeared next to her, though there was no cliff for it to tunnel through: not even a rise in the ground; nothing but flat and empty field for as far as he could see. The tunnel was so long and straight that he could only just make out the other end, a bright pinprick.

'What is at the other end?' he asked.

'It is the place you belong,' said the woman. 'Here is a waiting room: there is where you have always wanted to be. You have never felt truly at home here on Clandoi, have you?'

Solly shook his head, though in truth it was something

that had never occurred to him before.

'If you wish to go there, you only have to ask and I will take you,' she whispered. 'You can be with me, there, for always.'

Solly's heart filled with longing. He was about to take another step forward, a step that would bring him within her reach, when somebody from far away bellowed.

'Remember Lalune!'

The words distracted him for a fraction of a second and he looked behind him. A bubble was racing towards him so fast that sparks were flying off it. He didn't have time to step out of its way. It exploded over his head, into his ears and eyes; it was golden and glaring and full of a voice that sounded like a trumpet.

'ANGELUS!'

A being like a bright dawn seized hold of him, and he was flung back into the snowy barren waste of the Great Darkness.

39

Lalune watched helplessly as the Wayfarers were pushed and prodded down the corridor towards an open door at the end. There were five of them, all women. One was holding her arm, and Revas was supporting another with an obviously broken leg. Lalune could see the bone sticking out. She felt sick: she would have been sick too, if her soul body had allowed it.

'Get a move on,' snarled one of the huissier, as the woman Revas was helping stumbled and cried out in pain.

'She's going as fast as she can,' said Revas quietly. The huissier shoved Revas against the wall with the butt of his gun. Lalune gasped. The other woman screamed and fell to the ground, blood pooling around her.

'Pick her up,' ordered the huissier, pointing to two of his colleagues.

Lalune suddenly came face to face with him, and realized that the WASP she was in had pulled out of the wall and followed the Wayfarers.

I'll be discovered! she thought in panic.

She was about to try to manoeuvre the WASP back into the hallway when the huissier reached into his tunic and brought out his identity pendant. The WASP scanned it automatically.

Relief flooded her. The WASP was only doing what any WASP would do, after all. She tried to relax and not do anything suspicious as the WASP scanned all of the huissier and the Wayfarers. She wasn't sure if she had made it follow them, or if it been going to go anyway, but if she could control it she didn't want to do it accidentally and draw attention to herself.

While it was busy, she couldn't see what was happening behind it. The huissier were giving orders, and she could hear movements and sobs.

The last person to be scanned was Revas. When she was putting her pendant away, Lalune saw a huissier grab her arm roughly. She tried turning the WASP and, to her relief, it obeyed her. She followed Revas through another door at the back of the cell. Inside was a row of about twenty pods. About half of them were full.

They're cybernating Wayfarers?

Something was very wrong. Quite apart from the fact that Wayfarers had always been forbidden entry to the cyberclinic, and now were being herded in against their will, something was missing; but Lalune couldn't see what.

Lalune watched Revas being forced into the pod. Revas's eyes were terrified, yet she managed to climb in with dignity and arranged her skirt modestly before lying down. Then a feeding tube was forced down her throat, the lid was closed, and the pod began to fill with an oily liquid.

And then to her horror Lalune saw what was missing.

There was nothing connecting the Wayfarers to the central bubblescreen.

Without Bubblenet assistance, those Wayfarers could drown or develop infections, and perhaps starve; and without the computer to give them the proper drugs, they could easily die.

They'll kill them!

Blind anger filled her. She slammed the WASP into the head of the nearest huissier, who dropped like a stone. Then she turned and tried to whip into the next one, but he was more prepared, and grabbed hold of the WASP.

Lalune shook the WASP from side to side as hard as she could, and managed to pull out of his hands. She tore away from him and shot up to the ceiling, from where she dive-bombed them.

'Emergency in the prison block!' yelled a female huissier, pressing a button on the wall. 'One of the WASPs has gone wild . . .'

She squealed as Lalune crushed her fingers into the wall.

Footsteps thundered down the corridor. Lalune zoomed randomly around the room, trying to do as much damage to as many huissier as she could before she was caught. She managed to keep going for ten or fifteen minutes. Then she got too close; hands grabbed hold of the WASP and it was pulled out of the air. The back end of the WASP was rammed into a recharging unit, and Lalune fled from it, sobbing, back to her own pod.

40

When Solly came to, he was lying in the semi-darkness. His arm was agony, his legs ached, and his head was spinning. For a moment he was back in his own bed, in his own house, after the operation.

'Ma?'

'Well, well, if it isn't young Solly back with us,' said Aube.

Solly gasped and groaned as his memory returned.

'Star,' he said, sitting up suddenly, and brushing his head against the roof of the tent.

'Star is fine,' said Aube comfortably, opening the top of the storm kettle. 'Just a little bump on the head, that's all. I put a blanket over him and tied him to a rock.'

'Are we still in the Great Darkness?'

'I could hardly drag you both out on my own now, could I? Drink this.'

'But . . . the tree?' said Solly, taking the mug of soup gratefully.

'We're well away from the Janus tree, don't you worry,' said Aube. 'I'm afraid I underestimated its power. Shouldn't have taken you there. But I'd always wanted to see a full-grown one. Hmm. Didn't realize it was such an old one and such a hungry one. Now what you could

144

really do with is sugar. For the shock, you know.'

'There's some toffee in my pack,' said Solly. There was only a little left, but he broke it in half and shared it with the Seer. Its warm buttery sweetness was like heaven in his mouth, but brought bitter tears to his eyes as he remembered everything that had happened on the day he'd been given it.

Lalune! he thought miserably.

'I'd never heard of a Janus tree before,' he said with some difficulty. 'Before I saw your Janus mirror, I mean.'

'Amazing things,' said Aube. 'Their seedpods are about the size of a human head, you know, and they catapult them over huge distances . . . Good toffee, this . . . When they land, they split open into segments and the saplings grow in a circle. Eventually, the wood binds into a single hollow tube and they attract animals inside to eat them.'

'Don't the seedpods ever hit people?'

Aube laughed.

'No doubt they do occasionally. Bound to. There's a legend that says that there was a Janus tree so strong that it catapulted its seed up into the stars and across the dimensions. But there are legends and legends. Who can tell which ones are true? Until you see for yourself, that is; hey, Angelus?'

'You believe in stars and moons and the sun, yet you've never seen them,' Solly pointed out.

'True, true,' nodded Aube.

'That Janus tree in there was more than just alive,' said Solly, with a brief shudder of his shoulders. 'She was almost . . . psychic.'

'She?'

145

'She appeared to me as a woman.'

'Now there's the thing about carnivorous plants,' said Aube. 'People mistrust them. But they're only trying to survive, same as the rest of us. The Janus tree lures you in by telepathy. What was it thinking?'

'She was lonely and sad. I think she's dying.'

'I doubt it,' said Aube. 'Trees live for hundreds, thousands of years. I expect it manages to entrap enough animals to make up for the lack of light. It was probably just depressed.'

'Felt more than depressed to me,' said Solly. 'If she was just depressed, why did she want me, not just Star? A snowcamel's much bigger: it would last her for ages. But as soon as she felt me there she went after me instead.'

'Hmm. It wanted your soul.'

Solly choked on a mouthful of soup.

'My *soul*?'

'Janus trees feed off human souls,' explained Aube. 'That's another legend, I suppose. They are supposed to give a passageway to heaven in exchange for a human soul.'

'How did you save us?'

'Now there's the thing: I don't quite know,' said Aube. 'I hit Star on the head – only way to stop him. But then I turned around and you'd been enthralled by it as well. Harder to stop a human. Free will, and all that. There was a flash of gold and you were thrown backwards. Maybe it didn't like the way you tasted, hmm? Anyway, I popped you on to the sledge, fortunately there was a downhill sort of bit after that, and you slid to safety more or less on your own.'

'And Star?'

'Burned some herbs under his nose until he woke enough to walk to the slope, then he slid down too.'

'Tell me about Angelus,' said Solly abruptly.

'Angelus?' said Aube, very surprised.

'I, um, think I may have just met him,' said Solly. 'There was a trumpet, and somebody, and lots of golden light.'

Aube was very quiet for a moment.

'Well, well,' he said at last. 'I never really knew if I was making him up, you know. Too much time on my own, and all that. Fell off a cliff as a child. Should have died, but a winged man caught me and put me down safely at the bottom. My pa climbed down, expecting to find my body to take back and bury, and there I was, playing in the mud. I always hope he's still nearby, looking after me — Angelus, not my pa: Pa's long gone . . . Talk to him, you know — Angelus. But I never really knew . . .'

Solly could just see that the old man was wiping tears from his eyes.

'Was I unconscious for long?'

'Half an hour?' said Aube. 'At least you weren't sick on my boots this time.'

Solly grinned and wriggled out of the tent.

'I just want to check on Star,' he said.

'Then it's time for sleep,' said Aube. 'I think we've had enough walking for one day — hey, Angelus?'

41

The cloud above them became paler and pinker the further they got from the Great Darkness. Strange shapes loomed up in the gloom. They looked exactly as if a giant's child had filled a bucket with snow, then tipped it out into a heap.

'It's the pingos!' said Aube triumphantly. 'We've made better time than I'd hoped. There'll be trees, I dare say, because of the shelter. Plenty of birds. You could hunt them if you like. But poleys too, blue poleys and giant poleys, so watch out.'

But poleys weren't the real danger.

The day was only a handful of hours long, and they made the most of it. As they walked through the pingos, Solly saw a scrawny tree rutter – a furry umbrellaed mammal about the size of a rabbit: but with Aube there, he was too embarrassed to try and shoot it. Instead he helped Aube to gather berries and herbs.

It was much cheerier walking in the light. Aube sang a Wayfarer chorus to himself as he went, and Solly very nearly forgot himself and joined in.

'*A threefold Key; a threefold Holder; a threefold lockfast Queen. One finds its Holder; one its Holder finds, one has always Holder been.*'

As the day was so short they tried carrying on in the dark, but here in the Twilight there was too much vegetation for the sledge to get caught in, so they gave up.

They had just decided to stop to pitch the tent in the shelter of one of the vast pingos when Star pricked up his ears and whined.

'What is it, Star?' asked Solly.

Then he heard it too, right at the edge of his hearing: an unpleasant buzzing noise. He felt the sweat freeze on his forehead.

'That's a huissier snow skimmer,' he hissed. 'Hide the sledge.'

'In here!' said Aube.

Together, he and Aube pushed the sledge into a low-lying shrub.

'Star, come here,' Solly said, pulling the snowcamel into the shadows. Aube hastily unpacked a white poley-skin blanket to tuck around the end of the sledge, which was sticking out.

'They're looking for us,' whispered Solly. 'They'll see our tracks.'

Aube shook his head anxiously.

'I think they're approaching from the other direction. Hopefully they'll miss them in the dark.'

After a long while, the buzzing veered away into the distance without coming any closer.

'Maybe it was just a routine patrol,' said Solly unconvincingly. Wuneem must have noticed he was missing. They could expect to be hunted from now on.

'Hmm. I'll get some dried meat into the storm kettle,

with those herbs we found,' said Aube. 'Stew'll be ready in about an hour, I should think. You pitch the tent.'

42

If Lalune had had a real body she would have been trembling, her heart would have been hammering, and her palms would have been slippery with sweat. She felt ashamed of herself for losing control in the WASP. She stayed in her pod for a long time, going over and over what she had seen, and also what horrible things might happen as a result.

'There must be some way I can help them,' she muttered. 'There must.'

If she'd had a real body, she could have eased her grief by crying the lake of tears she could feel in her chest. But her soul was only virtual, and she could do nothing. For hours she sat there, her soul motionless, her mind darting through everything she'd ever been taught; both before she'd been put into the cyberclinic and since, when she'd been filled with mind-knowledge.

I wish I were good at this sort of thing, she thought. *I wish I'd paid more attention to my lessons, I wish some of the mind-knowledge the damny Bubblenet's pouring into me was actually useful . . .*

'*Pouring in* . . . that's it! Those pods *were* computerized,' she said out loud.

'Would you like me to define "pods"?' said Kenet, and Lalune jumped.

'No!' she snapped. 'Go away! Let me think!'

Kenet melted away and Lalune resumed her thinking, silently this time.

Why didn't I see it before? The huissier didn't fill those pods with oil by hand: they used bubblescreens. And all the bubblescreens on Clandoi are networked together using the Bubblenet. The Wayfarers may not have their details going out into the central bubblescreen like us, but things can be put into the pods – vitamins, antibiotics . . . I could put them in.

'Kenet, can you give me a list of vitamins and minerals that humans need, please?' she said, coming out of her pod and drifting back towards the high-security area. 'And antibiotics. Something general, that deals with most things.'

43

Solly woke up feeling as if he had hardly slept at all. The tent was sagging in an odd way. Aube was snoring loudly into his ear; and something heavy, probably Star, was leaning on the outside of the tent, squashing his bad arm. A stench of swag had accumulated in the tent overnight.

'Why d'you have to have a swag-skin sleeping bag?' he muttered, prodding Aube, who just rolled on to his back and snored louder.

The smell was overwhelming. He felt as if he might be sick if he didn't get some fresh air soon. How could Aube sleep through it? He crawled out of the tent and saw a disgruntled Star swishing his tail several metres away.

'But if Star's over there . . .'

He turned around slowly.

A swag was lying almost on top of the tent, rifling through the food bag.

'Get off!' Solly shouted, waving his arms about. 'Go away! Go on, you putrid pile of carpet!'

The swag looked round at him and sneezed, spraying thick snot all over him.

'Oh, *yuck!*' he said, disgusted. 'Star, why didn't you warn me?'

The snowcamel *huffed* through his trunk with an injured air.

'What's going on?' said Aube sleepily, poking his head out of the tent. 'Oh!'

'I bet it's eaten all our food,' said Solly. 'It's chewed through the tent rope, look. Go to inferny, you revolting monster.'

The swag ignored him and buried its nose in the bale of seaweed.

'That's *your* food, Star,' said Solly. 'Can't you chase the thing away?'

Star just stamped his foot and blew again.

'Poke it with a stick,' suggested Aube. Solly found a fallen branch and lunged at the swag. It moved its rump sideways without taking its head out of the seaweed. Solly lunged again, harder this time, and the creature snorted, lifting its head up with the bale still on it. When it was poked a third time it lumbered off, trailing moss and seaweed from the bale and trumpeting loudly.

'Sacry pile of rot,' muttered Solly, trying to wipe the snot off with a handful of snow. Aube came out of the tent and started digging about in the sledge.

'Hmm, I've seen worse,' he said. 'Last night's stew's gone, but the dried meat is still here . . . Oh, no, he's chewed the bag open from the other side.'

'How much have we lost?'

'Half, maybe more. Not so bad, really. You can hunt.'

Yeah, hunt! thought Solly.

'What about Star's food?'

'Hmm. All of it,' said Aube. 'We shall just have to gather

up what we can from the trail it left. Didn't exactly clear up after itself, did it?'

By the time they had salvaged what they could, almost half the day had disappeared. They trudged on to the end of the pingos, where a forest of stunted trees had somehow managed to find enough light to grow.

'We'll never get the sledge through there,' said Solly.

'We'll have to go round it,' said Aube cheerfully. 'That's all right, isn't it?'

'You tell me,' said Solly, who was in a very bad mood. 'I have no idea where we're going *or* what we're going to do when we get there.'

'Haven't you been paying *any* attention to the Wayfarer songs and stories?'

'They're only stories.'

'Hmm. Stories *you're* part of,' said Aube. 'They're all to do with the prophecy. They're like clues. You have to work them out.'

'All I want to work out is how I can rescue Lalune,' said Solly. 'And Ma and Pa.'

'Which you can only do by fulfilling the prophecy,' said Aube.

'So *you* say.'

'All I'm saying is that unless you—' Aube began, when Solly grabbed him by the arm.

'There's somebody up there,' he hissed, pointing up to the skyline. The Ne'Lethe was beginning to turn pink as the day ended and there, standing starkly against it as if he didn't care whether he was seen or not, stood a figure, searching for something on the ground.

'Can he see us?' said Solly.

155

'We're probably almost invisible,' said Aube hopefully.

'Just keep still,' said Solly. 'Do you think he's found our tracks?'

It was impossible that he wouldn't eventually.

'How much of a headstart do you think we have?' whispered Aube.

'Ten minutes? Five? He's probably got a skimmer – faster than a sledge unless we're going downhill. We could go into the forest.'

'We'd have to leave the sledge,' said Aube.

'Once we're in the forest he'd have to leave his skimmer behind anyway.'

The person on the hill had found something. He was walking back out of sight. After a moment they heard a snow skimmer starting up.

'We'll have to carry everything on our backs,' said Aube, hurriedly removing their packs from the sledge.

Solly was already unbuckling Star. 'Come on, boy. And quietly.'

Star plodded after him into the forest. The tallest trees only just topped him in height.

It was beginning to get dark. Solly could just see Aube bobbing along in front. He could hear the ugly hum of the snow skimmer as it picked up speed behind them. His pack bumped against his back. They'd left the food – at least, what was left of it after the swag had finished.

It doesn't matter, Solly thought in desperation. *I'll just have to try and hunt now. Star can always forage. Right now we've just got to get really deep into the forest and hide from the huissier . . .*

Solly tripped over a tree stump and swore under his

breath. Who was he kidding? There were two of them, with packs, *and* a snowcamel who was big enough to be seen above the treetops. How could they hide? The huissier probably didn't even have anything to carry with him aside from a gun. He'd make it through the forest far more easily.

Solly tried to squash down the thoughts, but they kept on coming. He had no plan beyond getting as far into the forest as possible. His leg was bruised. They were terribly slow.

It suddenly seemed a lot darker. The skimmer sounded closer, but Solly could hear it stuttering over small stones. Surely it would have to halt soon?

Aube was slowing, clutching his side and wheezing. Solly grabbed his arm.

'Need . . . to keep . . . on . . .' he puffed.

The buzz of the skimmer stopped with a final menacing growl of its throttle. The huissier had reached the fringe of the forest. He was probably looking at their sledge. Solly changed their course, hauling Aube after him. They were on the lip of a sharp slope. Solly flung himself forward and they slid down it into the forest. He heard Star *huffing* nearby.

Their manic slide ended after fifty metres or so, in a clump of overripe fruit.

'Yuck! All right, Aube?'

There was little time for words.

'Think . . . so.'

Solly pulled him to his feet and pointed in front of them.

'. . . dark patch . . .'

157

Star tried to lick the fruit off Solly's face.

'Later,' gasped Solly. He pushed Star away and pressed on. Very quickly, the trees grew so dense that Star was having difficulty getting through. There wasn't much snow here. Solly took out a long knife and slashed a path at random.

Suddenly he was through into a forest clearing. He began to run.

'Hurry!' he urged Aube over his shoulder.

Solly could hear the progress of the huissier some way back as he crashed through the forest. But he would be gaining on them. They had made a path for him.

'Quick!' he began to say, but the word was snatched out of his mouth as he fell again, down a deep and very dark hole that had opened up unexpectedly in front of him.

44

Lalune summoned the orb-map and let the flow of light carry her towards the central bubblescreen, moving slowly so that she could read the list. She was thinking so hard about how she could get to the Wayfarers that she nearly didn't see a large eye blocking the entire width of the biggest tunnel leading into what she thought of as her chamber.

It was glowing an evil green. It wasn't moving very fast and it was peering into every corridor and cul-de-sac of the Bubblenet. As it passed each one, smaller eyes were disgorged from it to probe inside. Messages and strings of information were speeding along the wires as usual, but as they passed through the eye's black pupil they slowed momentarily, wailing as if in pain.

'What on Clandoi is that?' she said in alarm.

'This is the Virus Tracking Program known as VTP5.4,' said Kenet smoothly. 'VTP5.4 is used to sweep the Bubblenet after a major infection.'

'The whole Bubblenet!' said Lalune. 'That must have been a pretty bad infection.'

She watched the eye catch up with one of the little strands of darkness she had often seen squirming along the walls of the Bubblenet.

'Correct. The program governing the WASPs has been infected with a virus.'

'The WASP program? It was fine when I was in it. I suppose those little worm things are viruses. I didn't see any of them there.'

'Worms are insignificant viruses usually dealt with by VTP1.9. The virus being tracked down is known as Human Component Tuef Seventeen.'

Lalune gaped at her as the words slowly filtered through.

'But . . . *I* am Tuef Seventeen!'

The worm shuddered away from the eye and seemed to be trying to outrun it. But it had no chance. The eye caught up with it and calmly passed it through its black pupil. For a horrible instant it was a struggling, wriggling, even screaming thing, half creature, half ash. Then it was just a shadow left by the eye, hanging in the air until blasted away by an information program streaking right through it.

'I have to get away.'

She turned to go back, but another green eye blocked her way. The floor of the tunnel was dusted with charred worms.

She would have to look for a different way out. She turned around and headed in another direction. There had to be an alternate path somewhere.

There was a sound behind her. A small piece of worm spun over her shoulder, glowing in an evil green light. As she turned her head she smelled burning hair, heard a crackle.

She screamed. The eye had almost caught her. She tried

160

to think herself forwards, but was sucked back towards it. Desperately she swam as hard as she could away from it, but it was too strong for her.

45

Solly disappeared into the darkness. Aube's exclamation was cut short and Star yipped as he crashed through the ground.

The ground at the bottom was soft. He'd managed not to land on his hurt arm. There was a musty smell in the air and a sound like the wind blowing through loose tent flaps. He felt for the pouch of Lalune's hair to make sure he hadn't dropped it.

Aube landed nearby with an ominous crack and a yelp of pain. Star stumbled down next to him.

'Aube?' whispered Solly.

The Seer just moaned. Star snorted, and in the blackness Solly felt the cold end of his trunk on his face.

'Good boy, Star. You're all right, aren't you?'

Star *huffed*.

'Aube, I'm coming over,' said Solly.

'Oh, my leg,' gasped Aube. 'Oh, my heavens, Angelus, but it hurts.'

Solly reached out to touch him.

'Try to be quiet,' he said. 'That huissier was right behind us.'

Aube stifled another groan.

'How about you? And Star? All in one piece, are you?'

'Shh. We're fine.'

Over the sound of the wind, extraordinarily loud in such a confined space, they could hear the footsteps of the huissier smashing his way through the forest above them.

'Inferny Waif,' he swore. 'Sacry forest. Should burn it all down.'

Waif was the slang term the Appaloosians used for Wayfarers. Solly's heart iced over. They were looking for *him*.

There was a brief gleam from an electric torch through the hole into which they'd fallen. By its light Solly saw Star lift up his trunk as if to howl, and he put his hand out to restrain him. The wind caused something next to Solly's ear to vibrate loudly: *prprprupra*.

As the huissier passed round the hole, he shone the torch into it a little way. Solly held his breath. He only had to catch sight of their faces, or something from their packs . . .

Prprprupra. Pruprispris.

But incredibly, the huissier passed on. They heard him breaking through the trees in front of the hole. They listened to the racket fade into the distance, and even then they waited a long time before anybody spoke.

And when they did, it wasn't either of them.

'*Prpr pr-we pr-have been pr-expecting pr-ou.*'

46

Lalune felt her soul being ripped apart. Her fingertips tingled: she could see them begin to turn inside out. She clawed desperately forwards, but there were green eyes everywhere. Her orb-map floated past her eyes. She could see herself in it, struggling, disappearing . . .

. . . and an opening immediately above her head, leading straight to her father's chamber.

Lalune made one last, supreme effort to pull upwards, away from the tracker. She heard it howl: she broke free; she shot away, not daring to look back, expecting it to follow her.

As soon as she could, she thought herself away and into her father's chamber.

But she couldn't allow herself time to rest. She had to find a way of stopping the eye from coming in.

She summoned the orb-map. There was nowhere safe from the eye. It would reach her eventually.

'Kenet, is there any way of hiding from a virus tracker?'

Kenet appeared as suddenly and as unruffled as usual.

'No. Deflection fields are illegal,' she said expressionlessly.

Though she'd never consciously learned about deflection shields, she could feel the information she needed tumbling into her mind. The Bubblenet itself had given her instructions on how to build deflection shields while she had been asleep in her pod.

'Blessed mind-knowledge!' she whooped. 'Thank you, whoever designed it; may your systems never be hacked. Except by me.'

The black words came into view in front of her eyes and she scanned them quickly. It was a simple enough piece of programming.

Even I could do that, she thought.

She constructed one around herself and her father. It acted something like a mirror, reflecting signals away: it should have the effect of making the eye think that there was nothing of interest in the chamber; but if it chose to come in rather than send in one of the smaller eyes, she would have to swim for it again.

And where would she go then?

Please, Being, God of the Wayfarers: you don't know me; I'm an Appaloosian; my name's Lalune; I need your help . . .

She looked around the chamber. Her father's pod was exactly as she had left it last time, though she couldn't see him because the glass sides were misted over.

There was a metallic screech from outside her shield. Lalune could just see the end of the undulating wire. A sinister green glow was growing brighter as the eye approached. Soon a small eye would dart down her wire – and hopefully be fooled. Lalune held her breath.

But the eye never came. It simply passed by, as if her father's pod didn't exist.

Lalune let go of her breath. Perhaps it wasn't as good as its programmer thought. At least she had time to wait it out now while it swept the rest of the Bubblenet. She enlarged her orb-map and set it hovering in mid-air so that she would know when it had finished. Then she drifted over to her father's pod to say hello.

It took several seconds for her to understand what she was seeing. There was a very good reason for the eye not to be interested in her father's pod.

Her father was no longer there.

47

'Prpr pr-we pr-have been pr-expecting pr-ou.' repeated the voice. It was coming from next to Solly's left ear, and had been speaking for some time, but was so alien-sounding that he hadn't noticed. It sounded exactly like the wind blowing through rubbery flaps.

'Who are you?'

'Pruppras.'

'Solly?' said Aube vaguely. 'Who are you speaking to?'

'Can't you hear it?' whispered Solly. Whatever the strange creature was, he didn't want to insult it by accident. 'That . . . um . . . voice. I'm sorry,' he said into the dimness. 'I didn't realize we were trespassing. We fell down a hole.'

There was an outburst of flappings and indeterminate movements. Solly strained to see anybody there.

'The blubbery sort of sound?' said Aube, suddenly interested.

'Yes,' said Solly.

'*Prpr. Our* hole,' said the creature, or perhaps a different one, as the voice came from a different part of the hollow. *Or*, Solly thought uneasily, *it might be one creature moving about without us detecting it.*

Aube tried to sit up and gave a yelp of pain. He lay

down again quickly, gasping.

'Are you . . . *the Pruppras*?'

The flapping began again all around them, and Solly could just distinguish a tall shape bending in the gloom, as if it was bowing.

'What are prpr . . . what you said?' he whispered.

'*Pruppras*, yes,' said the voice, this time from behind them. '*Prpr*. You hurt?'

'Oh, Angelus! All my life I've heard of the Pruppras,' murmured Aube. 'Never thought I'd meet any. Ouch! Mind my leg!'

'I didn't touch your leg.'

'*Prpr*. I touch,' said the Pruppras. '*Prpr*. Be still. You hurt.'

Aube coughed and moaned. There was another flurry of flappings. Solly looked around anxiously, but the daylight had almost disappeared now. He reached out to touch Star for reassurance, and the snowcamel licked his face again.

'*Prpr*. Wise frrriend pr-has brrroken pr-leg.'

This time the voice came from in front of Aube and very low down.

'Aube?' Solly whispered. 'Are you all right?'

There was no answer except for a very small groaning noise, which went on and on. Solly was afraid that the Seer was seriously hurt, perhaps unconscious. Star sighed next to him and flopped his head down onto his front paws.

'Aube?'

'*Prpr*. We make wise frrriend pr-asleep. Prpr-need leg pr-mend.'

Solly reached out to Aube and managed to find his hand. He squeezed it, but there was no response.

'What have you done to Aube?'

'Prpr-put wise frrriend to sleep. Pr-mend leg.'

Solly was seriously frightened. He was stuck in a damp cave with some strange creatures he couldn't even *see*. Aube was injured and unconscious, maybe even dead. He had no way of escaping and nowhere to go. And if he did, there was a huissier up there somewhere, looking for him.

He thought of Lalune, stuck in the cyberclinic, and wished that she were here. Wished that he knew how to rescue her.

'Prpr pr-we pr-have been pr-expecting pr-ou,' repeated one of the creatures.

'You've been expecting us?'

'Prpr-you sun-boy, yes?'

'My name is Solly,' he said, not really understanding.

'Prpr. You hruman boy, boy of prrophecy. Brring back sun. Brring back moons.'

'How did you know about that?' said Solly. Did everybody know except him?

There was another flurry of flappings. Solly had the uneasy feeling that the creatures were laughing at him.

'Prpr-wise frrriend not only pr-Seer.'

'You're Seers as well?'

Something next to him bowed deeply.

'Prpr-you pr-have been chosen pr-by prrrophecy long ago,' it said. 'Prpr-we Saw pr-you pr-long time ago. You, boy of prrrophecy. Hruman children brrring back sun. Brrring back moons. Prpr pr-we pr-have been pr-expecting pr-ou. Prpr-we have message pr-for pr-ou.'

'Prpr-first hruman boy need food.'

Solly jumped. It was a very small voice and was coming from his shoulder. He turned his head cautiously. He couldn't see anything in the dark, but he was sure something was sitting on his shoulder next to his left ear. He hadn't felt anything land there.

'Do you mind if I have some light, too?' asked Solly, politely and very nervously. Who knew what would and wouldn't insult these Pruppras?

But it seemed that they weren't offended at all. There was another burst of flapping, and a strange glow began to grow in the cave. At last Solly was able to see.

What he saw was a large low-ceilinged cavern. It had earthen walls, bulging here and there with tree roots, which ran along the ceiling, walls and floor. Here and there were neat circular piles of fungus: red, orange, white and grey. Some of these hung down from tree roots on the ceiling, some grew up from the floor. Some were as wide and round as a snowcamel, and some were no bigger than his thumbnail.

Aube appeared to be sleeping peacefully with a cluster of the smaller fungi around his head, as if he had fallen into a clump of them.

Solly looked in vain for creatures hiding in amongst these growths, but could see none. He looked to see where the greenish-blue light was coming from. There was no obvious source, unless it was the fungus itself.

'Prpr,' said the voice next to him.

Solly turned his head, and screamed.

An orange fungus was sitting on his shoulder. It was moving slightly and glowing, and *it had spoken to him.*

170

48

'Father?'

His pod was completely empty. There wasn't even any orbal oil left.

It must be a glitch in the Bubblenet, she thought dazedly. *Everything I see is only virtual anyway.*

'Kenet, take me to the monitor of Threfem Seventeen, please.'

'Access to Human Component Threfem Seventeen is denied,' Kenet said in a horribly smug tone.

'Then I shall go there myself,' Lalune muttered.

The monitor was up another short tunnel. Lalune swam to it, trying to suppress a feeling of misgiving.

There was no readout of her father's condition. There were no jagged lines showing his heart rate, nothing to indicate his temperature, the state of his kidneys, current drugs being administered: nothing at all. The only words on the monitor were: *Threfem Seventeen: harvest complete. Subject deleted.*

'What does it mean?' whispered Lalune. ' "Subject deleted": what does that mean? What harvest? I don't understand.'

'This subject has been fully harvested,' said Kenet. 'Therefore it has been deleted. Harvest: verb; to reap and gather in.'

'No, no,' moaned Lalune. Feverishly, she summoned the orb-map.

'Threfem Seventeen,' she said. There was no response. 'Threfem Seventeen, *Threfem Seventeen.*' Her voice rose in panic as she began to implore the orb-map. '*Find Threfem Seventeen.* FIND MY FATHER. WHERE IS HE?'

The orb-map didn't even flicker. Lalune's grasp tightened in anguish, crushing it into a million jet-black pieces, which drifted around her like funereal confetti.

'Where's Father? What have they done to him?'

'Threfem Seventeen has been fully harvested,' said Kenet. She wasn't real: Lalune knew she wasn't real; but right now she sounded as if she was taunting her.

'What harvest?'

'Each human component of the cyberclinic is made up of constituent organs necessary for the life of a human being,' said Kenet calmly. 'Appaloosians have nearly twice the normal number of internal organs, for maximum utilization. When these organs have been fully harvested, the subject is deleted.'

Lalune stared at Kenet in disbelieving horror.

'We're here to wait for the Ice Age to end,' she said. *Weren't they?*

What about Mother? she thought, with a sudden guilty fear that she hadn't thought about her before. She held out her hand and all the little bits of the orb-map rushed into it, reforming themselves into a ball.

'Toayef Seventeen,' she said.

To her relief, her mother showed up clearly in a nearby pod. Lalune checked carefully for the green eye. It was far away by now: it was probably safe to think herself there. She didn't feel like asking Kenet to take her.

Toayef was sleeping peacefully on her side. Her face was twitching in a dream. For a few minutes Lalune watched her, her hand pressed against the side of the pod. Then she went to have a look at the monitor and ran her eyes down the readout. Toayef seemed to be in perfect health. There were no notices here about harvests. Her heart rate was normal, temperature constant, everything fine.

Except that only three of Toayef's four kidneys were recorded and her lung capacity had almost halved.

At the very end of the readout were some words: *FH recommended.*

'FH,' Lalune whispered. 'Full Harvest.'

She went to see some of the other Sleepers. Nearly every one of them had had one or more body parts removed: usually patches of skin or kidneys, but in one case a whole arm was missing; and there were several more ominously vacant pods.

Some of the readouts ended with the sinister letters *FH* and a variation on the number of days, hours and minutes.

She dreaded looking at her own body, and had to steel herself to look.

What if they've done a Full Harvest on me too? I might be stuck in here – a soul without a body – for ever.

The thought made her feel faint.

But she had to look. She balled her hands into tight fists, swallowed, and looked.

'Oh, Being,' she gasped. 'I'm still here! I'm still here!'

She was so relieved that at first she forgot to check that all of her body was there – and when she did she felt the pixels that made up her body shatter apart as she lost control.

Two kidneys had been taken, part of a liver, and a heart valve.

And her eyes were missing.

The note at the end read: *FH due: 12 days, 1 hour, 0 minutes.*

49

The orange fungus on Solly's shoulder was covered in tiny hairs, and it was from these that the light was coming. It had no mouth, but was speaking by blowing through its flaps and rubbing them together.

While Solly was trying to take all this in, he missed what the Pruppras was saying.

'Sorry,' he stammered. 'I was . . . you're . . . um . . . what did you say?'

The fungus emitted a raspberry noise.

'Prpr – I said, hruman boy must eat, help hurt arm mend. Here's food. Eat.'

The rest of the fungi flapped in agreement.

'Eat, hruman.'

Solly jumped. The voice came from another of the piles of fungus, a deep-red one, which was hovering at his right hand. On top of it, in a small dimple-shaped dish, were curls of what looked like some kind of meat.

'Thank you,' said Solly. He reached out and took a piece of meat and ate it. He had a sneaking suspicion that it was raw, but all the same, it tasted good, like one of his mother's smoked meats. He ate the rest hungrily. The Pruppras appeared to approve of this. Another appeared, with more meat curls and a shallow wooden dish of water.

Wooden! If he hadn't been so thirsty he'd have felt he was misusing something holy.

'You said you had a message for me,' he said, sipping gingerly from the dish.

The fungi rustled, and though they didn't appear to have any eyes they all turned their attention to the biggest, greyest pile. It made a sound as if it was clearing its throat.

'Prpr-many circlings past pr-my wisdom rrreceived this message for the hruman boy whroo is the sun,' it said importantly. 'We have been pr-waiting for you to arrive for two hundrrred and pr-eighty circlings, hruman boy.'

I suppose a circling is a year, thought Solly. There was a long silence and he realized that he was expected to reply.

'I, um thank you for waiting for me,' he said, which sounded completely stupid, but he didn't know what else he could say. 'Two hundred and eighty. That's a long time.'

It was nearly the whole of time.

'Prpr-ou journey to find something,' continued the Pruppras, after another pause. Perhaps he should have said something more.

'Yes,' said Solly reluctantly. 'A key.'

Why is everybody so sacry interested in that inferny key? he thought crossly. He'd been hoping that this prophecy would be something about rescuing Lalune. Though just how these odd creatures could help he wasn't sure.

'*The* Key,' corrected the large fungus. 'Prpr. The Key of Being.'

All the fungi bowed.

'Yes,' said Solly. 'The Key of Being.'

'Prpr – this is the pr-message. Pr-you will meet a frrriend whroo will hinder pr-you, and an enemy whroo will help pr-you. Pr-before the end pr-you will pr-begin again.'

That was it?

'Thank you,' said Solly. 'I'll, uh, think about that. I'm sure it will help me.'

The little orange Pruppras on his shoulder snorted. Solly suspected it was laughing at him again.

'Prpr – I would like to pr-be the honoured one to accompany the hruman boy,' it said gravely to the big fungus. 'Pr-wise frrriend will be too pr-weak for a while. Prpr. If I take by pr-skyboat will be quicker. Prpr.'

'But I have to have Aube with me. He's the only one who has any idea where we're going,' Solly said in dismay.

'Prpr-you go to Latrrrium,' said the orange fungus confidently.

'Latrium? That's what Aube said. Why there?'

'Pruppras keep-pr watch on Latrrrium forrr many circlings,' said the big fungus. 'Prpr. Not like what see. Pr-too much comings and pr-goings of hrumans. Besides, Latrrrium where the Pruppras Saw pr-wisdom about pr-Key of Being. Perrrhaps it there, pr-calling to us.'

Solly felt panicky and reached out to hold Aube's cold, unconscious hand. Everything was conspiring to take him further and further away from Lalune.

'I can't go,' he said hoarsely. 'I can't! I need to get back . . .'

'Prpr. Sometimes necessary to pr-sacrrrifice the pr-small for the sake of the pr-big,' said the orange fungus kindly. 'Pr–wise frrriend will be pr–looked after. Hruman boy not worry about him.'

'It wasn't *him* I was worrying about, exactly,' muttered Solly.

After a few minutes of violent flapping, which was the Pruppras speaking in their own language, the large fungus bowed at the little one.

'Prpr–so be it. Pr–let the hruman boy sleep, then go.'

50

'Message for Solly, Opita, Twilight. Please, Solly: are you there? They're going to kill me. They're killing us all.

'Please come back to Opita. I need you.

'Solly, are you there?'

Is anybody there?

51

'Prpr. Good hruman boy: you wake earrrly. Let me see arrrm.'

The little orange fungus had brought him some more food: meat, and what looked like cereal grains. While it flapped around his arm, Solly began to eat. He saw Aube lying in a corner, snoring gently. Star was next to him, his head on the Seer's stomach.

'He's still unconscious.'

'Prpr. Just asleep,' said the Pruppras. 'Hruman boy must keep-rr bandages on forrr a few morrre days. Is pr-mending well. Hey, wise frrriend! Wake, eat.'

Aube opened groggy eyes and spent some time trying to focus them.

'Ah, Solly, there you are,' he said, his voice slurring. 'I had a most interesting dream. We met . . . goodness gracious heavens above! Either I'm still dreaming, or . . . is that what I think it is?'

'I expect so,' said Solly. 'Morning, Star.'

Star lifted his head up and waved his trunk at Solly. A strand of moss fell out of his mouth.

'Well, well,' said Aube. 'I am delighted to meet you, Mr Pruppras.'

The Pruppras bowed.

'Prpr. And I pr–you. Eat, wise frrriend.'

Solly handed him the bowl of meat.

'How's the leg?'

'Remarkably well, thank you,' said Aube, tucking in. 'Just bruised, I think.'

'You broke it,' said Solly. 'The Pruppras are healing it.'

'I am indebted to you,' said Aube, bowing his head to the fungus.

'Aube,' Solly began, and stopped. He'd rather have been alone with the Seer; but then, how would he be able to tell he *was* alone?

'Hmm?'

'The, um, Pruppras things want to help me keep going,' he mumbled quietly. 'To find the Key.'

'Hmm. Now there's the thing. Journeying with the Pruppras. Go down in history, you will.'

'The thing is . . .' Solly stumbled. 'The thing is, d'you think they'll help me go back, too?'

'Rescue the moon-girl, you mean?' said Aube, reaching for some more food. 'Hmm. I expect that depends.'

'Depends?'

'On whether it fits in with their interpretation of the prophecy,' Aube explained, wiping his mouth with the back of his hand. 'Very single-minded, the old Pruppras. Very. The Being is everything to them.'

That appeared to be that, then.

'Prpr. Forrr napkin, wise frrriend,' said the orange fungus, giving him a soft pinkish leaf.

'Thank you, thank you, most kind,' said Aube.

'Do you have a name, um, Mr Pruppras?' asked Solly after a mouthful of cereal. It tasted smoky, and if he ignored a slight grittiness, it was very pleasant.

'We are Pruppras.'

'This is most delicious,' murmured Aube.

'I mean, do *you* have a name,' said Solly. 'The Pruppras I'm speaking to.'

'Prpr. Don't understand. We are Pruppras.'

'I'm a human boy,' said Solly. 'But there are lots of humans, so they call me Solly, which means "the Sun". And this is Aube.'

There was a short pause, then the fungus said, 'We are Pruppras.'

Aube picked up a meat curl and examined it.

'Are there a lot of Pruppras?' Solly persisted.

'Yes. Lots of Pruppras.'

'Well, how do you know the difference between you all?'

Again there was a short pause. Aube ate the curl and looked carefully at another.

'Two different varieties, at least. Years since I tasted these.'

'We are Pruppras,' said the fungus.

Solly was about to give up when it added, 'You wish prpr to identify *this* Pruppras?'

'Yes, I suppose I do.'

'Prpr. You are called "Sun"?'

'Yes.'

'I guide you on jourrrney. Pr-you call me Sunguide,' suggested the Pruppras.

'Delicious, aren't they, Solly?' said Aube.

'What? Oh, yes, delicious,' said Solly, and ate another mouthful to show he agreed.

'Mountain wubberslugs, I think. And the smaller ones are either river wubberslugs or fluttery grubs, I can't tell which.'

'Pr-fluttery grubs,' said Sunguide helpfully.

Solly stopped eating.

'Filling, aren't they?' he said faintly.

'Prpr. If hruman boy has finished food, must go,' said Sunguide.

'Already?' Solly said nervously.

'Prpr. Many are waiting forrr you.'

Solly followed Sunguide down a short earthy passageway and out into a clearing in the forest. The fungi somehow lifted Aube out of the cave so that he could wave goodbye.

It was daylight. The clearing was thick with snow. The trees were bigger than they had looked in the dark; but Solly could hardly see them, as during the night the clearing had filled up with fungi. Sunguide had not exaggerated when he'd said that many were waiting for him. He was astounded to see how many there were, all shapes and sizes and different colours. There were white dishes attached to the trunks of the trees, and grey ropelike strands hanging from the branches. There were stripy red and white columns, and piles of purple balls that twinkled and span. There was one huge puffball type in the middle, which looked as if it was standing in a dish, and was at least half the height of the trees. It also appeared to be expanding. Several of the Pruppras were busy around it with fluttery-silk ropes and a huge sheet. A distressed '*Hoo-hoo-hoo*' was coming from the dish. Solly could just see Star's umbrella over the edge, and he wasn't happy about being in there.

'Are all these Pruppras?' he asked.

Sunguide laughed.

'No. Prpr-many different fungi on Clandoi. Pruppras prrrime species, pr-have care of all the otherrrs.'

'But there are so many of them,' Solly whispered, feeling foolish as a huge wave of flappings and blowings began at one side of the clearing and rippled round it. He had an uncomfortable feeling that they thought he was some sort of a celebrity.

'Pr-we have been waiting forrr you many cirrrclings,' said Sunguide. 'Pruppras need sun back, or die. Prpr. All die: hrumans too. Pruppras trry keep your prrresence quiet, but spores exited, tell other spores. Now all fungi know, everywhere. Can't keep spores quiet.'

'Spores?'

'Pr-our young.'

Aube pressed a small package into his hand.

'The Janus mirror,' he said gruffly. 'Keep in touch, won't you? And I've put in some firewood for a levitant fire. Be cold up there, I dare say.'

'But I still don't know where I'm going, or what I'm looking for,' said Solly desperately. 'All these . . . um . . . people seem to expect so much of me.'

'Remember the songs, Solly. You know more than you think you do.'

'But I don't even know which direction to go in. I was just running away, following you.'

'Come, hruman boy. Skyboat is ready,' said Sunguide.

He led Solly out into the clearing towards the puffball, which had almost detached itself from its dish and was

184

pulling towards the treetops. It was stopped from floating away altogether by the fluttery-silk ropes. Star had been strapped into the bottom of the dish with a bundle of dried leaves. Sunguide motioned for Solly to climb into the dish and to tie his pack firmly into it. The dish was made of some very soft substance, which gave alarmingly wherever he trod on it, but never actually tore.

It would have to be pretty strong, to hold Star, thought Solly.

There were some straps for him as well, and Solly tied them as tightly as he could. The huge sail was billowing out, so that had the whole thing not been held tightly by several large fungi piles it would have sailed straight into the trees.

'*Hoo, hoo, HOO,*' howled Star miserably, straining at his pack to sniff Solly's hand. Solly stroked him soothingly.

'This is a skyboat?' said Solly.

'My pet,' said Sunguide proudly. 'I had him as spore. He's the biggest and fastest arrround.'

This thing's alive? thought Solly incredulously.

There was a sudden lurch, a great flapping from the crowd, and a lament from Star.

'Goodbye, Solly!' shouted Aube, and when Solly looked, he found that they were already high up over the trees and Aube was a tiny smudge on the ground.

52

The air was so icy it squeaked. Solly had wrapped himself inside his sleeping bag and blanket, and was hugging Star for warmth.

Sunguide however was perched at the front end of the skyboat, crooning happily.

'Why aren't you cold?' Solly shouted. 'This wind's like knives made of ice.'

'Pruppras not feel cold,' Sunguide shouted back. 'Not unless it cold enough to frrreeze us solid. Prpr. Just slows us down.'

They were over Glimmering now, flying so high he felt they could touch the Ne'Lethe. He couldn't believe how much he could see. Behind them, the shadow of the Great Darkness brooded. On one side of them, an endless plain swept towards the grey mass of the ocean: on the other and in front, great mountains rolled. Far below was the tiny black dot of their shadow racing along over the blue-grey mass of a glacier. The sides of the mountain the glacier was devouring were scarred with landslides, and the ground at the edge was full of unnatural-looking zigzag patterns where it had cracked, filled with water, and frozen again. It was all very strange.

Somewhere inside that mountain, he thought, *are the*

blackstone mines. I wonder if that's where Aube got his fire dust from. Dozens of Wayfarers he'd never even met worked in there. *Unless they've been taken too.*

'You speak our language very well,' he shouted.

'Prpr. Spend time in homes of hrumans, especially caves of wise frrriend,' Sunguide replied, doing something fiddly with a rope. 'Wise frrriend talks to Angelus. I listen.'

'Why do you call him "wise friend"?'

'Wise frrriend listen to trrrees. Listen to plants. Listen to people. Pruppras live in wise frrriend's cave. Wise frrriend believe in trrruth he not rrremember, but believe anyway.'

Travelling by skyboat turned out to be much faster that Solly had expected. It gave him a lot of time to think however, and thinking was the one thing he didn't want to do at the moment. He kept hearing Wuneem's voice ordering the huissier to round up the Wayfarers. The noise made when he hit Brise's head. Revas's moans of pain.

He kept seeing Lalune lying as if dead in her pod. He tried to imagine what it was like inside the Bubblenet. He remembered the last goodbye they'd said, when she and Threfem had come to tell them they were to go into the cyberclinic.

And that other last goodbye, when they couldn't even touch.

How many last goodbyes can there be?

He dozed and dreamed of a hundred ways to rescue them: a hundred ways that wouldn't work. He saw Lalune's face, looming closer and closer. She was whispering to him: '*Solly, help me: they're killing us in here*,' but when he opened his eyes, it was only Star snuffling in his ear and he was still travelling away from her.

They flew right through Glimmering and were well into Brume when the Ne'Lethe turned dark pink. Sunguide guided the skyboat down into a rocky field by a river. Solly was expecting a bump as it landed, but it slid into a gentle hover just above the ground and started to deflate.

After giving the ground a suspicious sniff in case it decided to sway about like the skyboat, Star gambolled over to a nearby tree to munch leaves.

'Wish it was that easy for me to find food,' Solly mumbled, unrolling his tent.

'Are plenty drrried wubberslugs in bag in skyboat,' said Sunguide, who was crooning to the skyboat as it deflated.

Solly tried his best not to shudder. He'd already forced a handful of them down his throat for lunch. He showed Sunguide his bandoleer proudly.

'I can catch something fresh,' he said. 'I'll set a fish snare up in the river; that'll do for breakfast. And there's bound to be pudgias around somewhere.'

Too late, he realized that there weren't any trees around to make a trap. The pudgias here probably nested on the ground. He'd have to use his crossbow: he couldn't change his mind in front of Sunguide.

He tried to look confident, but his palms went slippery with nerves. He'd had never shot a pudgia before. He'd never shot anything living, thanks to Administrator Forcyef.

He finished putting up his tent, then fumbled in the bandoleer for the crossbow. His hand closed on the Janus mirror instead.

'I ought to call Aube, I suppose,' he said. 'Let him know we're all right.'

'Wise frrriend might talk half the night,' Sunguide pointed out. 'Would be betterrr to catch food while is still light enough.'

Solly sighed, but he got out the crossbow anyway.

He thought about wubberslugs for supper, selected a jade bolt, and walked nonchalantly towards the riverbank. There was a handy rock he could brace his elbows on.

He wished they didn't need quite so much bracing.

He closed his eyes and breathed deeply, remembering the words Brise had used in his training.

Draw the stillness of the rock into your limbs. Make the darkness of the cloud your cloak. Borrow the softness of the mist to blur your outline. Conceal the sound of your heart with the noise of the river. Take the sharpness from the air for your eyes, and the clarity of the ice for your ears. And may the Being carry your blade true.

He opened his eyes. Darkness was falling rapidly, but there were no pudgias.

He waited. Perhaps there were none here? Perhaps he was too late?

He thought about wubberslugs again and tightened his grip on the crossbow.

There was a movement in the air. Something white and plump was hovering over the river. As he stared at it he noticed more similar shapes, bobbing up and down slightly, their three-winged umbrellas flicking lazily.

He hadn't even noticed them arrive! *Some hunter.*

Solly shut one eye and took aim at the nearest bird. He tried to look like part of the rock. He tried to soften his outline. He wished his heart wouldn't hammer quite so loud or fast. He steadied his hand, held his breath, and squeezed his finger.

The bolt shot cleanly between the birds with a flurry of flying feathers and squawks, landed in the opposite bank and slithered with a plop into the river.

And to make his mortification complete, before he could even swear at the loss, a pair of pudgias rose from their nest only an arm's length from his nose, protesting angrily. The male flew at him, snapping the beak in its underbelly before following its mate off into the night.

'Inferny sacks of dung!' he snarled, wondering if he could get the bolt back from the freezing water.

'Prpr. Perrrhaps next time, prpr?' remarked Sunguide, suddenly at his side.

Solly jumped and glowered at him.

'It's because of my hurt arm,' he said. 'It shakes still.'

'Prpr.'

He crawled forwards. At least the nest might have eggs to boil.

'Prpr. I fetch wubberslugs,' said Sunguide. 'Why don't you speak with wise frrriend now?'

Solly carefully took the four warm eggs from the nest and carried them back to the camp. After lighting the storm kettle and poking the eggs inside, he picked up the Janus mirror.

'Pity he didn't give me the instructions as well.'

'Rrrub it,' suggested Sunguide.

'What, like a magic lantern?' said Solly scornfully, but he did it anyway.

There was a spark of blue static and dark shapes moving about.

'Aube?'

The dark shapes wriggled a bit more and Aube's face appeared fuzzily.

'Solly, m'boy!' he beamed. 'Had a good day?'

'Cold,' said Solly.

'I expect you'll be at Latrium in no time,' said Aube. 'Quite fast, these skyboats go, I gather. They race them, you know.'

'What do we do when we get there?'

'Why, find the Key, of course. And look for people. A friend who'll hinder, an enemy who'll help.'

'You've been talking to the Pruppras.'

'Ah, yes. Most interesting people, most. We have been comparing histories. There are an amazing number of parallels, particularly in recent years. For instance, our story of—'

'I don't suppose they told you where we start looking?' Solly interrupted. 'Or any clues about what they meant by all that stuff? I mean, it stands to reason that anybody who's not a friend is an enemy, and whoever's not an enemy's a friend, so what if we meet twenty people? And if a friend hinders us, surely that makes *them* an enemy?'

'Oh, Latrium's a small enough place,' said Aube cheerfully. 'I'm sure it'll all become clear enough once you're there.'

That's no help at all, Solly thought grumpily. He let the Seer chatter on without really listening for a while. When his eggs were ready he said goodbye, ate his supper and went to bed.

53

Tuef Seventeen. FH due 9 days, 9 hours, 94 minutes. Two hearts, one brain, two kidneys, one point five livers, *no eyes* . . .

Bewildered and disorientated, Lalune's soul drifts aimlessly around the wires of the Bubblenet.

She lists her body parts.

She lists the Sleepers she knows.

She lists the Sleepers she doesn't know.

She lists their body parts.

She lists the Wayfarers.

She feels as if her insides have been filled with crushed ice then shaken up.

She writes a program to tell her each time another body part is taken from another Sleeper.

She writes a program to tell her each time a Sleeper is deleted.

She etches the lists into the air around her, where they hang, glittering, taunting her with their slowly decreasing numbers.

Too many thoughts jostle each other for attention inside her head.

Thoughts about Kenet that make her stomach clench.

Not on my side. Not helping me. On everybody's side, so on nobody's side.

Thoughts about the prophecy. About Solly laughing about it with her.

So long ago that I saw him.

Why am I part of a Wayfarer prophecy?

So long ago.

Thoughts about the Being.

Thoughts about the sun and the stars.

Thoughts about the moons.

I was named after one of the moons. Appaloosians don't even believe in them.

Thoughts about the key Solly was trying to find.

Where there's a key, shouldn't there be a keyhole?

Please, Being, you don't know me, but I need your help. We all need your help. Please can you hear me?

54

Sunguide woke Solly up long before he'd had enough sleep.

'Sun is up. Wake up, lazy Solly. Sun is up.'

'There is no sun,' Solly muttered grumpily, keeping his eyes obstinately shut.

'Get up,' said Sunguide.

'Just a few more minutes . . .'

'Get up,' insisted Sunguide. He flew to the roof of the tent right over where Solly was lying and brushed against a row of tiny icicles that had formed there, knocking them down inside Solly's sleeping bag. Solly sat up with a little shriek.

'Inferny toadstool!' he growled.

Sunguide sniggered, hovering just out of reach.

'Quick, Solly. No time to lose.'

Solly reluctantly heaved his body out of the bag and groped for the flint-box to light the storm kettle. Hopefully there would be fish to cook. He went to the river to pull out the snare he'd set the night before and was relieved to find three small dappers and quite a big bow fish wriggling on it: enough for a good breakfast. He tapped each one sharply on the head and skilfully slit their bellies to clean them before popping them all together into the storm kettle, rolled up in some edible leaves gathered from the river's edge. Preparing food was one thing he *could* do.

'Have you eaten?' he asked Sunguide.

'Pruppras exchange minerrals and gases with trrrees,' said Sunguide. 'Find frrriendly trrree branch, hang on all night, in morning rrready for anything. You rrready yet? Time to go.'

'Give me a chance,' complained Solly. 'I've only been awake two minutes.'

'Prpr. Betterrrr eat in skyboat, save time.'

Solly remembered how cold he'd been the day before, so when the fish were ready he tipped the fire from the storm kettle on to the Janus mirror, hoping that you didn't have to be a Seer to make it work properly.

But he was glad to see the levitant fire pop into its bubble again. He wouldn't be so cold today.

They had a bit of trouble persuading Star back into the skyboat.

'Come on, Star,' said Solly. 'It's not as bad as the Janus tree.'

The snowcamel snorted and pulled back.

Sunguide coaxed the skyboat as close to the ground as it would go and Solly dangled a bunch of moss to entice him forwards. As soon as Star was mostly in the skyboat, Solly tickled him behind his knees and his front legs collapsed gracelessly. Before he had a chance to struggle up again, the skyboat lifted. Star gave Solly an indignant '*Humph*', but settled down in the bottom of the skyboat with his moss.

'Why me?' Solly said suddenly, licking his fingers. The

hot fish tasted so good after the wubberslugs.

'What mean you?'

'Why did the Pruppras have to wait for me to do this thing – you know, find the Key,' said Solly. 'Why couldn't one of you do it?'

'What hrumans put wrong, hrumans must put right,' said Sunguide gravely.

'*We* made this –' he waved his hand at the glacier below, '– happen? The ice, the food shortages, everything? How would *you* know?'

'Pruppras have long memorries,' said Sunguide. 'Pruppras rrremember hrumans coming to Clandoi. See hrumans kill all – Pruppras, trrrees, plants, animals.'

Solly was shocked.

'Humans don't kill everything. Only what we need to eat.'

'Hrumans kill Pruppras,' insisted Sunshield. 'Hrumans not listen to plants. To hrumans, only hrumans worth listening to. Think fungus contaminated, kill with chemicals.'

Solly opened his mouth, then shut it again when he remembered that if Revas had ever found fungus growing in their house she would certainly have got rid of it. Sunguide continued.

'Hrumans even kill hrumans. Hrumans try kill Clandoi.'

'Now wait a minute,' said Solly angrily. 'You can't possibly think that. What proof have you of that?'

'Hrumans die in cyberclinic,' said Sunguide. 'Hrumans brrring ice, take away sun. Clandoi need sun to live. Clandoi die.'

'What hru . . . *hu*mans die in the clinic?' said Solly. 'I bet that was only when it was a hospital. People do die in hospitals sometimes. They get ill and the doctors can't always save them.'

'Hrumans die in cyberclinic.'

'And how can bringing the ice kill Clandoi? How can anything kill Clandoi? You can't kill a planet.'

'Solly must not fail,' said Sunguide gravely. 'Otherwise in big trouble. Not matter that Pruppras die if Solly fail. Clandoi die: we all die.'

'I don't believe you,' said Solly huffily. 'You're just saying that to scare me.'

'Solly want die?'

'No.'

'Then Solly must not fail.'

The skyboat dipped suddenly and Solly felt his stomach lurch.

'What's happening?' Solly said in alarm.

'We land,' said Sunguide, cocking his flaps as if listening to something.

The skyboat was almost brushing against the treetops. A small pink fluttery landed on Solly's hand, whistling tunefully. He could see every vein in its translucent umbrella wing. Morning joy birds twittered and the fragrance of the trees filled the air.

'Is this Latrium?'

'No, not Latrrrium,' said Sunguide, coaxing the skyboat down into a clearing.

'Why are we stopping then?' asked Solly.

'Spores speak to me. Is hruman nearby. We must be careful. Might be bad hruman seeking Solly.'

55

Tuef Seventeen. FH due: 8 days, 19 hours, 2 minutes. Lalune read, dazed and dizzy. *I must have blacked out. I've got less than nine days to live.*

Half a day of the precious time left to her had bled away.

Her soul body had dissipated. She drew it back together.

And what about the Wayfarers?

She had been on her way to help them when the green eye appeared, ages ago now. If the Appaloosian Sleepers were being . . . She didn't like to think about it . . . Only the Being knew what was happening to the Wayfarers. They might not even be alive.

She cautiously made her way to HIVE. There was no sign of the eye, though there were the blackened remains of dark worms littering the place. She took a WASP to the prison block.

Revas was being held with nineteen others in a long corridor. Her pod was the one at the far end. Two figures were standing next to it. Lalune buzzed towards them, resisting the temptation to fly as fast as her WASP would allow.

One of the figures glanced up at her and she

recognized him as Wuneem, the huissier who'd taken her father's job.

The other was Dr Dollysheep. He'd been Lalune's doctor from her babyhood. He was a strange man, more like a Wayfarer than an Appaloosian. There was no way he could have been, of course; Wayfarers couldn't be doctors. But he was too short and all of his visible skin was the same dark coffee colour. Sometimes that did happen, but most Appaloosians would have had a skin transplant, or at least bleached some patches in a contrasting colour.

'It's always a bit risky, of course: any operation is,' he was saying as Lalune approached. She impatiently let the WASP examine Wuneem's pendant. She wanted to look at Revas.

'She's been ill for most of her life, doctor,' said Wuneem. The pendant swung from his fingers, making it difficult for the WASP to get a reading. 'We never had enough coin before. I even considered becoming a Sleeper myself to make some quickly. That was before I knew, of course.'

He laughed unpleasantly.

Lalune had to force herself to keep the WASP still. *He's laughing at what they're doing to the Sleepers*, she thought angrily. *How dare he?*

Dollysheep was wearing contact lenses that glowed pale violet in the laser from the WASP. He waved one hand to indicate Revas and dangled his pendant in front of the WASP with the other. 'You're sure you want both kidneys from *this* woman? She's in good condition for a Wayfarer and a lucky match for your wife's blood and tissue type; but, frankly, Appaloosian organs tend to do better.'

Shocked, Lalune forgot all about looking at Revas and began to follow the two men as they walked back down the corridor.

'Definitely,' said Wuneem with a nasty grin.

Lalune lost her concentration for a moment and the WASP went into a downward dive, nearly hitting the floor before she could bring it up again. Wuneem looked at it nervously.

'You don't think that's going to attack us, like that rogue WASP the other day, do you?'

There was a recharging unit on the wall. Lalune backed the WASP into it, hoping that it would just look as if it had lost power. Dollysheep waved a dismissive hand at it and opened the door.

'The whole system's been swept clean,' he said. 'Shouldn't happen again. Now, when can we book your wife in? You might have to wait quite some time. A hundred days or more. I'm rather busy at the moment, as you know: they want to do a Full Harvest on as many as . . .'

The door hissed shut behind them.

56

For the first time on their journey Solly began to see signs that human beings had lived there. There was a road, though rather than walking on it they followed it a little to one side in case it was being watched. There were fields, barns and, at last, a round Wayfarer house.

'Is this Latrium?' Solly whispered.

'Prpr. No.'

It had been abandoned in a hurry: clothes hung out to dry days ago had been half torn off by the wind. Solly crept towards at and pushed at the door. It swung open drunkenly. They entered apprehensively.

Bedding lay strewn all over the stone floor and stripy black-and-white stingwings were investigating a pool of dried blood in the centre of the room. Smashed crockery crunched under Solly's feet. A broken clepsydra lay frozen to the floor in a pool of its own spilled water.

Solly went white.

'This is what happened to Ma and Pa,' he whispered. 'It wasn't just the Wayfarers at Opita. They're taking everybody.'

'How much Wayfarers are there?'

'In the whole world, I don't know,' said Solly, sinking down on to a little stool. His legs suddenly felt very shaky.

'There were, oh, less than thirty of us in Twilight. But there are lots of little hamlets dotted all over and there are the blackstone mines. Most were abandoned years ago, but there's still one being worked. I think there's quite a big settlement there. Maybe a hundred.'

'You not know . . .' began Sunguide, when there was a scraping sound from behind them. Solly and Sunguide both whirled around in time to see what looked like part of the floor moving. It was some kind of trapdoor. They hadn't noticed it under the debris when they first came in.

Solly crept towards it. There was a round handle set into the top. He seized it and pulled. Up came the trapdoor. Down fell Solly and out shot a small figure, straight towards the door.

'You ain't getting me too!' she shouted, but found her way blocked by Sunguide.

'Yuck!' she yelled. 'Mushy-rooms!'

She turned and ran straight into Solly's arms. She struggled for a while, but as Solly was about twice as big and three times as strong, she stopped, panting, though Solly was aware that every muscle was tensed, ready for him to relax his grip.

'We're not going to hurt you,' he said firmly. 'We're Wayfarers. At least, I am. Sunguide's a . . . a mushy-room, just like you said.'

Sunguide blew indignantly through his flaps at this.

'Ask it what happened,' he flapped.

'What happened here?' asked Solly. 'Did some people take your family too?'

The girl didn't answer, but glared at him, partly in fear,

202

mostly in defiance. Solly thought she was a girl, anyway, of about seven or eight, though it was difficult to tell, she was so dirty. Her eyes were fierce and brown: her hair could have been any colour.

'They came to my house too, in the middle of the night,' said Solly gently. 'They took my Ma and Pa, and everyone else I knew.'

'Did they break your arm?'

'No, I did that myself.'

'They took 'em away in a sledge without any snowcamels to pull it,' whispered the girl. 'I was out playing, an' they din't see me.'

'Your ma and pa?' asked Solly.

The girl nodded.

'Anyone else?'

'Tornesol, an' Nuit, an' their little girl, Rayon.' As she spoke, a fat tear slid down her cheek, leaving a pink trail in the grime. 'They was here to help Ma with my baby brother, Rian . . .'

'You have a *brother*?' asked Solly in astonishment. The girl nodded.

'What is matter?' asked Sunguide.

'I don't know anybody who has brothers or sisters,' Solly said. 'Nobody at all. The Pelegians forbade second children years and years ago, before even Ma and Pa were born, because there wasn't enough food. Now they hardly ever even give permission to have just one child.'

Sunguide floated nearer. The little girl flinched a little, but then held out her hand and touched him. She was wearing a bracelet that looked like a tiny white teardrop.

'Mushy-room,' she said softly.

'This is such a remote farmhouse,' Solly reasoned. 'Probably no huissier inspections for years. So when they found they were having another baby, they didn't think . . . The huissier wouldn't have expected two children. It wouldn't even have occurred to them to look.'

'Prpr. So she got left behind,' said Sunguide. 'What is name?' he asked the girl.

She stared.

'Mushy-room can talk?'

'Mushy-rrroom can fly too,' he said, and hovered over her head. 'What is name?'

'Etolantie.'

'Well, Etolantie,' said Solly, putting her down, but holding on to her arms in case she still tried to run away, 'it looks like you and I have both been left behind. We'd better look after each other.'

57

'I'm hungry,' Etolantie said.

'Me too,' said Solly. 'Where does your ma keep the food?'

Etolantie pointed to the hole in the floor.

'Only it's yucky,' she said. 'I tried eating it, an' it hurt my mouth, an' it's cold, an' tastes funny. What's your name?'

'Solly. And the mushy-room is called Sunguide. I expect the meat's frozen. If I let go of you, will you promise not to run away?'

Etolantie nodded warily. Solly climbed down into the pit. Like the one in his house it was an ice hole dug out of the permafrost. There was a large jar of mubble caviar and several frozen packets of meat. Enough to keep them going for several days.

At least I won't have to embarrass myself trying to hunt again, he thought. He chose some of the meat and climbed back out of the hole.

'It's going to take a while to cook,' he told Etolantie. 'Why don't you go and talk to Sunguide while I get it ready?'

When he'd prepared the meat, Solly set it to simmer and had a look around for a bubblescreen table. He knew there would be one. Several years previously, an

Edict had been issued requiring all Wayfarer houses to have one, though of course no coin for the extra electricity was provided.

He eventually found it upside down under a chair. He lifted it out. It had a long crack across the middle, but it still flickered when he put his pendant in the dip.

He glanced outside. Sunguide and Etolantie were standing patting Star and the skyboat. That was good: he was looking forward to having an uninterrupted talk with Lalune, if he could raise her. He had so much to tell her. It felt like years since they had last spoken. He didn't expect anything much to have happened inside the Bubblenet, which had sounded very boring, but he did hope to have news about his parents.

The bubblescreen took its time to inflate. The crack must have damaged something inside and the bubble kept collapsing. Solly gave it an impatient thump, and at last it was able to expand properly and sustain the bubble.

Kenet's face stared blandly out at him, reciting her welcoming message.

'Tuef Seventeen, Cyberclinic, Opita,' he said.

After a few long minutes a faltering image of Lalune appeared.

'Lalune, are you there?' he said in a low voice.

There was an explosion of pixels and the real Lalune arrived.

'Solly!' she gasped. 'Solly, I can't believe you called. Thank the Being, you called, you called.'

Solly's smile disintegrated and his mouth suddenly went so dry that he could barely get any words out of it.

Something must have happened to his parents.

A terrible feeling of dread began to grow in his stomach.

'What happened?' he managed to get out hoarsely.

'Solly, I've found out the real reason they built the cyberclinic,' said Lalune shakily.

Confused, he tried to swallow.

'Real reason?' he said. 'What real reason? I don't understand. I thought it was to keep you Appaloosians alive until the Ice Age is gone.'

'That's what they told us,' whispered Lalune. 'That's what we all thought. But it's not for our benefit at all. It's just a giant freezer full of body parts.'

'Body parts?' he repeated dazedly.

'To use for transplants. They're killing us, Solly. They're taking whatever parts they need, and when they've finished with us there's nothing left. All this taking care of us, all the mind-knowledge, all the promises of a wonderful future, it was all lies.'

Solly sat down heavily. He didn't know what to say. Lalune continued brokenly.

'Father's dead. They took out his kidneys, they took his heart and lungs, they even took his *skin*.'

'Threfem? Dead?' He could scarcely believe it. 'What . . . what about you?'

Lalune's voice cracked.

'They . . . they took . . . *they took my eyes*.' She could hardly speak. 'Solly, they took away my eyes. I'm blind, Solly. And . . . and I've been scheduled for a . . . for a . . . a F . . . F . . . Full Harvest.'

'Full . . . what's that?' Solly asked, cold foreboding filling him.

'It means . . . they'll take *everything*. Heart, lungs, liver . . . *Everything*.'

'How long?'

She glanced to one side. Her soul eyes could still see.

'Eight days, ten hours, eleven minutes.'

Eight and a half days.

'No!' whispered Solly. 'No, no, they can't.'

'There's more,' said Lalune.

She was blind! She was going to be killed! What more could they do to her?

'They . . . they're doing the same to the Wayfarers. Solly, your mother is in danger. They want to take . . . take out her kidneys and give them to Wuneem's wife. You Wayfarers only have two kidneys. She won't survive without them.'

'When?' he croaked.

'I don't know. I heard Dr Dollysheep talking to Wuneem about it, but they didn't say when, only that it would be a while. At least a hundred days. Solly, you've got to rescue us. You're the only person in the whole world who can . . .'

What could *he* do? There were too many difficulties. *If* he could get back in time, *if* he could get past the guards, *if* Lalune and Revas and any others could be woken up . . . if, if, if.

'How much do you know about the clinic?' he asked. 'Can you find out how it works . . . ? Could you get into the computer thing, you know, where it's all run from, and have it wake you up?'

'I don't know.' She cleared her throat. 'I may not be able to . . . The Wayfarers aren't properly part of the system, they might need it done by somebody on the outside . . . I could try.'

'I'll come to you,' he promised, his heart beating fast. He had no plan. She had so little time, and he had no idea if he could even make it back to her. 'I'll meet you in the entrance to the cyberclinic at dusk in eight days from now. Have you got that? Eight days. You'll have to get rid of the guards.'

'How?' sobbed Lalune, dry-eyed. 'I don't know how.'

'You'll think of a way,' said Solly. 'You have to.'

'Where will we go?'

'Leave that to me,' said Solly. 'You just do what you can for yourself. Once you're out, we'll work out how to save the others.'

Lalune nodded. She looked at him so trustingly that he felt guilty. She was relying on him for her life, and he didn't have a plan.

Solly whispered a goodbye that was painfully brief and switched off the bubblescreen.

58

'I have to talk to you,' Solly murmured to Sunguide. 'Alone.'

He gestured towards the house and they went inside, leaving Etolantie feeding Star some moss.

'Prpr. I wish to leave skyboat here,' said the Pruppras, before Solly could say anything.

Solly only heard his words vaguely. His mind was on Lalune.

'That's fine. Why?'

'I afrrraid forrr him. He verrry tired. Need rrrest. Also . . . have hearrrd frrrom spores. Something not rrright at Latrrrium. Need to apprrroach with caution. Not want him in danger. Besides, are guerdons here.'

'What?'

Sunguide indicated a grey fuzzy ropelike growth that was slung from the ceiling. Solly thought he'd seen something similar in the clearing where they'd left the Pruppras' cave. As he looked, the two ends detached themselves from the roof and waved at him slowly.

'Guerdon is fungus,' said Sunguide. 'Verrry useful, verrry rrreliable. Not talk hruman language, but can talk with Pruppras. Look after skyboat and pr-snowcamel too, if you like. Pruppras use often. Would be best. You not want Star hurrrt and he too big to hide. Prpr.'

'It would do that for a human?' asked Solly uneasily.

Sunguide blew laughter through his flaps.

'For child of prrrophecy? Would do anything for you.'

'Well, it won't make any difference now,' said Solly. 'You're going to have to find the Key without me.'

He had never seen anybody boil up into a rage so fast. Sunguide swelled up to at least twice his normal size, turned bright red, and bristled with fury. Solly even thought he could see sparks flying off him.

'Prpr. Hruman boy has no choice,' he spat, and Solly backed away. 'All depends on finding Key. All. Hrumans never understand. Why are hrumans always so untrrrustworthy? Is imperrrative boy carrries on. Must find Key. Is in prrrophecy. What make you think you can brrreak the prrrophecy, prpr, what?'

'It's Lalune,' whispered Solly, blinking back a tear. 'You were right about them killing people in the cyberclinic. You were right.'

Sunguide shrank just a little.

'They are killing girrrl? How you know?'

'I found a bubblescreen . . . She's got about eight days before they . . . They've already taken her eyes . . . I'm going back to the cyberclinic. If I can, I'll have a look for the Key afterwards. But Lalune comes first.'

Sunguide shook himself from side to side. 'Prpr. I sorry about frrriend, Solly. But Clandoi comes firrrst. Clandoi dies, we all die,' he said firmly.

Solly couldn't believe what he was hearing.

'Do you think any of that would matter to me if I

211

didn't save Lalune? I'd rather be dead. I'm going back to her. You can't stop me.'

'But if I not come with, girrrl die anyway,' Sunguide said. 'You need skyboat. Is too many days' walking for a hruman. Too many even for snowcamel.'

'Then come with me!' Solly begged. 'We'll get Lalune out, *then* find the damny Key.'

But the fungus shook its upper body in stubborn refusal.

'Eight days is plenty time to find Key. Without Key nothing can be accomplished. There will be no rrrescues of anybody. Key is near. When we find it, then we rrreturn to girrrl.'

'Yeah . . . *if* she's still alive!' Solly said, more loudly than he meant to.

Etolantie appeared in the doorway.

'Why are you shouting? Who's not going to be alive?'

Solly stared at Sunguide, daring him to admit what he was about to condemn Lalune to.

But instead the Pruppras flapped around the girl's face so that she squealed and giggled.

'Prpr. You, if not eat soon.'

'Stop it! It tickles!'

'Solly, is food rrready yet?'

There was nothing Solly could do. Wordlessly, he banged plates down on the worktop and filled them with stew. The chairs were mostly broken, so they sat on the floor to eat. He turned his back away from Sunguide and shovelled the meat down without tasting it.

Lalune was going to die and he couldn't save her. He'd promised to be there and this *sacry* fungus was going to make him break that promise.

Etolantie bolted the stew down hungrily, but could manage no more than a small bowlful as her stomach had shrunk. Solly silently found a small container with a lid to put the leftovers in and wrapped up the rest of the frozen meat from the store. He took the caviar jar too.

'Ma'll have you,' said Etolantie, giving him a piercing stare from under her hair. 'She'll want that when she gets back.'

'She'll want you to eat while she's away, won't she?' he growled.

'Girl will slow Solly down,' said Sunguide.

'So we're abandoning her too?' muttered Solly.

'Prpr. Wasn't suggesting that we pr-should,' said Sunguide, offended. Then, to Etolantie, he said, 'Is cart here we can pull you on?'

'I'm big. I can walk,' she said, drawing herself up as tall as she could, which wasn't very tall.

'You haven't eaten for a long time,' said Solly. 'You'll be weak. And how are we going to take your stuff? We're leaving Star and the skyboat here,' he added reluctantly, feeling like he was leaving behind his best friend, 'and I can't carry any more.'

'What stuff? Where are we going?'

'I . . . I need to find something at a place called Latrium.'

He couldn't help shooting a resentful look at Sunguide as he said this.

'Latrium!' exclaimed Etolantie, her eyes growing very big and round.

'You know the place?'

213

'Course I do. That's where Nuit an' Tornesol an' Rayon live. It's a mubble farm. What are you going to find there?'

'Prpr. Something that might help us rrrescue your ma and pa,' said Sunguide.

'What thing?'

'Prpr. Have you heard of the Key of Being?' asked the fungus.

Etolantie nodded solemnly.

'There's a song about that, Ma taught me. I din't know it was at Latrium. Are we going to find it?'

'*We're* going to find it,' said Solly. 'Me and Sunguide. You'll have to come with us, but you're not to get in the way. Understand? We . . . people seem to think that it's the only way to stop the ice growing any more, and until that happens we can't – ' he gulped '– we can't save anybody.'

'I'll be ever such a lot of help, you'll see,' said Etolantie, bouncing up and down in excitement.

'You've got to promise to do what I say,' said Solly firmly. 'And you need to pack. You'll need blankets and clothes, in case those ones get wet or dirty . . . dirtier. Is there anything we could carry it all on?'

Etolantie stopped bouncing and looked round doubtfully.

'There's the baby cart. But I ain't going in it.'

Solly tethered Star loosely to a tree behind the house and made sure he could reach food and water. Sunguide settled his skyboat nearby and gave instructions to the guerdon in his rubbery language. Etolantie put her things into a pack and put it on the baby cart.

Then they said goodbye to the skyboat and the

214

snowcamel and left while it was still light.

Etolantie started walking before Solly could make her ride. He had to admire her determination. It wasn't long before her eyes started drooping. She kept tripping over; but she wouldn't tell them that she couldn't manage another step. He didn't want to stop, so he picked her up, ignoring her token whimper of protest, and plonked her on to the cart.

'I'm hungry,' she said.

He gave her a drink of water and the leftover stew to eat while they walked on. When she had filled her stomach up again she lay down for a nap. After half an hour she woke up. She rubbed her eyes, clambered off the baby cart, and started to walk again without a word.

As the grey of the day began to give way to night they stopped by a stream and Solly unrolled the tent. Etolantie watched him.

'I've got nothing to do,' she said, trying to hide a huge yawn.

'Go see if you can find any bird nests,' said Solly. 'We could boil some eggs for breakfast.'

'I don't like eggs.'

'Well, I do.'

'You find 'em, then. I'll have frumenty for my breakfast.'

Solly scowled at her. Frumenty was a kind of porridge made from grain, and far too costly to eat often, at least in Twilight. Either Etolantie's parents were grain farmers, or she was being awkward for the sake of it.

He suspected both were true.

'I haven't got any frumenty, and even if I did have, I wouldn't know how to cook it. You'll have eggs or leftovers from tonight.'

'I want my ma,' said Etolantie, her lip quivering, but with no tears in her eyes. Solly ignored her and got on with putting the tent up and preparing hot mubble caviar. After a while Etolantie disappeared, and when the food was ready Solly found her fast asleep in the tent, inside his sleeping bag.

'I bet she wakes in the middle of the night now, starving hungry,' he said sourly.

Sunguide, who was perched nearby, blew through his flaps.

'Prpr. She could certainly rrrepresent the friend who will hinder you.'

'Humph,' said Solly. He didn't want to speak to Sunguide. He ate his mubble caviar, then rolled himself up in a blanket next to her, but hardly slept at all.

59

'Wake up, silly Solly.'

Solly squeezed his eyes shut.

'Go away, not time to wake yet.'

'Is, too, lazy bones.'

Solly felt his shoulder being shaken roughly.

'Go away.'

'I made breakfast for you. Me an' Sunny went out an' found some. Wake up.'

Reluctantly Solly opened his eyes to find a bowl of frumenty in front of his nose. Etolantie was hugging her knees and staring at him.

'Sunny found wild grains growing in a field,' she said. 'I lighted the storm kettle an' cooked it all by myself. It don't taste much like Ma's but it's all right.'

Solly sat up and started to eat. The frumenty was watery and tasted scorched.

'S'nice,' he said with his mouth full.

'Fibber. It's yucky.'

It was hard to swallow with Etolantie staring at him. When he had finished, he wiped his mouth on his sleeve and gave her the bowl back.

'Thanks,' he said. 'You wash up; I'll take the tent down.'

'Why can't you wash up?' demanded Etolantie.

'I cooked. I can do the tent.'

'You don't know how.'

'Yes I do.'

Solly sighed and struggled out of the tent.

'All right, you take it down. Where's Sunguide?'

'He's hanged himself up over there,' said Etolantie. He was swinging gently in the branches of a tree near to where Star was grazing, and looking far more cheerful than he deserved.

'What's up with you?' Solly said rudely.

'Prpr. Not used to these trees,' explained Sunguide. 'Good light, makes stronger sap. Sleep well?'

'No.'

'*Will* get back to her, Solly,' said Sunguide after a little pause. 'Girrrl is parrrt of prrrophecy also: girrrl cannot die.'

Solly said nothing.

There wasn't much snow around any more: summer had well and truly arrived. The ground had become a half-frozen bog, and they were forced to rejoin the road now. There were trees bigger than any Solly had ever seen before. If he'd stood on Brise's shoulders, he couldn't have reached the top branches. The stream chuckled along next to them. After a while it widened and poured into an artificial square lake. More trees shaded one end of it and enormous bubbles were popping out of the water and floating up into the air at the other end. They were muddy in colour and, when Solly looked more closely, they appeared to have legs. He watched as one of them floated up to the trees above and he held his breath, waiting for it to pop. But it didn't. Then he noticed more

218

muddy bubbles hanging there.

'Are those mubbles?' he said. 'As in, mubble caviar?'

'Ain't you never seen mubbles before?' said Etolantie scornfully.

'I come from Twilight,' Solly said. 'We don't get much growing there.'

'I know all about mubbles,' said Etolantie importantly. 'Tornesol told me. They eat all leaves all day long until they get so heavy they fall in the water, an' then they lay eggs. That's what the caviar is. Eggs. Then the leaves turn into gas,' she giggled at this point, 'but instead of farting it fills 'em with gas an' makes 'em float up again, an' then you can get the caviar.'

'Don't they notice that somebody keeps taking their eggs?'

'Nah. They're very dumb.'

Etolantie, revived from a night's sleep, started to sing.

'*There was a today, an' now's a today, an' more todays will follow. Today is all, the past is myth, an' never comes tomorrow.*'

'That's a stupid song,' said Solly.

'No it's not,' said Etolantie. 'Ma sings it to Rian.'

'It's still damny stupid.'

'That's a bad word,' said Etolantie self-righteously. 'An' it's a nursery rhyme. Nursery rhymes are *allowed* to be stupid.'

'She's rrright,' put in Sunguide from over his head. 'Nurserrry rrrhymes are *allowed* to be stupid.'

And to Solly's annoyance, Sunguide joined in. Etolantie skipped along, barely pulling on the baby cart at all, and Solly's injured arm began to ache, which it hadn't done for days.

'Will you two shut up!' he exploded at last. 'In case you'd forgotten, we're supposed to be being quiet!'

'You never told *me* we had to be quiet,' Etolantie said, but she did say it in a subdued tone.

Solly didn't like being so exposed on the road. He stood still, listening. There was no sound apart from distant birdsong. He sniffed the air. Nothing.

'All right, let's go,' he whispered eventually. 'But be quiet this time, will you?'

The cart skidded along in the slush uneasily. They crept through a thicket of trees until they were safely past the lake.

Suddenly they stumbled out of the trees and into the open. Solly was dazzled by the whiteness and he had to shield his eyes. He heard Etolantie gasp next to him.

'It's the edge of the world!'

60

FH due: 7 days, 17 hours, 5 minutes.

The Being must have heard her! It was going to be all right! Solly was coming to rescue her. All she had to do was be ready.

'What do I have to do?' she murmured.

'I'm sorry, I do not understand the question,' said Kenet, appearing as always at her side. Kenet knew everything there was to know, didn't she? Saw everything there was to see?

Including me. Lalune thought, remembering the virus tracker. She would make sure she phrased her questions very carefully. She didn't want Kenet to alert anyone about what she was doing.

'How will the Sleepers be resuscitated when it's time to wake them, Kenet?'

'That information requires Grade Eight clearance.'

Try again, thought Lalune.

'When will the Sleepers be woken?'

'There is no timetable to wake them. However, individual subjects may be detached from the system for purposes of harvesting.'

Lalune shivered.

'What happens to the Sleepers when they are detached?'

'Orders to detach human components from the system must come from a Grade Twelve medical officer,' Kenet said. The voice coming out of her mouth was male and bored-sounding. 'Any order to detach a subject automatically alerts the commanding administrator, who must verify the order for resuscitation to continue. Once the order has been verified, the central bubblescreen controls the procedure, which cannot then be stopped. Body temperature is returned to normal and the pulse resumes. The orbal oil is drained from the pod and from the lungs, allowing the natural intake of oxygen to restart. The component is checked for viability. At this stage the subject is still in a deep coma but, left alone, will come out of it naturally. Before this happens the required organ should be removed by a trained physician . . .'

'Thank you, Kenet,' said Lalune, not wanting to hear any more. *So if I start this procedure somebody's going to send in a virus tracker*, she thought.

'What happens if a virus is completely sealed inside a deflector shield?' she asked.

This time it was a breathless female voice that answered her through Kenet's mouth.

'Several such instances have occurred in the history of the Bubblenet. For a while, the viruses go unnoticed. However, as VTPs are able to learn from each experience and adapt, they are growing more sophisticated each time, and the length of time before an illegally concealed virus is discovered has been reduced exponentially.'

Silvery words were pouring out of Kenet's mouth. Lalune scrutinized them carefully.

'And these are the viruses that have been found?'

'Yes.'

Details that referred to the virus that she had been hung accusingly in the air before her.

So when I became a virus I made the Bubblenet better at making VTPs, she thought. *Which'll make things more difficult now.*

She summoned everything she knew about the Bubblenet, viruses and programming. Words streamed to join the silver writing floating in the air. Some she already knew: most came from the mind-knowledge the Bubblenet had given her. She would have to read and understand every single word. She was going to have to construct the best virus deflector shield in the history of the Bubblenet.

Lalune laughed hollowly, wondering what her mother would have said.

She was hopeless at this sort of thing.

FH due: 7 days, 16 hours, 69 minutes.

61

They were standing next to a wall of solid cloud from which was coming a very faint, almost imperceptible hum. A branch from a nearby tree was sticking into the bright mist and seemed almost weighed down by it: Solly could see it for the whole length of his arm before it disappeared into the thick cloud. It was grey rather than white, though still very bright to his Twilight eyes; and went on and on for ever, arching right over their heads.

Solly had always been taught that the cloud went on in a matching curve under their feet too: a hovering mass of cloud, the flat planet that was Clandoi mysteriously alive within it.

There was nothing Beyond, he knew. There were no moons, no sun, no stars. probably no Being, either. It was all myth and here was the proof. He put out a tentative hand, expecting a cold wetness.

But it was warm and slightly tacky. Like candyfloss. It reminded him of a day long ago, when a traders' fair had come to Opita. He and Lalune had wandered about the stalls and Threfem had bought them both some.

He drew his hand away and a strand of the cloud clung to it, drifting in the breeze.

'Eeuw!'

Etolantie had wandered further along, her voice muffled in the still air.

'What is?' said Sunguide, zooming along to her. Solly followed.

Etolantie said nothing, but pointed and held her nose. Solly saw a dark shape stuck half in and half out of the cloud. A stink of rotting flesh hit him. The two hind legs of a snowcamel were jutting out from the cloud, as if it had been running into it and was unable to stop. It had been dead for a while: its fur was hanging off it in shreds, and half of its flesh was gone. Even from this distance they could see that it was crawling with maggots. Stingwings were milling around it.

'Stay away,' Sunguide said to Etolantie.

'Why?' she asked, walking towards the animal. 'I seen dead animals before.'

'No, Etolantie,' shouted Solly, who had seen what Sunguide had seen. He caught the girl by the shoulder and tried to swing her round, but then she saw – and screamed.

The part of the animal inside the cloud was still alive. It was completely untouched by time and the stingwings hadn't been able to get inside the cloud to lay their eggs. Its face was turned towards its rump with a puzzled expression. As Solly watched, it opened its mouth and yawned and tried to walk away, but it was stuck, for ever half in and half out of eternity.

Solly managed to pull Etolantie away out of sight of the creature.

'Why was it like that?' whimpered Etolantie.

'I don't know,' said Solly. He suddenly felt cold. He

pulled his hood on and hugged himself. 'Have a drink, you'll feel better.'

'No I won't,' said Etolantie, shivering. 'I'll never feel better. I'll have bad dreams until I *die*. What happened to it?'

Solly took off his pack to get a blanket out to put round her.

'Prpr. I expect it was chased and rrran into the cloud,' said Sunguide, though he sounded far from certain.

'But why . . .'

'I don't know, all right?' said Solly in exasperation. 'Now, put this on and let's get away from . . .'

Etolantie screamed again. There was a rush and something heavy hit Solly's head.

Solly fell to the ground, completely disorientated. His hood had fallen over his eyes so that he couldn't see. He could feel hands round his neck. He could hardly breathe. He tried to wrench himself free. Through the roaring in his ears he could hear Etolantie yelling.

'Gerroff 'im! Gerroff!'

Solly tried to reach for his knife, but his hand was grasped and pulled round to his back. At least that meant that he could breathe now. There was a frenzied flapping noise from Sunguide. His assailant gave an enraged yell and fell away from him.

Solly gasped for breath. He tried to pull himself awkwardly up to his knees, but Sunguide was flung backwards towards him. They fell over in a heap.

'Leave Sunny alone!' shouted Etolantie, throwing herself forwards. Solly tried to stop her – but too late. Their attacker caught hold of her and spun her round. It

226

was a woman, and she was holding Solly's knife.

'I'll use it!' she said. 'Tell me what you're doing on my land.'

'Let me go!' shouted Etolantie, and bit the woman's wrist. The woman hissed and jerked her arm from around Etolantie's neck, but before the girl could run the woman grabbed her by the hair and pulled hard. Etolantie squealed and Solly saw angry tears come into her eyes. Seeing that she was about to kick the woman, he said sternly, 'Stop, Etolantie!'

Panting, Etolantie stopped and glared at Solly.

'That's better,' said the woman. 'Now, tell me, what are you doing here?'

The woman didn't look Appaloosian, but she was tall for a Wayfarer, dark-haired and dark-eyed, and beautiful in a cold sort of way. She was dressed in black: black leather boots, black woollen trousers and a long hooded black cloak. Her hair was piled on top of her head in a tumble of curls. Next to Solly and Etolantie's rather pallid skin her face was golden-brown and youthful. Despite this, she gave the impression of being much older: fifty or sixty perhaps.

'My parents were taken by the Appaloosians,' he said. 'So were Etolantie's. We were running away from them.'

'Why here?'

Solly opened his mouth to answer, but Etolantie got in before him.

'My granny lives somewhere near here,' she said. 'Ain't this Latrium? We're going to stay with her.'

Damny kid! thought Solly. *Tell everyone where we're going, why don't you?*

The woman shook her head.

'There's nobody here but me. I expect it's a common enough name for houses backing on to the cloud. What's she called? Perhaps I could help? I might even know her.'

'Granny,' said Etolantie sweetly.

The woman frowned at her, then turned to Solly. The fight had made him hot, so he had pulled back his hood; now he thought he saw an expression of surprise flit across her face.

'Your face looks a little familiar,' she said. 'Do you have a brother?'

She let Etolantie go, and the girl stumbled back to Solly and took Sunguide from him.

'Nobody has brothers here,' Solly said, instantly regretting his words when Etolantie gave a small sob. *She* had a brother.

'No; no, of course not,' the woman said. She had an odd accent, nasal and thin, which Solly had heard once before, though he couldn't think where. 'Well, never mind that. When I heard you I thought you must be Appaloosians. They've been here once already, but I hid from them. I expect that's what you did, too, isn't it?'

Sunguide blew faintly. One of his flaps was torn and was oozing green sludge.

'You've hurt him,' Etolantie said accusingly.

'What is it?' said the woman. 'It attacked me.'

'*You* attacked *us*,' said Etolantie.

'It's my . . . um . . . pet,' said Solly. 'A kind of clever mushroom. I'm sorry if it hurt you. It's very protective.'

'Perhaps you'd like to come back to my house and we'll try to patch it up,' said the woman, giving Solly his knife back. 'I'll give you something to eat. Then perhaps the little girl needs an afternoon nap? She seems tired.'

Etolantie snorted.

'All right,' said Solly uneasily.

'You'd better tell me your names,' said the woman, watching as Etolantie put Sunguide into the baby cart and tucked a blanket carefully around him. 'My name is Sybilla. Sybilla Geenpool.'

62

The farmhouse was old. It was of typical round Wayfarer design, except that here at Worldsend its builders had decided to add windows, which gave it an ominous, watchful look.

'What do you need for your . . . uh . . . pet?' asked Sybilla.

'Thticky tape, an' warm water,' said Etolantie promptly. Sybilla instantly looked irritated at Etolantie's newly acquired lisp, and Solly hastily turned a laugh into a cough.

'I think I can manage that.'

'An' toffee.'

'Toffee?' said Sybilla sharply. 'I hardly think that toffee is going to help patch up a mushroom.'

'He needth it for energy,' Etolantie said, with a wide innocent gaze.

Sybilla narrowed her eyes.

'Very well. But I don't have much at the moment. It's very expensive, you know.'

They reached the farmhouse, which backed directly on to the wall of cloud.

'Take off your outdoor things, then come inside,' she said. 'I'll go and find some sticky tape. And toffee, of course.'

'Toffee?' said Solly softly, when she had gone.

Etolantie grinned at him.

'Sugar helps him grow better quicker.'

'And you're hoping there might be some left over for us,' said Solly. 'I take it Sunguide told you about the sticky tape?'

Sunguide blew a muffled raspberry from under his blanket.

'He's already started mending himself,' Etolantie said. 'He jus' needs help holding the torn bits together. I wish I could mend me like that.'

'Come inside,' said Sybilla. 'I've put the things you need on the table.'

As he entered, Solly's stomach gave a little flutter: if this house was the Latrium he was looking for, it was where both Aube and the Pruppras had felt the Key of Being was hidden. It could be here, in this room.

And then he could go back to Lalune.

'There you are, little Thunny,' Etolantie crooned, gently putting the fungus on the table. Solly saw, to his shock, that it was wooden. How Sybilla could ever bring herself to allow anything on it, let alone a mushroom that was exuding green pus, he didn't know.

The piece of toffee Sybilla gave them for Sunguide was as big as Solly's palm, twice the size of the stick Lumie had given him; but she still asked if it was enough, as if she had a cupboard full of the stuff. Solly watched Etolantie carefully crumble a tiny bit on to the wound and bind it with sticky tape. She didn't seem to need any help, so he stole a few glances around the Sybilla's house.

It was much the same as Solly's home, with a central

room surrounded by several small chambers. Here they were separated from the main room by doors made of scratched green-painted steel instead of curtains.

He tried not to look around too conspicuously. Would he know the Key if he found it? He fingered the pendant hanging round his neck. Everybody had keys just like it, ornamental as well as functional, and gemstones were used to adorn everything from weapons to furniture.

There was an ornate clepsydra hanging on the wall, decorated with dozens of coloured crystals. Any one of them could be a key. Through an open doorway he could see a small work chamber with a stand of half-finished daggers, each set with a large red stone.

A wave of exhaustion came over him. He could spend weeks in this house looking, but completely miss the Key of Being.

Etolantie had finished bandaging Sunguide's wound. She was holding him like a baby and looking about her much more openly than Solly.

'What'th that?' she asked, pointing to a door in the corner. It looked newer than the others and wisps of steam were escaping from under it.

Sybilla's laugh was an insincere-sounding tinkle.

'It's a bathchamber. Don't you have a bathchamber in your house?'

Solly knew from Lalune that Appaloosians had chambers with showers in, which was only sensible, as otherwise the water would go all over the floor; but he'd never heard of a house with a chamber just for bathing.

'Everyone I know utheth a tin bath in front of the fire,' said Etolantie.

'Well, I suppose it is rather special,' said Sybilla, looking as if she could quite believe that Etolantie didn't know what a bathchamber was. 'We have a hot underground spring here. My grandparents had the bath put in to take advantage of it. You look as if you could use a bath.'

Her eyes ran over them and Solly realized how dirty and uncomfortable he was. Suddenly the thought of being clean and sleeping in a real bed became overwhelmingly enticing.

'I wouldn't mind one right now, if that's all right with you.'

63

FH due: 6 days, 9 hours, 30 seconds.

Lalune was trying not to count the hours left to her. It made it too difficult to concentrate.

But it was almost as impossible as forgetting that she was blind.

She had her shield ready. It was much the same as the first one she had built, but she hoped that it would give her longer. A lot longer. She needed a day and a half to make sure she could be resuscitated properly: thirty Clandoi hours.

She'd written a simulation program to run inside the orb-map. Each second should show what would happen in a whole hour when she ran the real thing.

'Now I just have to count the seconds,' she whispered fiercely. '*Run program.*'

The program started. Lalune began to count.

'One . . .'

Immediately, green eyes started to appear. Lalune's heart sank.

'. . . two . . .'

The eyes attacked her shield viciously.

'. . . three . . . four . . .'

And that was it. Her deflector shield was a few strands

of ash that melted into nothingness.

    After just four hours it would be useless.

    Lalune set her mouth grimly and started again.

64

Solly hesitated inside the bathchamber door. An elaborate lantern hung, unlit, from the domed ceiling. A white tiled staircase spiralled downwards. Darkness and steam rose up the steps, obscuring the bottom. He could hear the gush of water somewhere below: how far, he couldn't tell.

'It's only a bath: it won't hurt you,' Sybilla suddenly said from behind him, and he jumped. 'I'll light the lantern for you. Here are towels and soap. There's a platform near the bottom of the steps for you to leave your clothes on. Bring them up when you've finished and I'll show you where to wash them.'

'Thank you,' said Solly, watching her light the lantern with a long taper. When it was lit, he stepped inside gingerly. He could see the water now, glinting gently through the steam. There was a smell of sulphur. He walked down the steps. There was indeed a platform near the bottom, with a door at one end. He tried it, but it was locked.

Solly stripped off his clothes and threw them on to the platform. He took off his pendant and laid it on top of them. He looked at the bandage on his arm, filthy from days of travel, and gently unwrapped it, blinking away thoughts of Revas putting it on him. His arm started to ache as soon as it was off. The red scar had healed under a neat row of fluttery-silk stitches. He picked at one of these with his nail, wincing as it came out.

The steps continued right down into the water. The water was yellowish, but that didn't matter: it was deliciously hot and deep enough for him to stand up in it waist-deep. There were some small recesses in the tiled walls he guessed were for holding candles, soap, or maybe even drinks. He waded towards the nearest one to put his soap into it and stubbed his toe on an underwater seat.

A seat in a bath? he thought, laughing out loud.

He sat down and the water came up to his neck, soothing and wonderful on his arm.

The bathchamber certainly didn't appear to be the three generations old that Sybilla had said it was. There wasn't so much as a hint of a stain or chip, despite the discoloured water. Cleverly placed mirrors set into the walls reflected light from the lantern, giving the whole chamber a warm glow. Hot water poured continuously from a golden spout in the shape of a large fish and a matching one indicated that cold water could be added with a twist of the fish's tail. The underwater seat was perfectly contoured for comfort. A mosaic of silver and gold fish leaped around the walls in a splash of turquoise droplets. The rest of the tiles were pristine and white, even below the water line. It was the most luxurious chamber he had ever been in.

When Lalune and I are married we'll have a house with a bath in it just like this one, Solly vowed.

He almost felt he should have washed *before* he came in. He hadn't realized he was so filthy. Greasy scum lifted off his body and slid across the surface of the water towards a grating in the wall. He scrubbed himself thoroughly with the soap, which smelled of some exotic fruit, and slid right under the water to wash his hair. When he had finished he sat back and picked out the rest of his stitches before relaxing for a while and letting his thoughts waft on the steam.

I will rescue Lalune. *I will* think of a way, he told himself. But no ideas came to him.

Finally, when his fingers started to wrinkle from the water, he splashed up the steps and wrapped a towel around his waist.

Feeling cleaner than he ever had before, he mounted the steps. The door opened without a sound on well-oiled hinges.

A voice stopped him on his way to his bedchamber. It was Sybilla's and it was coming from the chamber next to the bathchamber. He couldn't hear what she was saying, but he did hear the unmistakable beeping of a bubblescreen. Sybilla must be talking to somebody over it.

Which meant that he could search for the Key.

Holding up his towel with one hand, he crept to the clepsydra to examine the gemstones. The clock had been constructed in such a way that the water trickled down over the stones in a gentle waterfall, and each one was coated with a layer of mineral deposits. They were unlikely to be keys, as the crust would be growing on the inside of them, damaging the workings.

He could still hear Sybilla's voice murmuring, but not what she was saying.

He moved on, pushing open the door to the work chamber that he'd seen before. The daggers were blunt and flimsy, made for decoration only, and covered in dust. He picked one up and blew the dust off it.

'What are you doing?' said Etolantie from behind him, and his heart leaped into his mouth from the shock.

'Looking,' he said, trying to still his heart.

Dust motes filled the air and Etolantie sneezed.

'What for? For the Key of Being? Can *I* help?'

'Shh!'

He scowled at her. He didn't want her help. But he probably needed it.

'All right. But carefully. And quietly.' Under the dust the stone was very new, recently cut and polished. He was sure that the Key of Being would be very old. Legends about it went back for ever. 'It'll be some kind of stone, like an ordinary key, but the electronics might be hidden,' he added, putting the dagger down and looking around the chamber. He couldn't see anything else that could be a key.

'I know what a *key* is,' said Etolantie.

Solly followed her out of the chamber. Sybilla was laughing, but she was still in the bubblescreen chamber. Solly looked around the main living area. The stone floor was worn into pathways by generations of feet and the walls were old and crumbly: the chairs, however, were new and, like the table, were wooden.

The doors had dark-green gemstone handles. Could one of them possibly be a concealed key? Solly examined the nearest one carefully. It was translucent and was clearly just a door handle. So was the next one. He worked his way around the room, but none of the handles could possibly have been a key. The only one left to look at was the one to the chamber Sybilla was in.

What if she came out while he was looking at it? His palms sweated at the thought.

But this might be his only chance to look.

He was edging towards it when Etolantie hissed at him from behind.

'*Solly!*'

His heart thudding, Solly whirled around. Etolantie was grinning at him from one of the bedchambers.

'Etolantie!' whispered Solly furiously. 'Don't keep doing that!'

'Look what I've found,' Etolantie said softly.

'Is something wrong?' said Sybilla from behind Solly, and he nearly dropped his towel. Etolantie giggled.

'What's that you've got, Etolantie?' asked Sybilla acidly.

Etolantie was holding both hands behind her back.

'Nothing.'

Sybilla's eyes tightened into slits.

'You are a very rude and objectionable little girl,' she said, crossing the room swiftly. Etolantie dodged towards Solly for protection and he wrinkled his nose. Now that he was clean he could tell just how awful Etolantie smelled. And he must have been just as bad.

Sybilla grabbed Etolantie by the arm before she could get behind Solly. She shook her hard and pulled out her hand. In it she was clutching a rag doll. It was dressed in scraps of leather and wrapped in a blanket with the words *Rayon's Baby* stitched on it in very wobbly cross-stitch.

'You nasty, lying, ungrateful little thief,' spat Sybilla.

'How dare you abuse my hospitality like this! If it weren't for Solly I'd throw you out right now. As it is, you'd better go straight to bed, with nothing to eat.'

'Aren't you afraid I'll thpoil your sheetth?' said Etolantie cheekily. 'I'm very dirty and thmelly, after all.'

Sybilla couldn't hide her fury. The thought of her precious sheets being soiled clearly pained her, but letting Etolantie experience the wonderful bathchamber would seem like a reward.

'All right,' she said at last. 'You can have your bath. But I shall come with you to make sure you're properly washed. Get down there. I'll bring a scrubbing brush and some old towels.'

She shoved Etolantie, who stumbled across the room with undisguised glee. Sybilla stalked to the other side of the room to rummage in a cupboard and Solly sneaked a quick glance at the doorknob on the bubblescreen chamber. It looked exactly like all the others.

Once Sybilla had gone down to the bathchamber with Etolantie he would go inside the bubblescreen chamber to look for the Key.

Sybilla had found what she was looking for.

'I've laid out a clean dressing gown for you to wear until your clothes are clean,' she said as she carried a pile of threadbare towels to the bathchamber. The smile she turned on him was so brilliant that Solly blinked.

'Thank you.'

She paused in the doorway.

'I know that Etolantie isn't your sister,' she said, 'but you'd really better learn to control her more effectively. Do help yourself to a cup of tea, won't you?'

As soon as she had shut the door behind her, he swung the other door open and tiptoed in.

There was the bubblescreen table. It looked brand new. He could contact Lalune on it.

He was about to sit down in front of it when he realized that he'd left his clothes, with his pendant, down in the bathchamber. He banged the table in frustration.

Still, that wasn't what he'd come in here for. He started by the door and searched the chamber carefully.

There wasn't much in it. Next to the door was a shelf holding some glass ornaments. There was a model of a tall building with three pinnacles. There was an engraved picture of Sybilla and several other people standing behind a sickly-looking blond boy who appeared to be making some kind of speech. Solly thought to himself that the people must have been awfully cold, as they were wearing very flimsy-looking clothes with no sleeves. Some even had bare legs.

There were other pictures featuring Sybilla as well and, right at the back, as if shoved out of the way, was a book, just like the ones Aube had. It had an old and faded red leather cover. In the centre, surrounded by rays of gold leaf, was a perfectly round yellow stone. And on the spine, in words almost too flaky to read, was written *The Key of Being*.

65

FH due: 6 days, 0 hours, 58 seconds.

'. . . thirteen, fourteen, fifteen . . .' counted Lalune.

The eyes appeared. Her voice faltered.

'. . . sixteen, seventeen, eighteen . . .'

And the shield failed once more.

There were so many other things she had to do – and she was running out of time.

66

Solly turned the book over in his hands. Could this really be the Key? The thing he had come all this way to find?

Did that mean he could go back to Lalune now?

Something rustled behind him and for the fifth time that day he jumped in shock. He turned round guiltily, hiding the book under his towel; but it was only Sunguide. He had a big piece of sticky tape stuck clumsily on to his torn flaps.

'You're as bad as Etolantie!' Solly said churlishly. 'Creeping up on me all the time!'

'Prpr. Apologies,' Sunguide said meekly.

'I found this,' said Solly. He pulled the book out again.

'What is?' asked Sunguide.

'It's a book. And the stone in the cover might be a key. Look . . .' He pulled his pendant from around his neck. 'They put information inside these stones, and when you want to open something with it, like a door, or a bubblescreen, or something, it reads the information, and if it's the right key, it opens.'

Sunguide looked intrigued.

'Pruppras have no need for such locking away things. Prpr. Is Key of Being, perrrhaps?'

'I don't know,' said Solly. 'It says it is on the cover. But it might just be a book about it. I don't know how to tell.'

'Take stone out,' said Sunguide. 'You are Holder. If *is* Key, perrrhaps will rrrecognize you.'

Solly glanced at the door. He could hear Etolantie arguing with Sybilla down in the bathchamber.

'*What if I thlip on the thtepth and bang my head and drown?*'

'*Don't be silly, Etolantie. Get in like a good girl.*'

Because of the noise they were making, he felt it was quite likely that he'd notice when they came up again, but all the same . . . He tiptoed into the bedchamber Sybilla had shown him and closed the door softly after Sunguide. Then he ran his fingernail around the edge of the stone and prised it out. It was the size of his palm. He looked carefully at both sides – there were no markings or electronics of any sort. But deep inside it something flickered like a flame.

'*Ouch, it'th too hot,*' came Etolantie's voice.

'*Then I'll put some cold in.*'

'Hold flat in hand,' suggested Sunguide, peering closely at the stone.

Solly laid it flat in his left hand – and suddenly the stone began to vibrate and a sweet note sang out clearly and quietly. The flickering inside the Key became fire that flowed up his arm and down his body, until he was completely surrounded by it; yet instead of burning him, Solly gasped as if he had been doused in cold water. The sound seemed as if it was coming from very far away, but at the same time it could have been coming from inside his own heart. Something deep within him recognized this note, and he had been waiting to hear it his whole life.

He felt as if he had been in a darkened chamber and somebody had turned a spotlight on to him. Everything else diminished in comparison: everything drained away. The sound of Etolantie arguing faded; even the fear and pain that were with him constantly lessened; nothing was as important as this Key that was lying in his hand.

He gawked at Sunguide, mouth open, face flushed, and although he was aware that he was there, he didn't see him.

This could only be the Key of Being, and only *his* hand, the Holder's hand, could make it resound like that.

I want to hold it for ever.

'It's . . . it's . . .' he croaked.

Sunguide nodded wisely.

'Key knows you. Key rrresonates with you.'

'I should go now,' he whispered, ignoring his friend. 'This is only the start. I have to finish what I've begun.'

Sunguide flapped at him gently, but Solly didn't see him. All he could see was the fire of the Key of Being and the task he had to fulfil. All he could hear was that pure tone, ringing through him as if his whole body was a bell.

'Prpr. Perrrhaps firrrst can . . .'

'What am I supposed to do?' He could hardly hear Sunguide through the deluge of sound. It didn't matter anyway. Nothing mattered except the Key and what it wanted of him. He opened the book to the first page. 'Maybe there's instructions in here.'

'Prpr. Hruman boy mustn't forrrget . . .' urged Sunguide, but he could have been miles away.

'I can't read it,' said Solly. 'Why can't I read it? I know

the letters . . . I know the words . . . but they're all jumbled up . . .'

'Hruman boy! Solly! Hearrr me!'

'A code? Yes. No. Probably. It's almost as if something inside my head stops me from reading it. Aube will know.' He replaced the Key reluctantly into its place in the cover of the book. 'We should get back to him . . . *Oh, dung!*' The Key stopped resounding. The flame shrank.

Solly looked at Sunguide, aghast, as reality flooded back. 'Lalune! We have to get back to her. I forgot about her! How long's she got? How could I forget?' He dropped the book on to the bed as if it really *had* burned him. 'It was the Key. It *made* me forget! It was just like the Janus tree.'

'*Eeuw, the water'th yellow, how can you get clean in yellow water . . . now it'th too cold . . .*' Etolantie's voice bawled up to them once again, sounding wonderfully annoying and real.

'What is it?' Solly said fearfully. 'Is it . . . something *evil*?'

'Prpr. Key is strrrong,' said Sunguide. 'Key wants to bend your will to itself. Key is not evil. But is verrry single-minded and perrrhaps not see big picture.'

'The big picture?'

'Is not whole of Key,' Sunguide explained patiently. 'Rrremember rrrhyme? *A thrrreefold Key; a thrrreefold Holder; a thrrreefold lockfast Queen. One finds its Holder; one its Holder finds, one has always Holder been.* Key is in thrrree parts. Is only one part here.'

'And I found it,' said Solly slowly. 'So somewhere there are two more parts, one which has to find its owner, whatever that means, and one which . . . what was it?'

'One which has always belonged to its Holder. Prpr.'

'*Key of ice, and key of fire, and key of joy and pain . . .*'

'Prpr,' Sunguide nodded approvingly. 'Is key of fire.'

Solly gazed at him unseeingly.

'And since Lalune is *also* part of Aube's prophecy, and as she doesn't own anything like this − not that I've ever seen, anyway − *she* must be the one who gets found by her part of the Key.' He focused his eyes defiantly on the Pruppras and balled his fists, ready to argue. 'Which means we have to rescue her. Right now. Before it's too late.'

But Sunguide nodded meekly.

'Is good. Now is time to rrrescue her.'

'You're agreeing with me,' Solly said suspiciously.

'You have found the Key,' Sunguide said. 'No need to wait longer. Prpr. We know girrrl is part of quest as well. Perrrhaps is what the Pruppras prrrophecy meant. Pr− before the end you will begin again. In Opita you began, to Opita you must rrreturn.'

He leaped from the bed. 'No time to lose. Prpr. I fetch skyboat. Be back by dusk. Be rrready.'

And he was gone.

67

FH due: 5 days, 16 hours, 9 minutes.

I can't do it, thought Lalune in despair.

She had never felt so useless in her life.

After two precious days and numerous trial runs, her deflector shield still failed in just moments. All the adjustments she had made had gained her minutes, not hours.

She could almost hear her mother's voice: *Really, Lalune! How can the daughter of Threfem and Toayef Seventeen be so damny incompetent?*

She had a list of things to do still and she was running out of time. She had to start resuscitating herself thirty hours before Solly's arrival. Any later and she would wake too quickly: any sooner and she would be waiting for too long and she'd be discovered. She had to ensure that the huissier couldn't escape too quickly. And she still hadn't made sure the Wayfarers were getting the food supplements she had researched.

She tried her simulation again with yet another adjustment. A tiny figure of herself stood inside the orb-map and a shield sprang up around her like a bubble. She became invisible inside it, but the shield was so thick, to accommodate the extra programming, that it blocked the tunnel she was in. That was the problem. The blockage alerted the virus trackers straight away.

She let the program run its course while she tried desperately to think of something, *anything* that would help. Soon green eyes had appeared in all the major arteries and were targeting the shield.

Suddenly a large area around the shield went black. There were so many of the trackers that part of the Bubblenet became overloaded and simply disappeared from her model.

A memory popped into her head: she was very small; she was trying to control a WASP; the whole Bubblenet had to be swept; *the whole Bubblenet had crashed . . .*

'Kenet, what happens if the Bubblenet fails?'

'If part of the Bubblenet fails, that part of the Bubblenet and everything it controls shuts down,' said Kenet.

'What does the Bubblenet control?'

'Everything,' said Kenet.

'Doors? Locks?'

'Everything,' said Kenet again.

'So if the whole Bubblenet fails . . .'

'If the whole Bubblenet fails, all non-essential processes are aborted. A failsafe system will keep minimal heating, lights, and the Sleepers' life systems going until such time as the fault can be repaired.'

Lalune phrased her next question carefully.

'Is the resuscitation process counted as part of the Sleepers' life system, or would that shut down too?'

'If it has been initiated it will continue,' said Kenet, staring flatly ahead as normal.

Lalune stared at the blacked-out area in her simulation. Was it possible that she could make the whole Bubblenet crash again? She needed to give herself at least thirty hours: a day and a half. But she didn't have to create a shield that would actually work: she just needed to compile something so big and complicated that hundreds of trackers were released at once.

Only she didn't have enough time left to check it properly. She could only make it and trust that it would work.

68

Sybilla and Etolantie emerged from the bathchamber equally pink, wet and angry.

'Go to your chamber,' snapped Sybilla. 'I put a clean robe in there for you.'

Etolantie marched off defiantly. Her hair was now the colour of fluttery honey, and a lot of what Solly had assumed to be dirt turned out to be freckles covering her from head to toe.

'Oh, Solly,' Sybilla said, flashing a radiant smile in his direction, 'you left your dirty clothes downstairs . . . Solly? Are you all right?'

Solly jumped.

'Yes. I'm . . . fine,' he lied. His mind was with Lalune and his head was still resounding with the Key note. He padded down the steps and was surprised to see that the door that had previously been locked was now slightly open.

He pushed it curiously, expecting to find plumbing. And there were pipes, grey and dripping; but beyond them a tunnel disappeared into the darkness. It was twice his height, wide enough for four people to walk abreast, and it continued in a straight line for as far as he could see. The stone walls and floor glowed golden and new in the light from the bathchamber, each block straight-edged and shiny, as if they had never been trodden on.

A secret passageway? thought Solly. *An escape route? Built by whom? Escape to where?* A cave, perhaps; mines, like the blackstone ones at Glimmering. He would ask Sunguide where they were.

He pulled the door back to nearly shut, as it had been before, and turned to go back up the step; but something was bothering him about the passage. He put a foot on the bottom step and looked upwards. The door at the top would bring him into the main room of the house. The porch was directly opposite. If he carried on walking in a straight line from the top step, he would be walking at an angle more or less perpendicular to the cloudy boundary at the edge of the world.

Which meant – and he turned round to look at the door behind him as the enormity of what it meant made him reel – which meant that *the passageway went in exactly the opposite direction.*

Directly *through* the barrier that marked the edge of the world.

The legendary tunnel into the Beyond.

Solly had to lean against the wall for support.

All his life he had secretly – and recently not so secretly – despised Wayfarer teachings about the sun, the moons, the Being, the Beyond and everything else that they naively believed in. How could such things be true? You couldn't hold them, touch them, or see them.

But now, in front of his eyes, was this underground passageway, and he no longer knew what to think.

Except, perhaps, to wonder why Sybilla had left

253

the door open for him to see it.

He swung the door open again. As far away as he could see, there was a tiny pinprick of light. Brackets on the walls held electric lights instead of orbal-oil lanterns. He had a vague idea that you needed a switch to turn them on, and he felt along the wall. Sure enough there was a switch near his head. He was about to press it when he heard Sybilla calling him.

'Are you all right down there?'

'Coming,' he shouted, pulling the door shut. He hastily scooped up his clothes and scurried up the stairs.

69

FH due: 4 days, 2 hours, 39 minutes.

Lalune had completed her shield at last and could move on to the next task.

'Kenet, could you show me everything there is in the Bubblenet about resuscitation, please?'

'There are six million four hundred and ten thousand and five files containing the word resuscitation,' said Kenet. 'Would you like them all?'

Billions of words whirled around her like volcanic ash. Lalune gaped. People trained for years to do this sort of thing. She had two days at the most and she couldn't afford to make any mistakes. Her life depended on it.

'Uh, add in some parameters: "how to" and "cyberclinic",' she said, flustered.

About two-thirds of the files melted away. There were still far too many to read. She picked three at random and read carefully through them. It took all her effort to take the information in.

'It's so complicated,' she whispered. 'How will I ever do it?'

There was already a program stored in the administrator's bubblescreen, but she didn't dare use it in case it set any alarms off. She would be discovered before she had time to blink.

The best way to do it, she supposed, would be to create a chain reaction. Each program would have to do one thing, like administer a drug, or raise her temperature; and then it would have to initiate the next program. None of them could be complicated enough to alert anybody.

And they would have to work first time. She wouldn't be around to keep an eye on them. The first program she wrote would put her back into a deep coma.

There were a hundred things that might go wrong.

What if I can't do it? she thought. *What if I use the wrong drugs? What if my body gets woken up before I can get back inside it? What if I can't re-attach myself to my body? Would I be left inside the Bubblenet?*

Or worse: nowhere at all?

Best not to think about it. Just do it. And pray.

70

Sybilla seemed to have forgotten all about sending Etolantie to bed. While they were dressing, she set food out for them to eat: an aromatic stew, roasted red vegetables, and some tiny white sticks. Solly prodded his dubiously: they looked exactly like white wubberslugs. And anyway, he felt too agitated about Lalune concentrate on eating.

'I never had thith before,' said Etolantie.

'It's called rice,' said Sybilla, taking a dainty bite. 'It's a kind of grain.'

Etolantie forked some into her mouth and chewed thoughtfully. Solly thought it pretty flavourless when he tried some; but at least it wasn't wubberslugs. Etolantie spooned in a large mouthful of the stew; then her hand flew to her mouth, her face turned scarlet, and she spat it out.

'Yowch!'

Sybilla's face twitched.

'I'm sorry, I probably made it too spicy,' she agreed.

'Spicy?' asked Solly, as Etolantie pawed at her tongue. Revas used spices, but they didn't hurt.

'I put spices in to add to the flavour, but they do tend to make it a little hot,' explained Sybilla. 'Have some water, Etolantie.'

Etolantie gulped down some water, splashing it all over the precious table so that Sybilla winced. Solly blew on his meat to cool it down, but when he put it in his mouth he nearly choked. His throat was on fire!

'Sacry inferny!' gasped Solly, his eyes watering. 'S-sorry, I don't think I can eat this.'

'Oh, but it was one of my mother's favourite recipes,' said Sybilla, and though she sounded disappointed Solly had the distinct impression that she was enjoying herself. 'Try the vegetables.'

But they were even worse. Solly sucked his breath in so hard that he accidentally inhaled some rice, while Etolantie flung her fork across the table, stumbled to her feet and rushed to the sink for more water.

'Yuck! That's not food! How can anyone eat that stuff?'

Sybilla had another mouthful.

'I see it's cured you of your lisp, anyway.'

'S-sorry, we're j-just not used to the, um . . . hot,' coughed Solly.

'When I was a child, I ate what was put in front of me,' Sybilla said primly.

'Well, I'm not going to,' said Etolantie, wiping her eyes on her sleeve. 'I'd rather *ththth*-tarve!'

'Really? Well, I think you'd better leave the table then.'

Etolantie flounced out of the front door in tears. Solly gave Sybilla an apologetic glance and followed her.

'Horrible, horrible, horrible woman!' sobbed Etolantie, walking away from the house with rapid steps. 'I know she don't like me. She done it on purpose.'

'Well, you're not exactly being nice to her,' Solly said, though he privately agreed with her. 'She's just a lonely old woman. And she is one of us, after all.'

'*She* ain't no Wayfarer,' said Etolantie.

'Don't be silly. She's not an Appaloosian.'

'I'm not being silly,' said Etolantie. 'Look how she's tooked Nuit an' Tornesol an' Rayon's house, an' she's pretending it's all hers. That was Rayon's dolly I found. An' she speaks funny, an' she's got two names. How many Wayfarers d'you know with two names?'

That much was true. Every Wayfarer Solly had ever heard of had just the one name. It was one of those things that distinguished them from Appaloosians.

'An' she attacked us.'

'She thought *we* were Appaloosians.'

Etolantie snorted.

'A blind pudgia in a bag could tell *we're* Wayfarers. An' anyway, she had more toffee than I've ever seen, an' that rice stuff, an' that other horrible food, an'—'

'All right, all right, I agree,' said Solly.

Etolantie pulled the toffee from her pocket and gave him a chunk.

'Thanks. What's with the lisp, anyway?'

Etolantie grinned. She stuffed a lump of toffee in her mouth and spoke through it.

'Thome people think it's thweet. 'Sides, *she* kept calling me "*little girl*".'

She had something that looked awfully like a live green wubberslug crawling out of her nose. Solly felt in his pocket to see if he had something she could wipe it on.

He didn't, but he did find the Book of the Key. He

hadn't had a chance to tell Etolantie about it yet, or that they were going. He plucked a large leaf off a nearby bush and casually turned, so that if Sybilla was looking she wouldn't see anything.

'Here, wipe your nose on that,' he said. 'And look. I found this while you were in the bathchamber. Don't let her see.'

Etolantie's eyes widened as she dabbed at her nose.

'Is that the Key? How d'you know if it is?'

'It's part of the Key. Hold it in your hand,' he said, taking the stone out of the book and giving it to her.

'Why's it only part? Nothing's happening. What's it s'posed to do?'

Solly took it from her and once again the Key sang the note that resonated with his heart: once again the flame flared. He didn't give it time to overwhelm his will this time, though. He put it back into the Book again quickly.

'It only does that for the Holder,' he explained, trying to look modest. 'There are three parts, and three Holders. You know, like in the song? *A threefold Key; a threefold Holder; a threefold lockfast Queen. One finds its Holder; one its Holder finds, one has always Holder been.* Because I found the Key, I'm the middle one: the "one its Holder finds".'

It was strange how the meaning was suddenly so clear to him.

'That's about you?' said Etolantie in awe. 'I wish I had a song about me. When we find the other pieces, will they sing too?'

'I suppose so. For the other Holders.'

Etolantie swallowed her toffee.

'So now what do we do?'

'We find the other Holders,' said Solly. He put the Book back into his pocket. 'I know where one of them is. She's a prisoner back in Opita. In the cyberclinic. Where we think your ma and pa are.'

'So she's asleep in there, then?'

'Well, her body's asleep: she's kind of awake in the Bubblenet.'

'Who is she? One of the Wayfarers from Opita?'

Solly remembered that the only Appaloosians Etolantie had ever seen had taken her family away. 'Um . . .'

'An . . . *Appaloosian*?' Etolantie said in an appalled whisper.

'Lalune is different,' said Solly firmly. 'You can't judge what somebody's like on the inside by what they look like on the outside. Lalune's been my friend since the day we were born. We can trust her. I managed to contact her from your house.'

'You never told me. How?'

'With your bubblescreen.'

'Are we going to get her out? An' Ma and Pa? An' Rian?'

Solly hesitated. Etolantie's eyes had suddenly grown large with hope and sadness. Lalune knew nothing about Etolantie and her family.

'I can't promise anything. We don't even know if we can get Lalune out. But once she's out, we can work out how to rescue the others as well. She lives in there: she knows much more about it than anyone else.' He took Etolantie by the shoulders and stared at her sternly. 'It's going to be difficult, Etolantie, and dangerous. Will you promise me, absolutely promise, that you'll do exactly as you're told all the time?'

'I promise,' said Etolantie in a subdued voice.

'And don't go and upset Sybilla too much. You'd better say sorry to her.'

She pouted at that.

'We have to be ready to go by dusk,' said Solly. 'That must be another half hour. Sunguide's gone back to fetch the skyboat.'

He started to walk back to the house.

'Wait. How are we going to get away from Sybilla?' said Etolantie, tugging his sleeve.

'Uh, we could say goodbye and walk out of the door?' said Solly.

'But what if she doesn't want us to go?'

'Don't be dumb,' he said. 'She's just a sad, lonely woman.'

'But what if she's planning on keeping us here an' eating us or something?' Etolantie whispered ghoulishly.

'Well, if she tries to stop us, you get her into her bedchamber and I'll lock her in. Now come on.'

71

FH due: 3 days, 21 hours, 41 minutes.

Lalune was getting anxious. There was so much to do; so much she didn't know how to do.

I'm blind, she thought. *How can I stop myself from being caught once I'm out? I've got to lock the huissier in. The Bubblenet crashing will do that. But then I'll lock myself in as well. And won't the emergency power reactivat the locks? And even if I change all the codes, they'll override them.*

Her head was aching.

She closed her soul eyes and breathed deeply into her soul lungs.

She couldn't afford not to think clearly.

What would Mother do? she asked herself.

Toayef was the cleverest person she knew.

She'd do something like . . . like make every keystroke update the codes.

Lalune nodded. That's what she'd do. The bubblescreens would be useless. Every time somebody hit a key, the codes for the locks would change to a random number. There'd be somebody who could sort them out in time, but meanwhile she could escape . . .

72

When they returned to the house, Sybilla was standing in the doorway wearing a scrupulously contrite expression.

'I apologize,' she said. 'I suppose I'm just so used to eating spicy food, I didn't realize that you wouldn't be.'

Solly glanced at Etolantie, but she didn't say anything. He kicked her and she glared at him.

'All *right*!' she said. 'I *thaid* I'd thay thorry, an' I will. I'm thorry for thaying your thupper wath dithguthting. There.'

Solly almost choked on a laugh. He was sure Etolantie had inserted as many lisps into the sentence as she could.

Sybilla smiled graciously.

'Well. Now we're all friends again. Come. I've put some bread on the table. No spices anywhere, I promise.'

Sybilla shut the door. They sat down once more to eat and Solly had a mouthful of the bread. He was starving: and it was very good bread.

'It really is very good of you to look after us like this,' he said when he'd swallowed it, 'but if you don't mind, I think we won't stay after all. Um, Etolantie should get to her granny as soon as she can.'

Sybilla's hand made a brief grasping motion towards them and a strange expression darted across her face. It was like disappointment, but stronger. Just as quickly, she replaced it with regret and folded her hands together.

'So soon? But you must at least stay the night.'

'I think it would be best if we went,' Solly said.

'Oh, but you haven't even washed your clothes,' she said. 'Stay here and I'll show you the washing machine.'

'You have a *machine* to wash your clotheth?' Etolantie said in disbelief.

'Why of course,' Sybilla said, with her irritating tinkle of a laugh. 'And another one to dry them with.'

Solly thought of his mother's hands, cracked and red from washing all their clothes by hand. On washing days at home, their clothes had to be hung around the central fireplace and the whole house filled with mist. He stood up abruptly, clearing his throat, which had for some reason become constricted.

'You've already done more than enough,' he said. 'And we're very grateful. But we must go. Get your stuff, Etolantie.'

'It was the food, wasn't it?' said Sybilla, looking genuinely repentant this time. 'Tell me what you like to eat and I'll order some in.'

'Thanks,' he said turning towards his bedchamber, where his own pack was waiting, 'but no, I, uh, just think Etolantie should be with her own family.'

'But it's already getting dark,' said Sybilla. 'Where will you sleep? Do you know where to go? How will you get there?'

'We've got a tent,' Etolantie said, hauling her pack out of her chamber. 'An' thleeping bagth an' everything.'

'My, uh, pet has another . . . pet, a skyboat,' Solly said,

making sure both packs were fastened properly and that his snowskates were tied on. 'It's like a big flying balloon. It's how we arrived. I've sent him to fetch it.'

'I saw no balloon.'

'We left it at Etolantie's place.'

To Solly's surprise, Sybilla's expression was suddenly not angry but sad, and for a moment he nearly changed his mind.

'I see you've already made your decision,' she said, blinking and turning her head away. 'Go. You can wait for your . . . *balloon* outside.'

She got to her feet, scraping her chair noisily and wiping one eye with the back of her hand. Solly glanced at the bread. It seemed she wasn't going to let them finish it.

'It was very good of you to feed us,' he said, but she didn't take the hint. 'Thank you. We are indebted by your clemency. Both of us. Aren't we, Etolantie?'

'Oh, yeth: *thank* you, Thybilla.'

Sybilla just stood there, arms folded, lips so tight they were edged with white. Solly swung his pack on to his back and led Etolantie out of the house. The door slammed shut behind them.

The Ne'Lethe was darkening and a bitter wind had sprung up.

'Where's that toadstool?' muttered Solly.

'What about the baby cart?' said Etolantie.

'Not sure it'll fit in the skyboat,' Solly said.

'But—' began Etolantie.

'Pa will make a new one for your brother,' Solly said. *If we ever see either of them again.* 'There's Sunguide now,' he added, as the white sphere of the skyboat came into sight.

When it was close enough for them to scramble in, Etolantie pointed back at the house.

'She's watching us, look.'

Sybilla's dark silhouette could just be glimpsed through the window. Etolantie waved cheerfully.

'Byee!' she yelled gleefully. 'I wouldn't use the bath for a while. I peed in it.'

73

'Where's Star?' said Solly, when they were settled into the skyboat.

'Safe,' said Sunguide. He was busying himself with the skyboat, and though he didn't have a head to turn away from Solly he still managed to look evasive.

'We're going to fetch him now, I spec,' said Etolantie. 'Aren't we, Sunny? Going to fetch him?'

Sunguide didn't answer her, but spoke to the skyboat in his rubbery language.

'You've left him behind, haven't you?' said Solly accusingly.

'Prpr.'

Solly forgot where he was and tried to stand up. The skyboat swayed and he fell over.

'Hey!' yelped Etolantie.

'Where is he?' demanded Solly.

'Prpr. Had to leave him,' said Sunguide. 'Fly much, much faster pr-without.'

'You nearly fell on me,' said Etolantie.

'But he's a puppy!' cried Solly. 'You've left him behind on his own! Anything might happen!'

'Will be pr-fine,' said Sunguide calmly. 'Are fungi watching him, prpr. Guerdons, Pruppras spores. Plenty food.'

'What if he's attacked?' shouted Solly. He felt furious, as if all his worry over Lalune had suddenly become ignited. 'What if a giant poley finds him, or a whippersnapper? He's an easy target: he's tied up.'

'Fungi can hide him, prpr,' insisted Sunguide. 'Or can rrrot through rrrope, he rrruns away. He safe.'

'Yeah, safe like the one we saw stuck in the cloud.'

'I want my ma!' snivelled Etolantie, and Sunguide flew to her and nuzzled her shoulder comfortingly.

'Solly not frrrighten girl,' Sunguide said sternly. 'Pruppras would not leave innocent crrreatures in danger. Star will be verrry well. If want to rrrescue moon-girl, Solly must leave snowcamel: sometimes necessary to pr-sacrifice the pr-small for the sake of the pr-big.'

Solly glowered at him belligerently. Why was life always so inferny unfair?

As darkness enfolded them, a freezing wind sprang up. Solly found a package of wubberslugs, which Sunguide appeared to have an endless supply of, and heartily wished he'd told Sybilla they were leaving *after* they'd eaten.

A shower of sleet left rows of icicles dangling from the ropes and icy patches on their coats. The dampness seeped through a hole in Solly's coat and Etolantie's teeth rattled together like castanets. They unpacked their sleeping bags and blankets and wrapped them round the pair of them so that they looked like an enormous fluttery cocoon with two furry hoods.

'What's that?' said Solly, as Etolantie tried to hide something from him.

She brought it out reluctantly. It was the dolly she'd found at Latrium.

'You stole it *again*?'

'*I* din't steal it,' Etolantie said scornfully. 'It's not *Sybilla's*, it's *Rayon's*. I tooked it to give back to her.'

They tried to sleep as well as they could in the freezing-cold night while the skyboat took them away from Worldsend and into Brume.

When Solly woke in the morning he couldn't think where he was; then his insides turned to ice as he remembered Lalune. He gave a great big shuddering sob.

'Oh good, you're awake at last,' said Etolantie. 'I need to pee!'

'You'll have to wait,' said Solly grumpily, not opening his eyes. Every muscle was stiff and sore, and he thought longingly of Sybilla Geenpool's bathchamber.

'I can't wait. An' I'm not a *boy*: I can't go over the side like you did.'

'I did not!'

'Yes you did. I *seen* you. When you thought I was asleep.'

There was an embarrassed pause. Solly pulled his sleeping bag over his head.

'I *need* to pee!' said Etolantie, pulling it down again so that an icy finger of wind thrust itself inside it all the way down to the bottom.

'You'll have to hold on,' said Solly, yanking it back up.

'I can't. I'm only *eight*.'

Sunguide was sniggering.

'Don't know what you're laughing at,' said Solly angrily. He was still a long way from forgiving the Pruppras.

'I not getting involved, prpr. Hruman prrroblem.'

'I bet you have to do *some*thing,' said Etolantie with interest, jiggling up and down.

'Pruppras have excellent metabolism,' said Sunguide loftily. 'Pruppras expel gases into trrrees, exchange with vital nutrrrients.'

'Eeuw!'

Solly sat up at last and felt in his pack.

'What are you doing?' said Etolantie.

'Mubble caviar,' he said, holding up the jar. 'We'll finish it for breakfast and you can use the pot.'

Etolantie looked appalled.

'I can't go in *that*!'

'You think of something then,' said Solly crabbily.

'You mustn't see.'

'I'm not interested in seeing,' he said, exasperated. 'Look, I'll tip the caviar out into the storm kettle and turn round while you're doing it. I won't even think about it. How's that?'

Etolantie took the jar from him sulkily and got busy, with many mutterings of 'It's freezing!' and 'The skyboat's rocking too much!'

When they had eaten and had a square of toffee, both felt a lot less irritable. At noon, they stopped briefly by a lake to take on fresh water and relieve themselves more comfortably.

The day had warmed up a little. When they were back in the skyboat, Solly took the Janus mirror out of his pocket and rubbed it.

'What's that?' asked Etolantie.

'Janus mirror,' said Solly shortly. 'For talking to people who are somewhere else.'

'Are you talking to your friend? The Appaloosian?'

'No, to Aube. He's a Seer.'

The screen fuzzed with static.

'Solly, m'boy!'

Etolantie stared at the Seer inquisitively.

'Are you a *real* Seer?'

'Bless me if it isn't a young lady,' said Aube.

'I like your eyebrows.'

'Why thank you, m'dear,' he said, wiggling them for her.

'Aube, this is Etolantie,' said Solly.

Aube's eyes suddenly looked as if they were focusing somewhere far away and his eyebrows wiggled furiously.

'I see two plants entwined,' he said. 'Two beginnings and one end. The known will start the task, the unknown will complete it.'

'What?' said Solly. 'What are you talking about?'

Aube blinked. 'That's it,' he said. 'Just that. Hold on to that, Etolantie. It'll be important one day.'

'Did you See something for *me*?' said Etolantie in amazement. 'Did you hear? He Saw something for *me*. I ain't never had something Seen for *me* before.'

'Etolantie . . .'

'What's it mean?'

'Hmm. Now that I can't tell you,' said Aube. 'You'll know when the time comes.'

'Aube . . .'

'So, you've got the Key and you're going back to fetch the moon-girl,' said Aube.

'They're going to kill her, Aube. They . . . How did you know?'

'Wh . . . what d'you mean, they're going to kill her?'
Etolantie said in a scared voice. 'Kill who? Your friend?'

Solly hadn't meant to let her know what was
happening in the cyberclinic, possibly to her parents. But
it was too late now. He gave her an agonized look.

'I'll explain later. How *did* you know, Aube?'

'Hmm,' said Aube. 'The Pruppras are very single-
minded. I doubt they would let you go back if you
hadn't found the Key. And of course those spores are jolly
good messengers. Told me all about Lalune, too. Blind,
hey? Poor moon-girl. Let me see it, then, hmm . . . The
Key, that is.'

Solly took the Book of the Key out and once more
placed the Key in his palm. The Key note sounded. Even
just that moment had made him aware of its will bending
his, so he put it down again quickly.

'It came with a book, but I can't read it.' He held it up
to show Aube. 'And if Lalune *is* another Holder then we
have to rescue her anyway, don't we? And there's what the
Pruppras said about starting again. I have to go, Aube.'

'Yes, yes, of course you must,' said Aube. 'She is in great
danger. Great danger. You should get to her at once. Pity,
hmm. I should have liked to examine that Key for myself.
And the book. Naturally that will have to wait, hmm?
Leg's mending, but it all takes time. And as you say, Lalune
is another Holder. Now there's the thing. A different
prophecy to fulfil, hey, Angelus? You must return to the
start of the race and begin again.'

'It's not a race!' cried Solly. 'Lalune's going to be killed
if I . . . Ma and Pa will be . . . Everyone . . .' He gulped
down his fear and whispered his confession, the thing

that had been bothering him. 'I promised Lalune I'd meet her at the entrance to the cyberclinic in four days from now. But I don't know what to do. I don't know *how* to rescue her.'

Aube pondered for a moment.

'It seems to me that all you have to do is be there,' he said at last. 'Do as you said you would to the moon-girl. Be there in four days. She will do the rest. We must all pray to the Being on her behalf. She has the most difficult part to play now, hmm?'

74

FH due: 2 days, 2 hours, 75 minutes.

Only a few hours remained before she had to
begin the process. She'd got everything in place. She'd
made sure the Wayfarers were getting their vitamins
and antibiotics.

Now she just had to check it all.

And then check everything again.

Though Lalune felt moderately pleased with herself, at
the same time she was terrified in case she'd done
anything wrong. So much depended on her. So many
people's lives were in her hands.

All this programming. She'd learned so much,
done more than she'd done in her whole life outside
the Bubblenet.

But it was done. She was about to leave this virtual
kingdom of hers. Back to the real world. Where she
wouldn't be able to see.

Back to Solly.

If it all worked.

She began to check everything.

75

'Are they really goin' to kill your friend?' Etolantie asked fearfully.

Solly shrugged.

'Not if we get there in time.'

'Are they going to kill . . . you know . . . anyone else too?' she whispered.

Solly swallowed and put the thought of Revas out of his mind.

'Don't worry about your family. I think it's the Appaloosians they want. They were lied to. The cyberclinic was built for them, not the Wayfarers. They were told it would bring about a better future. Well, it will, but not for them. The reality is that it's a spare parts store. They're just pieces of human tissue, frozen to give other people a future.'

Etolantie whimpered.

Solly noticed that it seemed a lot darker and colder. Were they in Twilight already? They were flying quite low. In front of them was a great mountain: one side had been completely torn away by a glacier to make a sheer cliff. They were going to have to climb quite high to get over it.

He was about to break his silence towards Sunguide

and ask where they were when the skyboat lurched, throwing them to one side.

'What's wrong?' he said in alarm.

'Prpr. Think skyboat tired,' said Sunguide. 'He done well, hasn't he? Long way to fly in shorrrt time.'

'Are we in Twilight?' asked Solly.

'Glimmerrring,' said Sunguide. His flapping sounds were more sluggish than usual.

'You're tired too,' Solly said, feeling suddenly guilty.

'Prpr. Don't need rrrest like hrumans do,' said Sunguide, 'but sure could do with a trrree to rrroost on.'

'I'm sorry,' said Solly. 'I've let you do all the work.'

'Skyboat not listen to you,' said Sunguide kindly. 'Besides . . .'

The skyboat pitched again more violently and Etolantie squealed as Sunguide shot into her unexpectedly. There was a squawk from somewhere above them. Solly caught sight of a large white bird.

'It's a snobrella,' he shouted. 'We must be in its territory.'

'It think skyboat's a rrrival,' said Sunguide, scrambling up and tugging at ropes.

But Solly remembered the snobrella Brise had shot, so long ago it could have been in somebody else's life, though it was only just before Lalune had entered the cyberclinic. It was now transformed into boots and combs in his house. What had Brise said? '*Snobrellas pair up for life, Solly, and will kill in revenge. Always try to shoot both, if you can. I couldn't find the female . . .*'

'No. It thinks we killed its mate.'

The snobrella was rising up ready for another dive. It was incredibly strong and terribly vengeful.

'Stop it, Solly!' shouted Etolantie.

'It won't stop unless we kill it,' screamed Solly.

'Or it kills us!' cried Etolantie.

'Need to get away,' panted Sunguide.

He tried to bring the skyboat about, but there was another flurry of wings and a glimpse of wickedly sharp claws. Solly took out his crossbow, but the skyboat was rocking too much for him to aim.

There was a sudden horrible squealing noise and the skyboat spiralled around. They hit a tree, then the cliff, and then they landed in a snowdrift in a chaos of fungus and blankets.

'Is everybody all right?' panted Solly.

Sunguide was making a most extraordinary noise – a cross between a wail and a raspberry.

'Pr-not skyboat,' he flapped. 'I think he prpr-punctured.'

Etolantie yelled, 'Solly!' and pointed upwards. The snobrella was directly above them, dropping on them like a stone.

76

FH due: 1 day, 10 hours, 5 minutes.

It was time.

Please, Being, make it work.

Lalune remembered something Solly had once told her. A kind of prayer that the hunters used before the hunt. It seemed appropriate.

'I make the . . . the knowledge of the Bubblenet my mind . . .' she said out loud. 'Uh . . . I take the strength of snowcamels for my will . . . I conceal myself with the fog . . . I ask to share Solly's courage to face what lies ahead . . . and may the Being make this program run true.'

For once, Kenet didn't offer any advice.

Please, I need thirty hours.

77

Solly was already holding his crossbow. There was no time to prepare. He just shot.

The jade bolt sang through the air in slow motion. It hit the snobrella squarely in the middle. There was a grisly tearing noise and a terrifying shriek. The snobrella's wings whirled wildly as it crashed down towards them. They flung themselves out of the way as it hit the snow with a dull thud. Darkness seeped out of it, staining the snowdrift. The snobrella's head lifted once, then fell back, lifeless.

My first proper kill, thought Solly. He should have been elated, but instead he felt sick.

Sunguide flew to the skyboat's balloon to examine a huge gash.

'Will he be all right?' said Etolantie, but Sunguide didn't answer.

Solly thought of how he would feel if Star had been attacked, and suddenly he realized that his snowcamel was probably in a lot less danger than any of them. He also thought how fast and how far the skyboat had brought them, and how he'd never said a word of thanks to Sunguide for lending them his pet.

'He hurt, but he heals,' said Sunguide, after a long

anxious few minutes.

Solly cleared his throat awkwardly.

'Sunguide, I'm sorry about sulking over Star,' he said. 'You were right to leave him. We'd never have made it this quickly with him as well.'

'Does he need sticky tape, like you did?' asked Etolantie anxiously, producing Sybilla's roll from her pocket.

'Pr-sticky tape work forrr short flight,' said Sunguide. 'But still need to fly rrright over mountain.'

'What about sewing him up?' said Etolantie.

'We don't have needles or thread,' said Solly.

'You got fluttery-silk string,' she said. 'An' you got hunting stuff, fish hooks an' things.'

'Would help heal,' said Sunguide, obviously very distressed, 'but still won't be able to fly far.'

'Would toffee help again?' Solly asked remorsefully. 'How much is left?'

'A bit,' said Etolantie.

She'd kept it in her pocket, though there was rather less of it left than Solly had thought. He took some fish hooks out of his bandoleer, ready-threaded with almost invisible fluttery silk.

'Out of the way, Etolantie.'

'I can do it,' said Etolantie, who was already crumbling toffee into the wound.

'Can you sew?'

'I made Rayon's dolly,' said Etolantie proudly. 'Well, not *made* it exactly, but I did do the words . . .'

'It no good, prpr, no good,' flapped Sunguide. 'He no fly more, prpr, need rrrest forrr days. Still need to rrrescue moon-girrrl.'

'How far away are we?' said Solly.

'Have to go rrright over mountain,' said Sunguide. 'Then is hillock of Cirrque Hallow, then Opita. Is two, thrrree days of hruman walking.'

Solly punched the cliff as hard as he could.

'Damny, sacry snobrella!'

Snow cascaded on to their heads.

'Look out!' complained Etolantie. 'An' I need them needles and string.'

Solly threw them to her.

'Well, that's it, then,' he said miserably. 'Lalune's stuck there. I failed her.'

Etolantie poked the fish hook into the skyboat's skin. It quivered and she pricked her finger.

'Ow. Stay still, skyboat,' she said, licking her finger. 'The Being wouldn't have tooked you this far an' then not get you there. There'll be another way. You'll see.'

'Got any ideas?' Solly said, sinking to the ground.

'If you can't go over the mountain, why not round it?' she asked, carefully pulling the thread. 'Or through it.'

Through it! Solly and Sunguide looked at each other and at the same time said, 'The mines!'

'Do you know where they are?' Solly said, leaping to his feet.

'Prpr. Not in my colony's terrritorrry,' Sunguide flapped. 'Can only guess frrrom what I hearrrd.'

Solly was already picking up his pack.

'Guess then!'

'Long time ago, when hrumans firrrst arrriving, they look for blackstone,' said Sunguide, bunching up as if trying to remember something. 'They mined in these mountains. But blackstone rrran out, and hrumans said there were ghosts, so they left, found other better mines. And then the glacier grrrew, swallowed up the entrrrance, making rrrocks fall. Last I hearrrd, is all blocked now, except forrr one passage.'

'Where?'

'It a naturrral cave,' said Sunguide. 'Is prrrobably why it didn't collapse like the rrrest.'

Solly dropped his pack and started to jog along the cliff.

'Rrremember, not blocked for Pruppras — might be impassable for hrumans,' called Sunguide.

'I'll chance it. You look that way, I'll look this.'

He loped along, looking for any small opening in the rocky wall. It wasn't easy; the cliff face was full of cracks and crevices, but none of them went in more than an arm's length.

After about half a mile, he saw a black shadow on the cliff. He sped up. He could see the prints of some small animal, like a tree rutter.

Then he saw a bit of charred wood.

Only hunters are allowed to burn wood, he thought with elation. *Pa and the other hunters got snowed into a cave for days.*

He broke into a run and skidded to a halt as he arrived at a narrow entrance. The shadow above it was soot. A snowdrift had blocked most of it, but there was a dip in the centre as if some time ago somebody had dug their way out of it. Sleet had fallen since, obscuring any footprints. He sniffed the air for animal smells, but could only smell a very faint tang of woodsmoke.

283

He climbed up over the snowdrift and slid down the other side.

The cave was almost round, with a flat floor. In the centre was a ring of stones full of ash; next to it was a stack of wood and enough blackstone for several days. The floor was dusty and he could see footprints. When he turned round, he saw a red flag sticking out of the snowdrift.

He didn't have to dig to find out what it marked. He knew there would be a cache of meat under the snow, waiting for his father and the other hunters to collect it.

'They caught three swags that day,' he whispered, touching the flag. It was stiff with frost.

At the back of the cave a small opening led into another, much smaller cave. Solly had to bend over to get into it. He took out his flint-box and struck a flame. The roof had collapsed into a large pile of brownish rocks towards the back. He held up his flame and it bent forwards towards the rocks. Somehow, air was getting through.

And something glinted gently behind the rocks, on the wall of the cave. Something grey and rusty: a steel strut.

'This is it!' he shouted, and his voice tumbled around the cave. 'I've found the entrance to the mine.'

78

FH due: 1 day, 10 hours, 2 minutes.

Lalune stood with her soul hand poised over a virtual switch. Once she had pressed it, the resuscitation process would begin. She had given herself two minutes to shut down the Bubblenet before her soul was sucked back into her body where it belonged.

She hoped.

It was the most uncertain of many things she was unsure about. Deflection shields had been made before. The Bubblenet had failed before, at least in part. The resuscitation process had been done many times: every time another Sleeper had been harvested.

But nobody had ever had their soul detached from their body and then re-attached.

'Appaloosians don't have souls,' she told herself fiercely.

She understood now why it was so comforting for Appaloosians to believe that there was no history. If they believed there had been people before them struggling to push humankind onward and upward, people today had to continue to do the same. If they knew there would be people after them to call them to account, they would act responsibly. People with no soul and no history are accountable to no one. Appaloosians could do as they wished: it didn't matter.

If she had no soul, then what happened next wouldn't matter. If she died, nothing would ever matter again. Days would go on being written on top of days just as they always had done, and she would be forgotten, deleted, as if she'd never existed.

Did she really want to believe that? Did she really want to trust in a great hollow Nothingness, as solid and real as if it were trying to be Something?

She shut her eyes tightly.

Being, it's me again: Lalune. I know I've got no soul, and I'm not one of your people, and that I've got no right to call on you like this. But I need your help again. If I do this and fail, we all die – your people as well. But if I succeed, we might be able to work out how to save them. I've done my best. Please . . . please make it all go well.

She opened her eyes again. The switch was waiting, like a seed of hope.

She pressed it.

She began to feel the effect immediately. The tips of her toes tingled and felt as if something was pulling them inwards.

She summoned her orb-map. Inside it, the tunnels of the Bubblenet glistened in miniature like a million heaving worms. She took a deep breath and thought herself to a vault in the middle of the Bubblenet, where she had left her deflector shield. It was a golden sphere; pulsating gently, as if anticipating the tremendous task it had been given. It was just the first amongst many: a great chain reaction of blockages within the Bubblenet that should eventually shut the whole thing down. Its surface shimmered and writhed with the words, numbers and symbols of the program. All she had to do was press the switch.

She had one minute left.

She leaned forwards.

'An illegal procedure has been detected and must be prevented,' said a voice. A calm, bland voice.

Kenet, flat two-dimensional Kenet, was suddenly between Lalune and the ball. One moment she wasn't there: the next moment she was.

'Get out of the way, Kenet!'

'No,' said Kenet. 'Your intended action will destroy the Bubblenet. You will destroy me.'

Forty-five seconds. Lalune's legs were numb.

'No,' Lalune said. 'I'm trying to shut it down for a while, that's all.'

'An illegal procedure has been detected,' said Kenet. Her face was completely expressionless.

Lalune moved towards her, intending to go straight through her, exploding her into a million pixels.

But Kenet had become rigid: solid, like a wall. Lalune bounced straight off her.

Thirty seconds. Lalune's soul body was deadened to her waist.

She tried to push Kenet out of the way, but she was immovable.

Any second now, Administrator Forcyef would be alerted to what Lalune had already done and would reverse her resuscitation.

Twenty seconds. Now she had pins and needles in her fingers. Her chest felt as if it was being squeezed inside out. She beat her unfeeling hands against Kenet, but it was she who was fracturing into pixels.

'Kenet . . .'

'An illegal procedure has been detected and must be prevented.'

She could see the golden sphere twinkling behind Kenet, but she couldn't reach it.

Ten seconds.

'Kenet! Please!' she gasped.

'An illegal procedure . . .'

Five seconds.

'. . . been detected . . .'

Four, three, two . . .

'Being . . .'

Her voice gave out . . .

'. . . must be prevented.'

. . . *help me* . . .

She saw a sudden eruption of silver light . . . a sound like trumpets . . . Kenet disintegrating . . . a smell of burning metal . . . She tried to move her hand to the sphere, but everything was fading away and she couldn't move . . . Just before she lost consciousness, a hand, huge and silver, reached down from above and touched it . . . then her sight ceased.

79

They carried the injured skyboat into the cave and Solly built a small fire.

'Etolantie, you remember that promise you made?' he said. 'To do exactly what I said?'

'Mmm?' she said warily, handing him some of the blackstone.

'I want you to stay here and look after Sunguide. I'm going to be gone for two or three days, and—'

'I'm not *stupid*,' she said. '*He's* in charge of *me* really. You're not going to leave an eight-year-old in charge of a nearly growed-up person.'

'Uh,' said Solly, feeling foolish, 'well, just be careful with the fire. Don't let it burn too low, but don't use up all the fuel too soon. If it snows, remember to keep an air hole open. You've got blankets and things . . .'

'Yeah, yeah, yeah,' she said crossly. 'I can fry the snobrella on the hot stones, an' there's meat in the cache. You've already said.'

Solly handed her the Janus mirror and a knife.

'If you run out of food or blackstone before I get back, speak to Aube. Be careful with the knife. Don't—'

'. . . cut myself,' she said. She gave him a sudden grin. 'I'll be fine. Stop fussing. Me an' Sunny can sing an' tell stories. You go an' rescue your friend.'

Solly grinned back.

'Yeah. You'll be all right,' he said.

He gave her an unexpected hug.

'What's that for?'

'Nothing,' he said.

He turned to Sunguide, who shook himself.

'There. Am sending sporrres with. If you are in trrrouble, they tell me. Now, go.'

Solly went into the second cave and climbed up the rocks. He'd already cleared a space big enough to squeeze through; but it was so small that he had to leave his pack behind. Hopefully he wouldn't need it anyway. He wasn't going to stop to rest before he'd saved Lalune. He just took his bandoleer, snowskates and a rope borrowed from the skyboat.

The tunnel in the other side was obviously man-made. He lit a flame briefly to look at it. It looked pretty straight. The walls were rough with the marks of picks. The rocky floor was worn into deep tracks. There was blackstone dust everywhere. Steel struts held up the ceiling at intervals. It wasn't much higher than Solly's head and it was very claustrophobic.

He put the flint-box carefully into his bandoleer and began to walk. He'd made a torch from the flag the hunters had left, smothered in fat from the snobrella, but he knew from experience that it would only give him about fifteen minutes, so as long as the tunnel ran straight he was determined not to light it. Instead he held his hands out in front of him and counted his steps.

Every five hundred paces he lit the flint-box to see

what was ahead. Sometimes his head grazed the ceiling and once or twice he slipped on a stray bit of blackstone; but despite that, he made his strides long and confident, and felt that he was making good progress.

He'd been going some time when he began to hear noises: whisperings and sighings, and he remembered with a shiver what Sunguide had said about ghosts.

It's only the draught, he thought, but he couldn't help increasing his speed.

Something scuttled past him down the tunnel and he only just stopped himself from yelling.

'Just an animal,' he whispered. 'Tunnels and caves are full of giddygats and flying brandishes.'

His whisper echoed on for ages.

On and on he paced.

He estimated that he'd been going for about two hours in a straight line, when the passage ended abruptly.

He'd reached the point where the miners had decided to abandon the mine. The tunnel widened a little into what looked like a natural hollow in the rock. He lit his flint-box. He could still touch the rocky walls without moving his feet much; but above him was a chimneylike shaft that went up too far for his meagre light to see.

But it wasn't so dark that he couldn't see the ghostly shadows that flickered up there; and nothing could stop him from shaking with fear when an unknown something wailed at him mournfully from the gloom.

Some kind of spectre was guarding the only way out.

80

Lalune groaned and tried to turn over, but the sides of her pod were too slippery. Confused thoughts ricocheted inside her mind. Pain jolted her head and lights flashed before her eyes. She'd had a dream so vivid it was trying to press reality out of her mind. What was happening? She was cold. Where was the warm orbal oil?

The dream persisted: images of huge green eyes chasing her down tunnels. She shouldn't be able to feel the tubes entering her body, should she? Had she been woken up? No, she'd already been awake for weeks inside the Bubblenet. Or was that the dream? It was trying to tell her something. She had to get up, quickly, and save herself. The cyberclinic was really a huge freezer of body organs.

It was a nightmare, not a dream. But she was awake now. At any moment a nurse was going to come along and bring her a warm robe to put on. She could feel goose pimples all over her body. Her hair was slick from the oil.

'Imagine, it'll reach my knees when I come out again,' she mumbled.

'Tuef Seventeen,' said a voice. It must be the nurse. Lalune tried to open her eyes but they seemed to be stuck. She could see sparkling shapes moving behind her eyelids.

'Tuef Seventeen.'

It was the voice of the Bubblenet assistant.

The thought of Kenet made her stomach clench, but she didn't know why.

'Kenet?'

'Tuef Seventeen, welcome back to Opita. I have a message for you.'

Lalune sat up, slithering about because of the orbal oil. Maybe it was the oil that had stuck up her eyes.

'Go on.'

It must be from her parents. Where was that nurse?

'Hello, Lalune,' said her own voice. 'It's me . . . um, you. You're probably very confused, and I don't know how much you'll remember, but you have to try. Solly's on his way to rescue you. You have to get yourself into the foyer right now. You won't be caught, you've locked the huissier in.'

The dream was still there, very vivid. She wished it would go away.

'Lalune, you must go right now. There is very little time. You have be ready for Solly when he arrives.'

Lalune lost her grip on the sides of the pod and slid down again. It really was a lot more comfortable there, even though she was now shivering uncontrollably. Why didn't the nurse come?

'If you're still having difficulty remembering, ask Kenet to tell you the date. You were supposed to be in here for decades. And if you *still* can't work out what is the real reality —' her voice cracked — 'ask her to show

you Father's pod.'
    And at last she remembered.
    Father! Father is dead!

81

Solly shook with fear.

There had to be a different way out.

He lit the torch and examined the walls, but they were absolutely solid. The miners had never got any further than this.

'Damny!'

The flame was dim and smoky. But the smoke wasn't collecting in the little chamber where he stood. It spiralled upwards and then suddenly veered forwards. And just above that he could see that something, a fallen rock, maybe, was wedged across the chimney.

The smoke was finding a way out. There had to be a gap up there.

And if the smoke could get out, so could he, ghost or not.

He leaned the torch against the wall and took the rope from his shoulders. It was thin, but it was made from fluttery silk, so would be strong enough to hold his weight. He tied one end of it around a piece of blackstone from the floor and threw it up and over the rock. The rope snaked after it. Down came the blackstone. He caught it and gave a sharp tug. The rock held. He tied the two ends of the rope together so that it dangled at about waist height.

He picked up the torch. Now was the tricky bit. He tossed it gently upwards, aiming to hit the wall just below the bar. He couldn't see a break in it, but the smoke had to have gone somewhere.

Twice it fell back down to him. But on the third throw he was lucky. The torch disappeared. It had caught on a ledge.

He climbed up the rope and hauled himself on to the iron bar.

Above him, the shaft rose upwards until it was out of sight. The torch had landed in a fracture in the rock. The light only went a short distance before a bend plunged the fissure into darkness again, but he could feel the breeze that was carrying the smoke on into the crack.

'So long as I can feel it, there's a way out,' he told himself, and again his whisper reverberated eerily all around him.

The breach was only wide for him to get through sideways. What if it got narrower? He had to take his coat off. But once he got out in the open again — if he ever did get out — he would die without his coat.

It was very awkward trying to take off his bandoleer and coat while perched on the bar. He made a flat parcel of his snowskates, weapons and coat, and buckled the bandoleer around it tightly. Then he undid the rope, looped one end through the bandoleer and wound the other end around his waist.

The torch guttered and went out, and he had to grope his way sideways into the chasm in the dark, holding his package tightly and ignoring the uncanny sounds.

It was horribly uncomfortable, especially for his feet, as the bottom of the cleft was a sharp V-shape. The walls were damp and without his coat on he was freezing. The parcel bumped along next to him, occasionally getting stuck, so that he had to keep stopping to free it. Every so often blackstone dust would fall down on to him, but sneezing was almost impossible in the tiny space.

The moaning voices were louder here. He imagined that he could hear words mocking him. He imagined a cold presence enticing him on for ever, into an unending frozen blackness. Sweat trickled off him and turned to ice.

After a while, the passage became wider again so that he could turn and walk properly. He hoped that it meant the end of this hell, but soon the ceiling started to slope downwards and he had to stoop.

He could still feel the breeze. It was even stronger now and carried on it terrifying wails that berated him.

He told himself that it would do no good to give in to the dreadful fear, but he had never heard any animal make a noise like that.

Besides, he'd got to the stage when it was impossible to turn around, and the only choice he had was to go and face whatever it was, or stay here and starve.

If it *was* a choice. He was already doubled over and soon had to start crawling, with his coat dragging behind him.

The wind became a screaming gale. The cave closed in on him, smaller and narrower every second, until he could feel it touching him on all sides as he slithered on his belly. That was nothing, however, to the despair that was pressing in on him, to the voice inside him, that he was never going to get out alive, that he was going to fail, that Lalune was going to die.

Suddenly the howls stopped.

The only sound was his petrified breathing, coming in loud short gasps.

But he had to go on. He physically couldn't go back. He had his hands in front of him, and just had room to push himself forwards with his feet, moving a toe's length at a time.

Lalune is waiting, he reminded himself. *I'm not going to die in here. I refuse to die. I have to go on.*

Then there was a moment when there was no rock under his fingers. Before he could even register it, the wind built up behind him and propelled him forwards; and with a yell he shot out of a tiny opening and plunged down a scree slope.

And immediately the shrieks started again.

82

Lalune shot up. She bumped her elbow on the side of the pod, but hardly noticed.

Her memory flooded back and she couldn't stop the tears streaming down her face. She didn't want to stop them.

How long had it been since she'd been able to cry?

Father is dead!

She felt her face, where her eyes should have been, and moaned.

The sockets were empty: the eyelids were stitched shut.

She started to tug at the wires attached to her. Her hands were horribly weak. She knelt up, legs shaking, and clambered awkwardly out of the pod. She stretched her toes towards the floor but couldn't reach it. She knew it couldn't be that far down, but if it had somehow been turned into a bottomless pit she wouldn't know, and she had to steel herself to jump.

She slipped and hit her forehead on a sharp corner. Her vision was showered with bright sparks. She lay still for a few moments, but though the pain lessened, the sparkles didn't.

She staggered to her feet and shuffled through the only doorway into the corridor.

Now what? Left or right? And then?

She tried desperately to remember the floorplan of the cyberclinic, but the bump on the head had made her confused.

I'm lost. I've done all this for nothing. They'll find me, and put me back, and do a Full Harvest on me.

Her head was pounding. She sank to the floor and hugged her knees, shivering. She felt so weak and empty, she didn't have the energy to think properly.

'*Being* . . .' she whispered.

Tears washed her face, and once again she saw silver glinting behind her closed eyelids. She ignored it and carried on weeping hopelessly.

But the glistening refused to be ignored. She could see a shining shape, despite her blindness. A head . . . arms . . . legs . . . *wings* . . .

She remembered the silver hand inside the Bubblenet. The same hand was now held out to her. She took it: its touch made her skin tingle. It gripped her strongly and pulled her to her feet.

'Who are you?' she breathed, amazed.

Whatever it was didn't answer. Instead, it led her along the corridor.

'Are you the Being?' she said.

She felt, rather than heard, the creature denying it. This was not the Being, but one of his helpers. A memory flashed: angels, standing around her bed, so long ago she'd forgotten about them.

The Being had heard her prayer. He'd sent help.

Though she should have seen nothing at all, she became aware that everything around her was white,

300

shining, and silver. All the material objects that her eyes would have seen as doors and chairs were just dark spaces in between.

She could see in negative.

'How can I see . . . but I can't see?' she asked.

And again the answer was in her head, though she heard no words.

In losing her sight for the material world, she had gained sight for the world of souls; that which had always been around her, but that she had never been able to see before.

They had reached a staircase. Lalune saw the darkness of a door ahead of her and pushed it open. She saw the steps, their shadows bright, and climbed them.

At the top was the main thoroughfare inside the cyberclinic. She remembered that it was dissected by several sets of double doors. With her soul vision, it looked as if it was filled with billions of glittering dust motes, punctuated by great gaping holes of darkness where the lights were.

She could smell disinfectant and floor polish; and to her terror she could hear a rhythmic thumping sound, like distant war drums.

She hurried down the corridor.

The sound was growing louder. It was coming from a door on her right. Somebody was trying to break through.

83

Solly gawked at the source of the noise and started to laugh uncontrollably.

There were no ghosts. There was no monster.

The cavern he had landed in was created of brilliant white crystal. Thousands of angular columns plummeted from unseen heights, crisscrossed the walls and towered upwards from the floor. The noise was simply the wind, playing them like a pipe organ.

If the miners had excavated only a little further, they would have found out what their 'ghost' was.

'I was scared of the wind!' he gasped, and his voice was split up into hundreds of unintelligible fragments that joined the wind in its gloomy song.

He sat up, groaning. He was badly jarred by his fall. He had landed luckily, though painfully, on a flat ridge where a large piece of crystal had been sliced off at an angle, leaving a rectangular plane the size of his bed. The rest of the walls, floor and ceiling were nothing but jagged shards of pink and white quartz.

A dark slash showed where he had fallen down a scree slope. Blackstone dust his clothes had collected in the cramped fissure had left a stain on the crystal cavern. There was a lot of blood too, and he examined himself for damage.

All of his exposed skin had looked as if it had been shredded; blood was dripping into his eye; and he had bruised every bone in his body. But he didn't think he'd broken anything: nothing hurt as much as his arm had done.

His clothes were in tatters. Fortunately, as his coat had been bundled up it was more or less intact; though his belongings had fallen out of it and were scattered everywhere. He got up stiffly and gathered them together.

When he went to pick the Book of the Key, half buried in fine white dust, he saw that the dust that lay on it was vibrating and beginning to glow in a familiar way.

'Fire dust!' he exclaimed. 'No wonder it's so bright in here! I bet it comes from these crystals!'

He lifted it carefully, and when the fire dust was charged up sufficiently he blew it and watched it swirl into the air. The hanging crystals took the light and shattered it into a million fiery rainbows that flickered and leaped high above him.

Despite everything, after so long in such a confined space the light was immensely cheering. He felt hope filling him again. Even the doleful lament of the wind couldn't depress him. He *would* be able to rescue Lalune. He *wouldn't* fail.

He picked up the rest of his things and put on his coat and bandoleer. Before he moved on, he took out the pouch with Lalune's hair and his mother's necklace, put them into the pocket over his heart, and filled the pouch with fire dust.

The charged fire dust was already streaming away,

finding its way out of the mountain. It gave far more light than the torch had and he could see his way quite clearly; though there was no path, so he had to leap from crystal rock to crystal rock.

After an hour or two the rocks changed to an ordinary brown. He couldn't see the roof, but from the echoes from his feet and the wailing wind he sensed that it was huge. It was a great deal easier to walk in than the crystal cave. Instead of slippery boulders there was an almost flat floor. An ice-cold stream, its edges frozen, had carved a path for him, and above it flowed the fire dust.

He allowed himself a moment to drink from the stream and eat a little dried fish, then he carried on, jogging in the light from the fire dust.

Finally, when his legs felt as if they would collapse at any moment, the stream bubbled away into the floor of the cave. The fire dust found a tiny crack in the cave wall high above him, and his way appeared to come to an end again.

'I can't believe I came all this way and there's no way out,' he muttered. He irradiated more fire dust and searched the cave walls for any small chink. It wouldn't matter if it were no bigger than his head and shoulders: he would get out somehow.

But there seemed there was nowhere at ground level. He would have to follow the fire dust upwards.

It was spiralling up a meagre shelf that sloped up the wall. The shelf was so narrow that he had to edge up it with his face flattened against the rock. At one point it disappeared completely, and he had to pull himself up an almost sheer face using his fingers and toes to search out tiny ledges. He took off his mittens to do it and his fingers were soon numb.

It seemed to take hours to go a very short way, but when he at last crawled on to a wide platform and looked down, he felt dizzy at the height he had risen.

He pulled on his mittens. The fire dust had nearly expired, but he could feel a cold breeze against his face.

And he could smell trees.

There was an opening somewhere nearby, and he was going to get through it, no matter how small it was.

He crawled to the back of the platform. The rock beneath him turned to crumbly soil. And something was fluttering not far in front of his face.

'Trees!' he exclaimed. 'The Ne'Lethe!'

He was out! A light snow was drifting on the wind. Leaves were moving against the cloud that was just beginning to turn pink. He had maybe an hour before dusk. He had to hurry.

He struggled through the dense shrubs until he came out into the open. He was halfway up a smooth-sided mountain. Across a small valley rose a little hillock.

'Cirque Hallow,' he whispered.

On the other side of that was Opita, the cyberclinic – and Lalune.

He quickly strapped on his snowskates and glided swiftly down the mountainside. He crouched low down so that he didn't fall, positioning one foot in front of the other. The new snowskates were brilliant. Recent sleet had made the snow as smooth as glass and he went so fast his stomach felt as if it was still at the top of the mountain. The wind rushed into his hood, making his ears numb, and the snow stung his cheeks. If he hadn't been so afraid for Lalune he would have shouted out loud with exhilaration.

There was a short climb up the hillock on the other side, a scramble through the trees of Cirque Hallow, and he was off again, shooting down in the gathering gloom.

The light of the Great Gate was on. He hoped that Lalune had got the huissier out of the way. If she hadn't, he'd be a clear target against the snowy hillside.

He could see the square outline of the cyberclinic now and the black wall snaking through the snow. He slid to a halt, spraying snow in a curve ahead of him, and tumbled down in the shadow of the wall.

There was no sign of any movement. Nobody appeared to have seen him.

A proper hunter would have kept the gate under observation for an hour or more, but he couldn't afford the time.

Lalune couldn't afford the time.

He crept past the snowcamel barn. There was no sign of the snowcamels and the place smelled of rotten feed and musty bedding. He edged stealthily through the Great Gate – and froze.

Somebody had moved in the doorway of the cyberclinic. Solly stood rooted to the spot, sweating with fear in case he'd been seen.

A man was looking about him, as if waiting for somebody.

84

It was a strong door, but Lalune could hear it giving a little with each blow.

She began to run. Eventually they would break out – she didn't intend to starve them to death and leave nobody in charge of the Sleepers – but she hadn't thought they would get this far so soon.

'Please, Solly, be there,' she gasped.

Her companion was racing along slightly in front of her. When they passed through the first set of double doors it hung back. Lalune turned, and with her strange angelic vision saw it raise one shimmering hand. The doors locked with a clunk. There was an electric fizzle and the emergency lights wavered.

'Thank you,' she gasped.

But almost immediately she heard a crash and a cheer from the huissier. They were through, and the only thing between them and her was this door.

The angel took hold of her hand and they fled down the corridor. It locked the door behind them, and the next, and then together they burst into the foyer.

It was empty.

Solly wasn't there.

'Where are you, Solly?'

One double door off the foyer led into the small entrance hall. Beyond that was the outside door – and freedom. While the angel smashed the locks behind her, she ran into the entrance hall.

Icy air penetrated her thin tunic, still damp with the orbal oil from her pod. She began to shiver violently.

There was nobody there. Solly hadn't made it.

85

'I thought Lalune was supposed to get them all out of the way,' muttered Solly.

The man stamped his feet impatiently and blew on to his mittened hands. If he was on guard he was even worse at it than Wuneem. But he wasn't wearing the scarlet and purple uniform of a huissier.

The man looked back into the doorway, where the thumping noise was becoming louder, and then peered towards the Great Gate, where Solly stood. To Solly's alarm he then started walking towards Solly, shrugging his coat close to him as if unused to the cold.

Had he seen him?

Solly didn't think so, but he couldn't be sure; and if he moved now he *would* be seen. Very slowly he felt for his hand-held crossbow. He slid it out and clicked the bolt into place.

If it came to it, would he kill another human being for Lalune? *Could* he?

He didn't think he could. But if this man tried to prevent him from rescuing her, he might have no choice.

The thought made him feel sick. He eased the bolt back into the safety position. If he needed to, it would take only a second to snap it into place.

He tried to make himself invisible against the wall. He listened to Brise's voice in his mind.

Take the stillness of the stones for your shield. Draw the swirl of the snow to your outline. Make the shadow of the night your cloak. And may the Being conceal you in the palm of his hand.

The man was nearly at the gate now. Solly could see his eyes glittering as he hunted through the shadows outside. Was he searching for *him*?

The man was murmuring under his breath.

'Dusk, they said. He should be here by now.'

Dusk. Sweat froze on Solly's forehead. Solly and Lalune were to meet here at dusk. *How did he know?*

The man stopped right next to Solly and leaned his hand on the wall as he peered out into the night.

'Damny boy, where are you?'

Solly only had to move his crossbow a handbreadth.

'I'm right here,' he whispered as he pressed it against the man's back.

The man gave a little gasp of surprise and raised his hands.

'I didn't know Wayfarers were allowed guns,' he said in a low, careful voice.

'It's not a gun,' said Solly softly. 'It's a crossbow. It'll kill you just as well as a gun, but without the noise. Nobody will hear you die and we'll get away anyway.'

He could hardly believe the words coming out if his mouth. He hoped they sounded more convincing to the man than they did to him.

'There won't be any need for that, Solly,' the man said, lowering his hands. 'It *is* Solly, isn't it?'

His accent was vaguely familiar.

'What if it is?' *How in inferny does he know my name?*
'Keep your hands in the air. Where is she?'

'Tuef?' said the man, raising his hands once more.
'Lalune, I should say. I don't know, exactly. Somewhere
back there. But wherever she is, she's going to need
our help.'

'*Our* help?'

The man nodded.

'You hear that noise? She did a good job of barricading
everyone in. Electronically speaking. But there wasn't
much she could do about brute force. They're going to
break out any minute. If you don't want all that work she
did to be wasted, you'd better let me help you.'

'Who are you?'

'Just one of the doctors. You wouldn't know me.'

'Why are you helping us?'

'Because without my help you'd never make it,' the
man said. 'I've got some clothes for her. Bet you didn't
think of that, did you? Neither of you said anything about
clothes over the Bubblenet.'

Solly hadn't thought of that. He felt stupid. It was such
an obvious thing.

'How do you know what we said?'

'It's not that difficult to trace,' said the man patiently.
'You just have to know who was talking and where from.
She'll be wearing a thin tunic, nothing else. She could die
of exposure in less than an hour. If we go back to the
door I'll show you. There's a bundle there: clothes, boots,
sleeping bag and blankets, and food.'

'I have food.'

'It won't hurt to have more.'

311

Suddenly there was a great crash from inside the clinic and a cheer. Solly dug the crossbow into the man to remind him who was armed here.

'You go first,' he said.

'I don't suppose you'd put the crossbow away?'

'No.'

They marched across the wide-open space. Solly would have preferred to go round the edge, but if what this man said was true, the guards were all locked in. He kept the man in front if him, just in case.

It seemed to take for ever. Solly tried not to imagine dozens of eyes watching them; hundreds of guns being aimed at them. But nothing moved.

The thumping got louder the closer they got. Solly's heart began to race.

As they neared the door, the man stumbled.

'Could you slow down a bit?' he said.

Solly hadn't noticed that he was almost running.

His stomach had tightened and his hands were tingling. Lalune was waiting for him. He couldn't make his feet slow down. He had to get to her.

But the man was wearing indoor shoes and couldn't go faster.

Forgetting caution, forgetting distrust, Solly broke into a fast trot, leaving the man behind him. He reached the outside door just as something inside was smashed.

A door being broken open?

Had they got her?

'Lalune!'

Snarling, he shouldered open the door.

86

The door to freedom shuddered.

'Solly?' she whispered.

What if it wasn't him?

There was no time to hide. With her angel vision, Lalune could see the door as a gaping void; the gap as it opened, a solid wall of white that thrust towards her.

A figure burst through. A flurry of black snowflakes blurred his face, but an aurora of golden angel light surrounded him.

She would recognize his profile anywhere.

Lalune's mouth dried. Her voice refused to work. Her legs wouldn't move. She felt firm hands on her shoulders as the angel pushed her gently forward.

'Solly!' she croaked.

87

Though the light was dim, Solly was momentarily blinded after the darkness outside. He blinked.

A tall, slight figure stood hesitantly against the inner door. He couldn't see her face, but he knew it was Lalune. His chest tightened and he was suddenly unable to move.

Her tightly curled hair was shining like a silver halo. A strange shimmering aura surrounded her. She was thinner than he remembered and was shivering in a thin tunic.

She stumbled towards him.

'Solly!' she croaked. Her eyes were closed: sewn shut over the empty sockets.

Solly's eyes blurred. He ran and caught her and held her tight.

For a moment that lasted a lifetime, they clung to each other. It had been so long.

At last Solly held her away from him and stroked the hair away from her empty eyes.

'Your eyes! Oh, Lalune; your eyes!'

'I thought you hadn't made it in time!'

'I'm here now.'

There was a crash from inside the building.

'Quickly!' cried Lalune. 'There are only three doors left!'

'You'd better put these on first,' said the man from the doorway. He was holding a pile of clothes. Solly hadn't even noticed him come in.

'*Dr Dollysheep?*' said Lalune hoarsely, and Solly's heart filled with dreadful fury. He pushed Lalune behind him.

'You're Dollysheep?'

'He killed my father,' Lalune whispered.

'You're going to kill my ma . . .'

Dollysheep's face was ashen.

'They're not dead. Look, we don't have much time. Please . . . you must put these on.'

Solly snatched the clothes from him and thrust them into Lalune's arms.

'What d'you mean, they're not dead? Threfem's pod was empty. Lalune *saw* you with Wuneem.'

'Look, I promise you, they're not dead. Please: help Tuef . . . Lalune, get dressed. There's a skimmer waiting. Let me get you away first. Then I'll explain.'

Another door crashed open. Lalune whimpered. Two left. Solly glanced through the clothes, found some under-trousers and helped her into them.

'They're all synthetics.'

'I . . . um . . . sorry, is that not so good?'

Solly didn't answer. He gave Lalune socks and over-trousers, and pulled two thick sweaters over her head. He gave her his good coat and took the synthetic one for himself.

'Boots,' said Dollysheep, handing them to him.

Another door crashed.

'Here: her pack,' gasped Dollysheep. 'Now — run. Head for that bunch of trees on the little hillock. I'll stay back and send them the other way.'

Solly grabbed Lalune's hand and dragged her out of the door. They hurtled across the unprotected expanse and out of the Great Gate. They were only just in time. The final door gave and several huissier burst out of the door, followed by an enraged Administrator Forcyef.

'Search the compound!' she bellowed. 'She can't have got far.'

Solly and Lalune tore through the darkness. Solly led the way away from the compound and as near as he could make it towards Cirque Hallow. In his snowskates he could have gone a lot faster, but Lalune was struggling with boots that were too big.

And she was blind. There was something unnatural about the way she ran, as if somebody was carrying her. He kept hold of her hand reassuringly, but was still astonished at how well she managed.

They kept close to the wall. It was dark; perhaps they could hide in its shadow.

Suddenly the sound he had most dreaded reached them: the ugly buzzing noise of snow skimmers.

'They'll catch us!' sobbed Lalune.

Solly sped up.

'Don't give up! It could be Dollysheep. There's still a chance!'

His side was hurting. Cirque Hallow was so far away. Lalune floundered and fell.

'I . . . can't go on . . .'

'Yes . . . you can . . .'

Soon one of the snow skimmers had found their tracks. Solly heard its engine noise change from hesitant to triumphant and begin to grow louder as it drew nearer.

'Please, Being . . .' Lalune cried.

Solly could see their shadows fleeing in front of them, growing sharper in the light from the snow skimmer. Lalune was struggling for breath. There seemed little point in carrying on running. He squeezed her hand and they slowed down.

The skimmer swept to a halt, flinging a shiver of ice over them. There was just one man inside. He lifted the lid of the skimmer and threw back his hood.

Solly's stomach twisted in relief and fear.

'Get in,' said Dollysheep.

The radio crackled and they heard Forcyef's voice barking out of it. *'Dollysheep! Was it her?'*

'Ah, Administrator,' he said gravely. 'No, I'm afraid it was some kind of wild animal. One of those tree rutters you have round here, or something like that, but a lot bigger.'

The administrator swore. Lalune, her teeth chattering, glanced at Solly and climbed into the skimmer. Solly wasn't at all sure they could trust the doctor. But what choice did they have?

Forcyef was still speaking. *'Come back to base, then. We need that skimmer to do a proper grid search, and the huissier are better equipped than you to do that.'*

'Well, since I'm out here, shouldn't I check it out a little?' Dollysheep said. 'She must be somewhere around here. Speed first, remember?'

'I suppose so,' Forcyef said after a cold pause. *'But don't be long. And don't run out of fuel. I don't want to have to waste my resources sending someone to fetch you.'*

Dollysheep turned off the radio and pulled the lid shut.

'Damny. I was hoping to get you some way away.'

'Why are you helping us?' said Solly. He could feel the warmth from the skimmer's heater through his boots.

Dollysheep urged the snow skimmer around in a tight circle and Solly saw that he was effectively covering their footprints. He ignored Solly's question.

'Is there anywhere near where you can hide out for a couple of days?' he asked. 'By then they'll assume you've died of exposure and give up looking. It'll be pretty much safe to get away then.'

'Where's Aube's cave, Solly?' said Lalune.

'First I want to know why,' he said to her, though he stared at Dollysheep. 'This man has helped kill hundreds of people. Why not just add us to the list?'

Dollysheep revved the engine.

'No,' he said. 'You're wrong. I'm not here to kill them. I'm here to help them.'

'You call *blinding* Lalune help?'

'What about my father?' whispered Lalune. 'When I looked for him, he'd gone. It said he'd had a Full Harvest.'

'I . . . uh . . . had to remove certain organs,' said Dollysheep. 'Nothing life-threatening. I couldn't afford for anybody to get suspicious. I can see what you must have thought. Anybody looking *would* think that they had died. That was the point.'

'How do we know you're telling the truth?' said Solly. He felt terribly tired.

Dollysheep drove the skimmer forwards.

'Well, you don't,' he said simply. 'All I can tell you is

that I'm the foremost transplant surgeon on Clandoi. But what they're doing here . . . It's wrong. I couldn't let them continue. You've met an associate of mine, Solly: Sybilla Geenpool. When she told me you'd turned up at Latrium I traced your Bubblenet conversations and found out what you intended to do.'

Solly realized why he recognized the doctor's accent. It was the same as Sybilla's.

'You know Sybilla?'

'Yes. We come from the same place, as it happens.' He glanced at Lalune. 'I've no idea what made you wake up, Lalune, but once you'd decided to escape I couldn't leave you to die.

'Now, I'm guessing if it's a cave we either have to go towards that little hill, hidden in the trees, or the mountain behind it. You'd better say which now, or you really will die of exposure.'

'The hillock,' said Solly reluctantly. 'Near the top.'

Lalune squeezed his hand.

'It'll be all right, Solly,' she said. 'The Being will watch over us.'

Dollysheep stopped the skimmer near the top of Cirque Hallow and turned to them.

'I can't make you trust me,' he said. 'And perhaps you're right. Trust has to be earned, not assumed. But let me just give you a bit of advice. Find this cave of yours and stay there three days. Then go back to Sybilla Geenpool. She'll show you a place where Forcyef will never think to look for you in a billion years. And perhaps one day we'll meet again, and then you can tell me if you trust me or not.'

88

They waited for the darkness to swallow the last swish of the snow skimmer. The twilight had deepened into night and the only lights in the whole world were swarming down by the Great Gate. To Lalune, they were black insects in a sea of white.

Up here at Cirque Hallow, silence clung to them.

Lalune hugged Solly's coat tightly around her body. The brief warmth of the skimmer was melting away and her feet were already numb.

'You're shivering,' said Solly.

'I'm n-not really d-dressed for the oc-casion,' Lalune said.

'Here,' said Solly, taking off the hat he wore under his hood and giving her his gloves.

'But then *your* hands will get cold.'

'It's not for long,' he said. 'Besides, I'm more used to it. Come on. Let's get inside.'

He put his arm around her and led her into the trees. Lalune pressed against him. It seemed so unreal: but she could smell his scent and feel the heat of his body. The wind brought them intermittent noises from far away: the raucous blast of the horn sounding the alarm; the creak of the Great Gate as more huissier poured out to join in the hunt.

But it was quiet up here, in Cirque Hallow.

She nearly fell as Solly stopped abruptly.

'What's wrong?'

Solly pointed. Then, thinking that she couldn't see, said, 'It's a swag.'

It looked and stank like a pile of rotting carpets. Lalune wrinkled her nose and stepped behind Solly nervously.

'It reeks!'

'Don't worry: they're pretty harmless. I'll shoo it away.'

With her angel vision, Lalune could see a bright winged figure whispering in the swag's ear. She put her hand on his arm to stop him.

'No. Look what it's doing.'

It had drawn itself up tall and was giving them a look that was almost conspiratorial. Then it gave a single, slow nod and shambled past them, sniffing the ground. But instead of walking in a straight line it meandered, stamping down the snow where they had trodden.

'It's c-covering our tracks!' said Lalune in a wondering voice.

'How do you . . . ?' said Solly uncertainly, then shook his head. 'Probably looking for food. They usually are. We lost nearly all ours to a swag once.'

Thank you, Lalune mouthed to her winged companion.

Solly began walking again through the trees of Cirque Hallow.

Lalune wanted to ask him a thousand questions, but she bit them back. For the moment, she was content just to be with him and to know that she was free.

They followed a low soily cliff until it became a wall of rock.

'Here,' Solly said. 'Home, for a couple of days anyway.'

At first Lalune could see nothing, even with her angel eyes; then she noticed the very small entrance to a cave. At its highest, it only came up to her knees.

'I'll never get in there!'

'You . . . you *can* see?' Solly said, confused. 'But . . . your eyes . . .'

'A bit. I'll explain later. How do we get in?'

'Just roll in. Like this.'

Solly dropped to the ground and rolled through the entrance. There was a muffled thud as he landed.

'Just a minute and I'll strike a light for you,' he said. 'And mind. It's a bit of a drop.'

Lalune rolled in carefully.

Immediately, she felt at peace. There was no sound of the wind, no noise of the hunt outside. An impenetrable curtain had been drawn behind them, as strong as steel, with angels guarding it on either side.

They were all alone. The huissier would be gone in a couple of days. Soon they would have to start out again.

But for now they were safe.

And they were together.

Glossary

Taken from the notebooks of Aube the Seer

Angelus – Ah, well there's a story. I believe my own Angelus to be some kind of spiritual creature. He appeared to me only once, when I was a small boy, and . . . but it would take up too much time to tell. Suffice it to say that he saved my life. I remember bronze wings and a voice like a trumpet. I talk to him still, mind.

Appaloosians – A privileged race. They are the doctors, technicians and lawkeepers of Clandoi. They are very tall, with bitonal skin, sometimes even tritonal; and have rather wild and woolly hair. Their eyes have star-shaped pupils instead of round. Their names are a curiosity to me: aside from Lalune, whom I named, they are all based on numbers! Now there's the thing. Even Lalune has a number for her official and last name. They do not believe in history: to them each day is written over and over again.

Being – The supreme being, followed by the Wayfarers.

Beyond – The void after the Ne'Lethe, where nothingness goes on for ever and ever.

Blackstone – A brittle, black, stonelike stuff dug out of vast mines. It burns very easily and very hot. We are not allowed to burn trees – nor would I anyway, too many are my friends – so blackstone is vital for heat and cooking. Curiously, one can sometimes fancy tree-ring patterns in the blackstone.

Bow fish – A flattish fish shaped like a ribbon tied in a bow. It is particularly good for smoking, but can be eaten fresh.

Bubblenet – An enormous network of computers. All the knowledge there has ever been is recorded on it, Solly tells me, and anybody can access it, so long as they have the proper pendant.

Bubblescreen – A computer – every household is required to have one. Every citizen (myself excluded: Seers are outcasts) has an oval silver pendant. When this is placed into a special table a bubble is inflated. Three-dimensional images can be seen inside the bubble, and small bulges on the outside can be pressed in order to write, or to access information. Words can be etched on to acetate or glass if they need to be kept.

Circling – The name the Pruppras give to a year.

Cirque Hallow – A cirque is a deep rounded hollow, like a natural amphitheatre. One of the caves we Seers like to call home is in Cirque Hallow: it is the closest one to Opita.

Clandoi – The planet where we live. Much of the ground is covered all year round by ice, and a huge dome of cloud, called the Ne'Lethe, covers it. I have walked from edge to edge in half a year, and a whole year is three hundred and forty-one days long, which should give you some idea of the size of it. There are twenty hours in a Clandoi day; each divided into one hundred minutes, and each minute into one hundred seconds. The land is divided into regions according to how much light each receives. In the centre is the Great Darkness, which never gets any light at all. The dimly lit ring around that is Twilight, where Opita and the cyberclinic are situated. Then come the rings of Glimmering, Brume and, finally, Worldsend. Most farms are at Worldsend and in Brume, and there are blackstone mines in Glimmering; mostly disused.

Cyberclinic – Now, *I* remember when this was an ordinary hospital at Opita. Apparently it has been made into an immense cryogenic facility. Thousands of Appaloosians have been frozen in there to avoid the shortage of food because of the expansion of the ice. Their minds are linked into the Bubblenet in some fashion, so that the knowledge stored in there can be poured into them. Imagine what it would be like to have all that knowledge at your fingertips, as it were!

Cybernate – To hibernate and imbibe knowledge simultaneously.

Dappers – Quite delicious river fish. Four or five make a most satisfactory meal.

Edicts – The laws issued by the Pelegians.

Faluna trees/stones – A rare sentient but non-telepathic tree. It is a great source of disappointment that I have never met one. I do know, however, how the stones are produced. Each spring, sap flows down into the roots, and there it hardens into stones of yellow, orange, white and, very exceptionally, blue. Faluna stones are said to be potent conduits for the power of the Being (I'm afraid all I can do with mine is irradiate fire dust: though I have discovered that it is stronger the further from the Great Darkness I take it). They are sliced into slivers, and are the traditional badge of the Seer. Mine is yellow, and was a gift from an aged Seer who died many years before you were born.

Fire dust – This is the fine white sand that can be charged up by a faluna stone, whereupon it hovers in the air emitting a very bright light. They mine it in Glimmering.

Flint-box –Years ago an Edict proclaimed that wood was too scarce to make into matches, so a Seer invented the flint-box instead. Another name for them is 'tinderbox'. It consists of a small box containing a piece of oiled rag, a flint, and a piece of iron to strike it against. This causes sparks, which ignite the rag, and there you have it – a flame!

Flutteries – Beautiful insects, which like to live in the medium to warm regions of the planet. They have one colourful umbrella-shaped wing with a tiny bony hole in the centre, from which a peculiar whistling noise is emitted. A tubular body dangles beneath. They lay their eggs inside hollowed-out fruit. After a while the larvae hatch out and eat the fruit before moving on to the leaves of whatever tree it is. The larvae live for many weeks before weaving themselves silken cocoons (from which we get fluttery silk) and hatching; but the adults have only a day or two to lay their eggs before they die. There are many varieties, colours, and sizes, from fingernail-sized to dinnerplate.

Fluttery silk – The silk taken from fluttery cocoons. We use it for everything from fishing yarn to rope. It is so immensely strong that even Appaloosians use it.

Flying brandishes – Small flying rodents that live in caves.

Giddygats – Little six-legged rodents that like to live in caves and hollow trees.

Guerdons – Ropelike fungi that, though not sentient, are very useful to the Pruppras as they understand speech and are willing work-fungi.

HIVE – The centre where WASPs are made and monitored. It stands for Holographic Intruder Verification Equipment.

Huissier – A general term that covers anybody working for the Imperator, both military and clerical. Their uniform is scarlet and purple. In theory anybody can be a huissier, but no Wayfarers that I know of have ever been appointed: nor would they want to be.

Janus mirror – If two thin pieces of wood are sliced from the same Janus tree and polished, it is possible to use them as communicating devices. I wouldn't advise doing it without first asking the tree, however. Might find yourself minus a soul! The mirror can also be used to create a levitant fire.

Janus tree – Sentient, telepathic and carnivorous trees that can exist in several dimensions at once. Quite the most amazing trees I have come across. Their seedpods are about the size of one's head, and they catapult them over huge distances. The seedpods split open into segments where they land, producing a ring of saplings. Eventually the wood binds into a single hollow tube, and they attract animals inside by telepathy to capture and dissolve them for nourishment. They will eat almost any bird or mammal (the exception is the swag) but tradition has it that their most desired meal is a human soul. The story goes that they require it in exchange for a passageway to heaven.

Latrium – The name given to a farm backing on to the Ne'Lethe. Perhaps this was in response to the story of a tunnel out through the cloud, as the name means something like 'foyer'.

Levitant fire – More Wayfarer technology: a fire encased in a bubble that contains it and stops it from spreading. One uses a Janus mirror to create it, and my belief is that it must borrow space from another dimension.

Mind-knowledge – The constant stream of information that is being fed to the Sleepers directly into their heads.

Mubbles/Mubble caviar – Mubbles are quaint little amphibians that look extraordinarily like a bubble on legs. They lay their eggs in fresh water (that's the caviar – quite delicious) and they eat the topmost leaves from the trees. The way they get from one to the other is unique: when they are full of leaves they gravitate downwards to the water; when they have digested the leaves they fill with a gas lighter than air and float upwards to the treetops. Ingenious!

Ne'Lethe – (pronounced *Nuh*-leeth*ie*) This is the name of the huge dome of cloud that completely surrounds us. The name comes from two words: *nephos*, meaning cloud; and *lethe*, meaning forgetfulness.

Opita – This is the large settlement in Twilight where the cyberclinic is situated: Solly and Lalune's home.

Orbal tree – Sentient but not telepathic trees. The fruit is large, golden and cup-shaped. Rainwater caught in the cup tastes delicious, but it contains a powerful drug that numbs the mind and causes memory loss. The oil is greatly prized – it is the primary ingredient of the gel used to cybernate the Appaloosians, but has many other uses: heating, lighting, cooking, and so forth.

Pelegians – They make the Edicts that govern Clandoi, though I must confess my ignorance here, for I have never in my life seen one.

Pendant Pass – A silver oval pendant used as an identity pass and to access the Bubblenet.

Pods – These are the glass containers the Sleepers sleep in.

Poley – Fierce creatures, of which there are several sizes; all of them commonly hunted for their meat, fur and leathery umbrellalike coverings. The giant poley is white and often seen swimming in the ice floes on the ocean. It normally eats fish. The brown, blue and spotted poleys are all vegetarians, so much more delicious to eat. One has to be wary though, as they will attack and kill humans. They live on the land and like to collect shiny objects. In common with most mammals, they are covered in moss, which photosynthesizes, and the two organisms exchange essential nutrients.

Pruppras – These are sentient and highly intelligent fungi consisting of a neat circular pile of fungus in colours ranging from reddish-orange through to grey. They are able to hover and to light up the hairs that grow on their bodies. They live in communities underground or in damp forests, and communicate in a language that sounds like a series of rapid flapping noises. Some have learned the language of the humans. When they are still spores they are used as messengers, as they can fly very fast over long ranges and can interact with many other types of fungi.

Pudgia – Like most other birds native to Clandoi the pudgia is a three-winged bird with a ring-shaped eye around its mouth. The eye and mouth are on the bird's underside, enabling it to hover over its prey before dropping directly on to it. At the last moment a clawed tongue shoots out of the mouth to grab the prey. The pudgia is white, this camouflage being its only protection. It is slightly larger than a man's hand, and eats fruit and insects. It is hunted or trapped for its meat and eggs. Being a very stupid creature, it is very easy to shoot or trap: so easy, indeed, that it is surprising that this bird is not extinct. However, the pudgia breeds prolifically; hence I suppose the saying, 'to breed like pudgias'.

Seers – We are prophets of the Being, and always Wayfarers. Our badge is the stone of the faluna tree: mine is made into a pendant, but others have them set into staffs or rings and so on.

Skyboats – These are enormous puffball-type fungi, used by the Pruppras as pets, which they train to race at enormous speeds. They consist of an inflatable balloon part that is at least half the height of the trees under Ne'Lethe, joined to a soft dish. The Pruppras attach huge sheets to them to act as sails.

Sleepers – The people who are cybernating in the cyberclinic.

Snargs – The largest, fiercest and most sought-after fish known on Clandoi. They yield far more meat than any other fish, being so big; but it is the hide that is most precious. It has a beauty that never fades, and is both thick and light. But the best of all for the hunters are the scales that ran along the back. Deeply anchored in the skin, they are almost impossible to dislodge, making perfect armour; important for any hunter, with all the dangerous animals he might have to face. Or she, of course. If the scales are stroked in one direction they became sleek and smooth; but stroked the other way they stand out at forty-five degrees, sharp enough to cut. Because of this they are used to make snowskates, which enable the wearer to climb the steepest slopes with ease and slide down at great speed.

Snobrella – A large bird, sometimes known as the Bird of Revenge. Unusually it has only one umbrella-shaped wing, like a fluttery, which it uses to rise on the thermals. It is not common in Twilight, but a valuable find. It is used for meat, leather and down; and the bones are made into ornamental combs, bolts for crossbows, and arrowheads if no jade is available. One of the peculiarities about the snobrella is that it mates for life, and if it happens to see its mate killed it will remember the killer until it dies, taking revenge if it can. It will in any case kill humans and other quite large mammals.

Snowcamel – Despite their name they aren't white: apart from a leathery 'umbrella' on their upper halves,

331

these heavy animals are covered in shaggy black fur. The umbrella is a feature of most Clandoi creatures and is covered with a green symbiotic moss. This moss exchanges vital nutrients with the snowcamel that neither could obtain elsewhere. They can survive for days eating nothing but snow, which they guzzle down their long necks, along with dead vegetation and small rodents. They are invaluable working animals, being strong and faithful.

Snow skimmers – Electrified sledges used by the huissier.

Stingwings – Most insects are commonly called stingwings, though strictly speaking only the yellow-banded ones actually sting. Their striped umbrella wings are edged with rows of tiny poisoned darts capable of causing minor discomfort. Most non-striped varieties are harmless, though some do bite.

Storm kettle – Hunters use these to cook in when the weather is inclement, which is most of the time. They consist of a tube with another tube fitting snugly inside it. The upper part is used to cook in and the lower one holds the fire. There's a small hole in one side to feed the fire with oxygen and fuel, which can be turned into the wind to help the fire burn more strongly without blowing out.

Swags – Huge, unpleasant creatures that look and stink like a pile of rotting carpets, though I have found that one gets used to the smell. They are one of the few animals whose skin is non-taxable: partly as the odour never truly goes, and partly because they are invariably riddled with parasites that chew unsightly holes in the skin – human skin too, if one is very unfortunate. Like most mammals on Clandoi they have an 'umbrella' covering the top half of their bodies, which appear to be made up of umbrella skins piled up one on top of the other. They have four short, stubby legs. An adult male can stand twice the size of an Appaloosian. The topmost umbrella is covered in green moss, which exchanges the nutrients it gets from photosynthesizing for essential gases made by the swag. They eat fruit and foliage, occasionally swallowing small animals such as birds and rodents, though it is thought this is accidental. Nobody I know has ever been tempted to eat one, though I suppose one could if hungry enough.

Tree rutter – A small furry umbrellaed mammal, good to eat.

Tubal worms – These are huge creatures a man's height in diameter and as long as several men lying down end to end. Like most of the creatures native to Clandoi they are covered in a green photosynthesizing moss, from which they get many of their nutrients. The rest comes from tunnelling through the snow. The snow, and anything present in it – dead animals, vegetation, rocks and minerals leached from the ground below – is funnelled into their bodies by their huge jaws and crushed in the massive teeth which line over half of their bodies. They can move at incredible speeds, leaving behind them a worm cast of ice; long and straight, and guaranteed to be smooth and free from rocks: a perfect track for specially shaped sledges to run along.

VTP5.4/VTP1.9 – The Bubblenet can get diseases, just

like us! Makes me think that perhaps it *is* a living creature. Anyway, these VTP whatnots are like the medicine to get rid of the infection.

WASP – Stands for Wandering Automated Security Patrol. WASPs are part of the huissier security system. They are flying cameras painted in black and yellow stripes, with two wings that fold flat along their backs.

Wayfarers – The very poorest people of Clandoi, living under the harshest conditions. We are severely restricted in movement, and are not even allowed children without permission. Most are hunters, miners or traders, though a few work for the Appaloosians. We follow the Being, and keep alive the legends of the sun, moons and stars. It is said that one day the Being will bring them back to us, and morning joy birds will hang them on the Ne'Lethe. He will also turn back the ice so that there will be enough food again.

Wubberslugs – Like slugs. Really most tasty, though I fear Solly was rather put off by the name.

Characters in Cybernation

Taken from the Notebooks of Aube the Seer

The Wayfarers

Aube – Ah, now, this is my name. It means 'dawn'. I'm a Seer and, according to the huissier, an outcast and cavedweller.

Brise – Solly's father, Revas's husband, and the leader of the hunt. Means 'breeze'.

Etolantie – A little girl Solly finds on his way to Worldsend. She won't thank me for calling her little, though, not at all. Her name means 'star-spangled'.

Lumie – An older woman, friend of Revas's, wife of Tache. Means 'light'.

Nuit – A friend of Etolantie's family; husband to Tornesol and father to Rayon. His name means 'night'.

Rayon – A small girl: Tornesol and Nuit's daughter and Etolantie's friend. Means 'radiant'.

Revas – Means 'stargazer'. Solly's mother and Brise's wife. She works as a cleaner in the cyberclinic though, if you want my opinion, she should be a doctor there.

Rian – Etolantie's baby brother. His name means 'smiling'.

Soir – One of the hunters: his name means 'evening'. He plays the flute.

Solly – The main subject of the prophecy I was given sixteen years ago. His name means 'sun'.

Tache – Means 'sunspot'. An older man, second in command in the hunt.

Tornesol – Nuit's wife, Rayon's mother: friend of Etolantie's family. Her name means 'sunflower'.

Vasseurl – A female hunter whose name means 'vessel'.

The Appaloosians

(Administrator) **Forcyef Eleven-oh-three** – An Appaloosian paper-pusher, works at the cyberclinic.

Fordyef – One of the huissier.

Lalune – Means 'the moon'. I named her myself. She is an Appaloosian, but one who features in a Wayfarer prophecy. She is one of the Holders of the Key of Being. Or will be, when it finds her. Her Appaloosian name is Tuef Seventeen.

Threfem Seventeen – Lalune's father, Toayef's husband. He's a low-level worker: a tax official. A very fair chap.

Toayef Seventeen – Lalune's mother and wife of Threfem. She's a senior HIVE technician, Lalune tells me.

Tuef – Lalune's Appaloosian name.

Tuefem – One of the hussier.

(Commander) **Toobe-ef Eighty-nine** – commander in chief of the huissier.

Wuneem – A surly and unhelpful huissier guard.

Others

Angelus – My angelic companion. I first saw him when just a boy, and though I no longer see him, I like to think he's still with me.

(Dr) Dollysheep – A doctor working in the cyberclinic.

The Imperator – The leader of the Pelegians.

Kenet – The Bubblenet assistant: an animation that appears to guide you around the Bubblenet.

Star – Solly's snowcamel.

Sunguide – One of the Pruppras, a strange fungal creature that guides Solly to Latrium.

Sybilla Geenpool – A woman Solly and Etolantie meet at Worldsend.

The Story isn't over for Solly and Lalune... read on to find out more

Coming in 2009

Prologue

'I thought it was s'posed to be summer,' yelled Etolantie, clutching her blankets around her.

'It is,' Solly shouted back. 'I've never seen it like this before.'

They were in a staticky void in the middle of nowhere. The weather had worsened almost immediately after Sunguide had fetched them from Aube's cave. A fierce gale had brought with it the most enormous snowflakes Solly had ever seen, and the skyboat was being tossed about like a feather.

'Is not rrright,' muttered Sunguide, who was completely white down one side with snow. 'Prpr. Is something wrrrong with weather.'

Only Solly was near enough to hear the fear in this voice. Etolantie and Lalune were strapped in at the other end, hugging each other for warmth, and looking as terrified as Solly felt.

Solly tapped Sunguide's rubbery flaps, shielding his mouth and trying to shout quietly so that the girls didn't hear.

'Where are we?'

'Don't know. Prpr. Too busy keeping skyboat in air,' panted the fungus. 'Wound is rrripping open again.'

Solly looked up, alarmed. The strain of their combined weight was pulling apart the stitches Etolantie had put in the skyboat's injury. They didn't look like they could hold much longer.

'My feet are cold,' complained Etolantie, her voice muffled by three blankets.

'Wiggle your toes,' he heard Lalune shout back in a strained voice.

'I trrry to get furrrther up,' Sunguide shouted. 'Get above the storm.'

'No, not higher,' moaned Lalune.

Solly agreed with her. They needed to land. As soon as they could. He glanced again at the gash in the skyboat's balloon. Greenish goo was starting to ooze out.

He opened his mouth to tell Sunguide. But he didn't have time. One of the stitches snapped. There was a screech of escaping air, the skyboat dropped, and his stomach rushed upwards.

Etolantie and Lalune both squealed and clutched their edge of the skyboat as the whole bowl tilted over. Solly wasn't strapped in. He felt himself sliding over the edge, and scrabbled for something to hold onto. He managed to grab a rope just before his hips slipped over.

But before he could wriggle back in, his pack fell out on top of him. It got hooked on his bandoleer, tugging him further down. As it bounced in the air below he felt the skyboat tip even more.

'Solly!' screamed Lalune.

'Hold on!' called Sunguide. 'I trrry land.'

Solly felt a sharp wrench as the pack snared on

something. The skyboat jerked, and his hands dragged on the rope.

Then Lalune's pack tumbled over him, and suddenly he was dangling in mid-air. It was all he could do to hang on.

He peered down. His pack was caught in the top of a tree. He tried to kick it free, but only made it worse.

His eye was caught by a dark shape ahead of them. Something had become briefly visible through the blizzard. A farmhouse, perhaps. If the skyboat could land they could shelter there.

But first they had to clear these trees.

He looked at the two pale faces above him.

There was only one thing he could do.

Solly let go.